AUG 1 2 2002

SANTA ANA PUBLIC LIBRARY

D1008499

SKELETONS

Also by Kate Wilhelm

Desperate Measures (2001)

The Deepest Water (2000)

No Defense (2000)

Defense for the Devil (1999)

The Good Children (1998)

Malice Prepense (1996)

A Flush of Shadows (1995)

The Best Defense (1994)

Justice for Some (1993)

Seven Kinds of Death (1992)

Naming the Flowers (1992)

And the Angels Sing (1992)

Death Qualified (1991)

State of Grace (1991)

Sweet, Sweet Poison (1990)

Cambio Bay (1990)

Children of the Wind: Five Novellas (1989)

Smart House (1989)

The Dark Door (1988)

Crazy Time (1988)

The Hamlet Trap (1987)

The Hills Are Dancing (with Richard Wilhelm) (1986)

Huysman's Pets (1986)

Welcome, Chaos (1983)

Oh, Susannah! (1982)

A Sense of Shadow (1981)

Listen, Listen (1981)

Better Than One (with Damon Knight) (1980)

Juniper Time (1979)

Somerset Dreams and Other Fictions (1978)

Fault Lines (1977)

Where Late the Sweet Birds Sang (1976)

The Clewiston Test (1976)

The Infinity Box (1975)

City of Cain (1974)

Margaret and I (1971)

Abyss (1971)

Year of the Cloud (with Theodore L. Thomas) (1970)

Let the Fire Fall (1969)

The Downstairs Room and Other Speculative Fiction (1968)

The Killer Thing (1967)

The Nevermore Affair (1966)

The Clone (with Theodore L. Thomas) (1965)

The Mile-Long Spaceship (1963)

SKELETONS

KATE WILHELM

St. Martin's Minotaur
NEW YORK

MYSTERY WILHELM, K.
Wilhelm, Kate.
Skeletons
31994011242226

SKELETONS. Copyright © 2002 by Kate Wilhelm. All rights reserved. Printed in the United States of America. No part of this book may be used or reproduced in any manner whatsoever without written permission except in the case of brief quotations embodied in critical articles or reviews. For information, address St. Martin's Press, 175 Fifth Avenue, New York, N.Y. 10010.

www.minotaurbooks.com

Library of Congress Cataloging-in-Publication Data

Wilhelm, Kate.
    Skeletons: A novel of suspense / Kate Wilhelm.—1st ed.
       p.   cm.
    ISBN 0-312-30075-1
       1. Photographic memory—Fiction. Ku Klux Klan (1915 -)—Fiction.
    3. Housesitting—Fiction.   4. Grandparents—Fiction.   5. Young women—
    Fiction.   6. Lynching—Fiction.   7. Oregon—Fiction. I. Title

    PS3573.I434 S58 2002
    813'.54—dc21

First Edition: August 2002

10   9   8   7   6   5   4   3   2   1

PART ONE

1

It was never easy being the daughter of Teresa and George Thomas Donne. That day it was harder than ever because I had to tell them I would not be graduating. I had put in my four years, but I had changed my major three times, and there weren't enough credits in any of my chosen and abandoned fields to warrant the magic piece of paper that said I was finished. Tess— she had insisted I call her that from the time I could speak—said bitterly that she had also changed her major three times but, on the other hand, had three doctorates. And Geo—George Thomas to the rest of the world—had a doctorate in economics and was adviser to presidents, kings, the chairman of the Federal Reserve Board, and CEOs. My brother, Ben, would start his internship almost immediately after graduating from medical school in June. And my grandfather was a world-renowned Shakespearean scholar. I was an appendix in a family of brains.

"I'll call you back," I told Tess, and hung up the telephone. Then I cursed.

Casey, my roommate, was grinning, listening. When I paused for breath, she said, "You're getting better, baby. Mama in a snit?"

"God, you wouldn't believe what she wants now."

"She'll spring for a mail-order diploma."

"Don't laugh." Casey could afford to laugh at me. She had just finished her master's degree in computer science and had been accepted to the doctoral program at CalTech. She was mocha colored with short, nearly black frizzy hair, tall and lanky, all arms and legs and big brain. And she had beautiful eyes, almond shaped, slanting, brown with light flecks. When we filled out our census form two years earlier, she had come to a stop at the entry about ethnic origin. "How do I know?" she said after a moment. "I got so many races running in me, I could be a one-woman marathon." She entered *Martian*.

At the moment she was lying on her back on the floor, with her legs on the decrepit sofa that had stuffing leaking from one arm; we patched it now and then with Band-Aids. I looked from her to the rest of the room—boxes everywhere, some packed and taped, most not finished yet. It looked as if the Vandals had moved in, made a mess, and were getting ready to leave.

"Tess said since I don't have anything better to do, and nowhere to go, I might as well house-sit for my grandfather."

"Oh yeah? I thought he never left home."

He had never spent a single night away from home that I was aware of. I sat down on the floor. No chair was without a pile of stuff.

"He's been invited to lecture at Oxford. On Shakespeare. Tess said he probably won't go unless he knows he has someone reliable to watch the house. Me, reliable? Hah!"

"Wow! Really?" Casey swung her legs off the sofa and sat facing me. "Baby, that's incredible! Of course you'll do it. What else do you have in mind?"

The question of the day. My mother had asked it, now Casey, and I had no answer. My job at the bookstore did not pay enough to keep even this tiny apartment, and all Berkeley rents were fierce. Maybe I could find a new roommate, but probably not until the fall term, and I couldn't hang on that long.

Then I was thinking of the day I had arrived there to find Casey looking things over. The housing administrator had said there was someone willing to share an apartment, no more than that.

"Angela Casada?" I asked that day, ready to turn and run.

"Yeah, but call me Angela and I'll cut your throat. I'm Casey. Who are you?"

"Marilee Donne. Call me Lee."

"Merrily done?" She laughed. Her teeth were very white and large. Then she turned and waved at the apartment. "What do you think?"

It was small, two rooms. The bedroom was jammed with two narrow beds, two chests of drawers, two desks and chairs. The other one we named the Everything Else Room; it had the ancient green sofa, sink, stove and fridge, and a minuscule table with a faded and cracked red Formica top, plus everything else we owned.

"Listen," Casey said, leaning forward, all serious now. "You can't live on the street. You'd be like cotton candy on the midway, gone without a trace by the end of the first hour. You won't live in your mama's house. You can't stay here. The YWCA? That's where they house women with crazy men on their tails, gals on parole, addicts, shit like that. Why won't the old man just close up the house and take off the way other folks do?"

"Haven't you got it yet, after all these years? My family is nuts, crazy, wacko. I don't know why."

"Okay. Okay. Would he pay you?"

"Tess said he would, and the utilities and stuff are all on an automatic payment schedule through his bank."

"So you get room and board plus something. For how long?"

"He would go in July, start his lecture series in late August, and stay until around Thanksgiving."

"Five months of freeloading. Doesn't sound too shabby." She reached out and patted my knee. "And, baby, you need some thinking time. Come fall, you could go to the university there and take a couple of classes, finish things."

Things were always simpler for Casey than for me. She had known what she wanted to do from the day she saw her first computer. She called me her Renaissance pal—dabble in everything, commit to nothing. And I had broken up with my latest boyfriend, the one who was supposed to be for good, just a month earlier. I dabbled in life, too. In fact, I didn't have anything better to do than house-sit for my batty grandfather.

"Want to come and hang out after you visit your folks?"

"You bet. I told Pop I'd work in the store for a couple of weeks, give him a break; but then I'll head up your way before I check in at CalTech." Her family lived in Phoenix, where her father owned a small variety store. They had lived in Chicago until Casey was ten or eleven, when her mother became asthmatic. Casey hated Phoenix; she was doomed for a sojourn in hell, she had said morosely when she made her plans.

I picked up the phone and dialed my mother's number.

I spent a week in Seattle with my great-aunt Luella, my grandfather's sister, who had been more of a mother to me than Tess ever was. Aunt Lu was seventy, and she greeted me like a grandchild, fussed over me, and generally made me welcome.

"Child, you're skin and bones! Are you sick?"

"Nope. And I'm not thin. You're too fat."

"Not!"

"So."

We laughed at the long-grown-stale exchange, then gossiped while she prepared dinner. She and my grandfather were fourth-generation Oregonians and had jointly inherited the house he still lived in. She had been widowed during World War II and for years afterward had managed his household, home for her and her two sons and my mother. Aunt Lu had remained with Grandfather for years, but finally she had been unable to resist moving closer to her sons, their wives, and her five grandchildren, all in Seattle. My brother and I had spent many summers in Aunt Lu's care while our own mother was off here, there, everywhere.

Entering her house in Seattle felt like going home. A good feeling.

I had unwound at Aunt Lu's house, but I could feel the coils tightening again as I approached the door of my parents' condo in Bel-Air. Geo was not there, Tess had told me; he was in Hong Kong, attending an important economic conference.

"Darling, you look wonderful!" Tess exclaimed when she opened the door and held out her arms to embrace me. It was a lie. I was bedraggled; she looked wonderful. She always looked wonderful.

In truth, I was jealous of my mother. She had brains, beauty, a rich husband, a part-time tenured teaching position, security she had not yet examined. They had the condo and an apartment in New York. They traveled to London, Paris, Vienna, Rome. . . . And now Geo was in Hong Kong.

Tess was slender and vivacious, always moving, always thinking and talking. Blond, as were most Landorfs, she was determinedly, seriously blond; her hair would forever remain as gold as honey. Mine was already darkening. With big blue eyes, and a dimple even, she was the most unlikely-looking woman ever to be endowed with a good brain, ambition, and drive enough to get the maximum out of life. Sometimes I wondered whether Geo found her energy as tiring as I did. I was already tired and I had not yet reached my room.

"What I thought we would do is shop first. You'll need a few things, I suspect, and then I made an appointment for you with Dr. Sandersson. You know, my therapist. Such a dear. If you'll just talk to someone about your problems, you'll find it helpful. I know I did. That's why I went into psychology years ago, trying to unravel the riddle of my existence. I learned that you can't do it alone, darling. No one can. Even the best of us needs outside guidance and counsel. I learned that I had to work through the abandoned-child syndrome, but I couldn't see it until someone else pointed it out. That's how our minds betray us, hiding us from ourselves."

Tess never let me forget that although deserted by her mother at an early age, *she* had struggled and prospered and made something of herself.

We had reached the guest room; I opened the door, then paused. "Tess, I am not going to your therapist."

"We'll talk about it tomorrow, darling, after you've rested."

She would talk about it, and I would listen—or more likely not—but she would do her motherly duty by me.

She had gotten her Ph.D. and then dropped psychology. She did not want to work with crazy people, she had explained. Instead she had gone into history, then dropped that, because all those people who made history were dead. She had settled finally for sociology, which she taught now and then at UCLA. She had written a book somehow linking urban planning with the eclipse of feminism in the new society, and she went on lecture tours spouting nonsense for which she was well paid.

The condo was beautiful, and held nothing of mine. When I was still at home, we had had a house in Sherman Oaks, which they sold the day after I left for school. I never asked what they did with my possessions. I had learned very early that to ask Tess a question was to be subjected to a lecture, and any question put to Geo ended up weirdly connected to economics.

"What it all comes down to is power," he said on my last visit. "Who gives the orders and who takes them. Feminism"—that had been the starting point of his discourse—"is the same. Who gives the orders, who takes them. Middle-class white women hire black women to do their dirty work here and in Europe. But in Africa, middle-class or upper-class black women might well hire a poor white woman to do the same chores. When they're equally middle or upper class, watch to see who gives the orders, who submits. Power struggle. And money wins. My two million lord it over your one million. Power equates with money every time. Even great armies with all the weaponry conceivable yield to richer nations."

At that point Tess interrupted coldly, "We were talking about feminism."

"So am I," Geo said.

For the next week I assumed the role of dutiful daughter to Tess's dutiful-mother act. I listened to her lectures, to her description of my brother's graduation. I listened to exhortations about seeking professional help for my "problems," with many hints that she knew perfectly well what they were, but discretion compelled her to remain silent. Then she flew to Hong Kong to join my father, to do some shopping, followed by a little trip to Tokyo.

After her departure I began the process of unwinding again. But I was starting to feel oppressed by the condo: the sleek, beautiful furnishings, all pale wood, metal, and matte black, with flaming red cushions strewn here and there, a royal blue Persian rug strategically placed, brilliant orange-and-green chair covers in the dining room. . . .

I missed Casey, our squalid hovel, Berkeley, my books. Grandfather's house was looming up more and more often in my mind, and I realized I wanted to get on with it, to go there, as much home as anywhere else on earth.

At first the idea had been incredible. Five months in Eugene, Oregon, alone in the house of a nutty old man? Me, the heroine of a Brontë novel? Ridiculous. Now I was more than ready, even eager, to get there. At least Grandfather never threw out my stuff the minute I walked out the door.

2

My family was gifted. Seeing everything in terms of power, which he equated with money, my father found the world simple to understand and master. My mother sometimes boasted that there was nothing she could not learn well enough to ace any test. The fact that she retained so little was of no consequence, she said; she had the basics. That she confused Aristotle with Archimedes, or Jung with Adler, or Napoleon with Hannibal was of no matter; she recognized important names and knew how to look them up if necessary. Her gift was her passion for whatever she was involved with at the moment; it might prove transitory, but while it existed, it was all that mattered.

My brother, Ben, had known since adolescence that the brain was the great undiscovered continent, one that he would map and conquer through brain research.

My grandfather was no exception. He had been taken to a Shakespeare play when he was six or seven, had been enraptured, and had remained under the spell ever after. He was on intimate terms with the entire oeuvre—the sonnets, tragedies, histories, all of it—and could and did recite obscure lines that few others had ever heard.

For my family the world had been simplified; I saw how one great idea could make the world smooth out, could master the conflicting, contradictory confusion that beset me at every turn.

I had no obsessive passion, no compulsion to do anything or be anything. My gift, if it could be labeled that, was an eidetic memory that seemed to retain a visual representation of things that I had seen. A glimpse of a butterfly landing on a sunflower ten years ago was like a snapshot that came to mind as if I'd just seen it. The arrangement of books on shelves; the flare of last light at sunset that turned the world gold and silver before it swiftly became dusk-blurred; snapshots in a photo album of people I did not know; the quirk of an eyebrow; beads of sweat on an upper lip; Casey's long, bony fingers with oversize knuckles; my mother's restless feet or boneless-appearing fingers.

If I entered a room I had been in before, I was aware if a chair had been moved, a picture hung or taken down, a lamp replaced. . . . I did not consciously or deliberately recall what had been, but past and present coexisted as distinct images in my mind.

As a gift it was useless, but I never really thought of it as a gift, which is something one can enjoy, or at least admire, or even trade for something else. For years I had assumed everyone had the same kind of visual memory that I did, and was greatly surprised to learn that it was not so. If I ever saw a crime being committed, I would make a wonderful witness who could describe in minute detail everything that happened, what the suspect wore, exactly what he or she looked like. And no one would believe me. I had learned that lesson, too. Perfect pitch is widely known and accepted, a perfect visual memory is not. When my brother and I compared our memories of childhood, I was amazed at how false his memories were, while he denied the truth of mine and clung to his own.

"Did it ever occur to you that you could be wrong?" he demanded once, and I shook my head.

Those were my thoughts as I flew into Eugene, Oregon, that day in July, believing I would not leave again until late in the fall.

Grandfather was waiting for me at the airport. I saw him from the top of the escalator, standing a bit apart from a mob of people down below awaiting the passengers. He had not changed much since I last visited, the same stoop, gray hair thinning, but no thinner than it had been then, a distracted expression, as if wondering why he was there. He was not a large man, five feet nine, slightly built, with a paunch that made him look soft. He was dressed in his summer outfit: chinos, a plaid sport shirt unbuttoned at the neck, brown suede shoes. In the winter he wore either a gray suit or a brown wool tweed. All of his socks were black, all identical. He could have bought a lifetime supply at an early age and never varied.

He was still gazing about with a nearly uncomprehending expression when I approached him at the bottom of the escalator. When I said, "Hello, Grandfather," he gave a start of surprise and looked me over as if he had never seen me before in his life.

That did not alarm or surprise me. When Ben and I stayed at his house as children, he often looked at us at the dinner table—Aunt Lu, her two grown sons when they were there, Ben, and me—as if he had not a clue about who we were or why we were having dinner with him.

Now he examined me as if checking, then belatedly held out his hand. We shook hands. No hugs and kisses from my grandfather.

"I didn't know you," he said. "You're all grown up."

Of course, I had changed over the past few years, but still. . . . I nodded, and we began walking toward the baggage area. He asked about the flight, about Tess and Geo, about the weather in Los Angeles, obviously trying to make small talk to cover the awkwardness between us. I understood that he did not have an idea how to treat me now that I was no longer a child to be tolerated. And he kept eyeing me with a puzzled look, as if trying to reconcile memory with reality.

As a child, I had been intimidated by him; he had appeared so distant and forbidding, so ill at ease with children about, and so unapproachable. Aunt Lu made up for him in every way, and we had come to accept that we were visiting her, and he just happened to be there, too. Now, for a week, until he left for England, there would be just the two of us in his house, and already I was starting to wish I had remained at the condo for a few more days.

We retrieved my suitcase and walked out, through the vast parking lot, to his car in silence.

"You have a new car," I said when he motioned toward a black Accord. "Nice."

"You remember my old car?"

"A green Taurus?" I asked, but not to confirm anything. I knew what he had had in the past.

"You're probably right," he said after a moment. "Frankly, I don't remember what it was."

He drove out of the lot, toward town, now and then casting a quick glance my way, still checking. Then he said, "I have a strange memory flaw. Faces escape me. Usually, even with the same people I see every day, I don't remember their faces and it's

like meeting them anew each time. And I practically never asso-
ciate a name with a face. It makes it difficult to teach, of course.
One would expect to be remembered after a term, but one rarely
is. Their work is remembered perfectly, but not the person or
the name. Strange." He looked at me, away. "You will have to
put up with it, I'm afraid."

"I could wear a name tag," I said. To my surprise, he laughed.
For the first time in my life I felt a sort of kinship with him, and
sympathy. "It must be hard with your colleagues, too."

"Yes. I suppose. It's not a rare condition; many people share it
to one extent or another. My colleagues are used to it, and most
of them are kind and helpful. They say their name and department, and that's all it takes. If they fail to do that, I have learned
to be quite blunt about it and ask. With each year one can shed
more of youth's inhibitions, I have found."

"I'm Lee Donne," I said then, and he nodded, and his hands
loosened their white-knuckle grip on the steering wheel.

My sympathy deepened. I suspected that he was dreading his
upcoming trip as much as he was looking forward to the opportunity to discuss Shakespeare with British scholars. "Yet," I said,
"you've probably memorized every line Shakespeare ever put on
paper."

"Very likely. It just happened, however. I didn't attempt such
a herculean task; it happened. I read a page or two a time or two,
and found that I had retained it."

We were approaching a Y intersection and he was slowing
down, looking bewildered. I remembered that Aunt Lu had said
he would get lost in his own backyard one day, and I said, "You
stick to the left."

We didn't talk much after that, and he drove with more confi-
dence as we drew closer to his house. I had never spent much

time in Eugene during my visits, but the streets were in my head, a built-in map. I could never get lost anyplace I had ever been, and now I could recognize changes here and there. A store gone, another in its place; a missing restaurant, fewer trees downtown, but wider streets . . . We drove through town, past the university grounds and buildings, past the millrace, home to countless fat ducks, and then headed south on Franklin until we reached Mason Loop, a few miles out of town. He needed no prompting to make the turn. This was his daily trek back and forth to the university where he taught.

The first Landorf to arrive in Oregon had intended to clear forested land and create a ranch, but he never got around to the ranch, although he cut down trees and sold the timber. At that time the property had been about a thousand acres; succeeding Landorfs had sold off parcels bit by bit. My grandfather's father had put in rows of noble firs, planning to sell Christmas trees, and we all knew what happened to his plans. Black Monday, the stock market crash, the Great Depression. Aunt Lu had told us all about those hard days. They had expanded the small kitchen garden to grow enough food to have produce to sell. What they couldn't sell, they used as barter goods; and what they couldn't barter, they gave away. They cut down the fir trees and burned them, and sold firewood when there was a buyer. My grandfather and his father hauled stones from the south fork of the Willamette River and rebuilt a fireplace, big enough to heat much of the house. They closed off some of it, huddled in the rooms they could heat, and got by.

When World War II broke out, Aunt Lu and her young suitor married, and she went with him to San Diego when he joined the navy. Three years later, the day after Grandfather graduated from high school, he joined the army. He was part of the armed forces that landed in Italy; Aunt Lu's husband served on a destroyer in the Pacific and was killed when his ship went down in a kamikaze attack.

We were passing a strawberry field, depleted of berries now in July. Across the road a cut-flower farm flourished brilliantly, and farther along goats and sheep grazed. South of the small farms Mount Pisgah rose, heavily forested, as if no saw had ever touched a tree there. Grandfather's property was three and a half acres now, and most of it in trees. Aunt Lu had kept a kitchen garden, but even that was gone.

As the acreage shrank, the house had grown over the generations. A two-room cabin, then four rooms, now at least ten, possibly twelve, depending on who was counting and what was being counted as a room. There were small enclosed areas, too small to be useful except for storage, with doors curiously placed as if at one time they had been necessary, but no one could remember why any longer. Ben said that the Landorfs were crazy and always had been, and they built a crazy house. If they decided they needed a room for something—a sewing room, for example—instead of knocking out a wall between two useless rooms, they just added a whole new room.

It was a house built for hide-and-seek games, and it was glorious for that purpose.

After the war, after school at Tulane, then UCLA, and finally Princeton, Grandfather had come home with a young wife and child, and although the wife did not stay long, he had never left again.

The first thing he did at home was add a garage and wall off the rear of it to make a darkroom. For a brief time he was interested in photography, but had long since given it up. The darkroom was still there, of course. It was the last addition to the crazy house that the crazy Landorfs built.

It was late in the afternoon when we arrived at the house, which looked exactly the same as always; even the same weeds appeared to be thriving along the front walk, the same fir needles banked against the house foundation. It needed a paint job, but it was no worse than it had been before, so I assumed that it had been painted at least once since my last visit. Inside, nothing had changed, I thought at first. More books, but that was normal; there were always more books on each visit. To the left of the entry foyer was the parlor/sitting room that was rarely sat in. A chair on the wall across the room blocked a door that led to the common room, or what we now called the family room, where people watched television or listened to music, played board games or played the piano.

In my cursory glance into the sitting room, I saw that a skull had been removed from the fireplace mantel. My gaze always had gone to it first when I came to visit. I loved it: a yellowing ivory skull mounted on a base of highly polished granite, with the single word engraved on it, ALAS. A large chunk of petrified wood was in its place. As far as I could tell, nothing else was different.

I had my mother's old room with rear-facing windows, a heavy oak four-poster bed with a lovely heirloom quilt my great-grandmother had pieced together. A dresser and chest of drawers, chair and table, even a small writing desk, and a closet bigger than our Everything Else Room had been at Berkeley. My boxes had arrived and were lined up against the wall.

We had a busy few days. Grandfather introduced me to people at the credit union where he banked; we opened an account for me and established a line of credit in my name so I could pay the bills that were not on automatic payment and pay for any emergency that might arise. The property tax would come due in November, he cautioned. He authorized my signature on his credit card. At home he showed me fuse boxes and other necessary household features, like how to turn off the water and how to start the furnace.

And he showed me how to operate his security system. He watched me program in my own password and activate it. The next day he had me change it without instructions, watching closely again to make certain I understood what I had to do. The next day when he asked me to change it yet again, I rebelled.

"Grandfather, what am I supposed to be guarding? It might help if I had a clue."

He looked around vaguely, shrugged, then said, "Nothing, I guess. But you never can tell."

That night I pondered: There was nothing of obvious value in the house. Most of the furniture was very old, antiques, but not valuable antiques. Much was handmade, heavy oak pieces of the sort that crowded every used-furniture store in the country. A rare book or two? I doubted it. There were thousands of books, but they were for reading, for studying; he was a pack rat, not a real collector. Besides, he could have put something like that in a safe-deposit box. The few items that could be carried off and sold were all covered by his homeowner's insurance, I felt confident—his computer, the television, an ancient stereo system.

I was getting ready for bed and stopped in the process of folding down the quilt. Now, that was priceless, I thought, and irreplaceable, yet he used it as if it were from a Wal-Mart sale table. He had no sense of the value of anything. Whatever he was guarding was not something that could just be picked up and taken out. He was gone for hours every day; someone could have stolen something already, and unless it was something that he used regularly, I imagined that he would never notice its absence. I gave it up. He was a crazy Landorf; maybe that was all the reason he needed for whatever he did.

3

Grandfather had never flown before, he mentioned on our way to the airport, and that alarmed me. I hoped he would not get lost in the terminal at San Francisco or at Kennedy, but there was little I could do except worry. "Call me when you get there," I begged him, and he nodded in his vague way. I suspected he would not give it another thought.

He had become more and more uneasy about going away for months. I promised not to leave without notifying him well in advance. And I offered to catalog his many books. It was a tentative offer. I understood that some people did not want anyone to move a single thing; they knew exactly where everything was in the midst of chaos. But not Grandfather. He admitted he didn't know where anything was unless it was under his nose. When his flight was called, he marched through the boarding gate and out of sight like a soldier going to battle.

Over the next few days I introduced myself to the neighbors: The strawberry lady, who worked in a department store as a tailor part-time and tended the strawberry fields. Her husband, she said, had a bad back, and she didn't say another word about him. I met the goat couple; middle-aged, with grown children, they were considering getting a few emus, maybe a llama or two. They told me about the milking schedule, every twelve hours, and if you start that regimen at five-thirty in the morning, you're stuck with it. And I met the flower lady and her live-in boyfriend, both also middle-aged, and I suspected they were growing more than just flowers. I glimpsed a couple of pretty big greenhouses behind a windbreak of shrubs. She made a point of saying they kept busy but she would like to drop by my place sometime, have a cup of coffee maybe. I decided I would not be seeing much of any of them.

I wandered through the house, eyeing the many books, some shelved, some in stacks on the floors of various rooms, on tables everywhere, and I realized that it was going to be more of a job than I had anticipated when I made the offer to catalog and arrange them. I didn't start yet; that could wait until after Casey's visit.

Poor Yorick now rested on a shelf in Grandfather's study, looking as disconsolate as ever. The books he had replaced were on the floor. I patted him affectionately.

On Thursday Mrs. Hawkins came to clean. I had told Grandfather that it wouldn't be necessary, but he insisted that she come as usual, or he might lose her, and he could not go through that again, trying to find a housekeeper. So she came, a stout, kindly woman in her fifties who did whatever needed doing, she said cheerfully, and went right to work. I got the message: She did not need any input from me.

My days were falling into a routine of sorts by the end of my first week alone. Up at about eight, breakfast and read the newspaper, tidy up from the night before—a popcorn bowl in the family room or several books on the kitchen table to be put away, little things that took little time. Take the car out to shop, rent movies or return them, buy some envelopes . . . I found some errand to go out for nearly every day, and I welcomed each and every one of them.

I started piano lessons. I had played the flute for a few years and was not very good, but I had learned to read music. I began weeding the front walk and around the house, in no rush to finish; the weather was too hot for much outdoor work that I wasn't used to. Dinner about seven, a little television, or more likely read some more, and bed soon after eleven. A nice simple life. I was surprised at how agreeable it was. I had needed simplicity, I realized, had needed to stop chasing myself in circles, trying to do what? I never had an answer, but I felt that I had stopped running, and I liked it.

On Friday night, a week after Grandfather left, I woke up thinking it was pouring rain, or even hailing; a fierce storm must have moved in. Then I sat straight up. Not in July, and it wasn't rain. A pattering of something on the roof? Had the wind loosened shingles? I got up, listening intently. The noise stopped, but as I walked to the windows to look out, it started again, farther away.

I didn't turn on a light but stood at the window, trying to see something. There were outside lights that came on automatically at dusk and went off at daylight. Everything was calm, but the pattering was on the roof.

I slipped on a robe and started to walk through the hall, trying to locate where the noise was coming from. It kept stopping, then starting somewhere else, so faint at times that I had to hold my breath to hear it. I paused at windows, carefully moved blinds or curtains to peer out—nothing. Pools of dark and light. I had reached the kitchen, and now the sound seemed to be coming from the sitting-room roof, but this time I remained at the kitchen window, waiting to see if anyone would appear. I felt that someone was tracking my movements, doing something on the roof, or to it, then moving away when I got to that part of the house and starting again somewhere else. Leading me by making noise. The pattering stopped again, but I stayed at the kitchen window. And I saw a shadow dart across one of the most dimly lit areas and vanish.

Shaking, I groped my way to the sitting-room window, from which I could see the front of the yard and the road beyond. There were many trees out there, but if headlights appeared on the road, I would see them. I didn't move again until a deer strolled into a pool of light. No headlights came on; there was not another sound.

It was three-thirty and I didn't know what to do. Call for help? Call the sheriff? For what? Whoever that had been was gone. If I had called as soon as it started, there might have been a point, but not now. No one had tried to break in; the security system was on, the green light steady, undisturbed.

I huddled in the family room until the sky began to lighten, and convinced myself finally it had been the work of kids out for a bit of fun. Frighten someone and hightail it out before anyone caught them, I thought angrily. How pleased they would be to know that it had worked.

On Saturday, tired and irritable, I stalked about the property, not really expecting to find anything out of the ordinary, and I didn't. Trees, a thicket of brambles that would take over completely before too long, weeds, wild laurel bushes . . . Then I thought of Mason Loop.

I knew there was a turnoff to the Arboretum, a wildlife refuge and natural area, but the road continued past that and ended up at a subdivision on the outskirts of Springfield, Eugene's sister city. Hopeless, I thought. Kids could well have come from there or from Eugene.

On Saturday night I made up the couch in the family room in order to spend the night there and, I hoped, get some sleep. There was no telephone in my bedroom, and if they came back, I intended to call the sheriff. At two they came back.

When the pattering started over the garage, I hit the dial for 911. In a near whisper I told the dispatcher that someone was throwing rocks at my house. The sound was over the distant bedrooms then.

"Can you speak up?" the woman on the phone asked.

"No. Someone's outside throwing rocks. I'm alone in the house. I don't want them to know I'm calling the police."

I gave her my name and address, and she asked if they had tried to break in or threatened me in any way; making conversation, I thought. "Are you going to send someone out here?" I demanded.

"I put out the word," she said, "but it might be a little while before anyone gets there. Why don't you turn on a lot of lights and see if they take off?"

I hung up. The stones were right above me in the family room. I went to the window as before and tried to see something. Hopeless. There were too many trees and bushes they could duck behind. I didn't turn on lights and let them know their scheme was working. I waited in the dark and listened, and when things got quiet again, I lay down on the couch and tried to go back to sleep, and failed until daylight.

I had been frightened at first, but on Sunday I was simply furious. I was tired, sleep deprived, and feeling put-upon; someone was playing a cat-and-mouse game with me, and nobody cared. A deputy sheriff came by mid-morning. I could have been dead and stiff by then, I thought as I admitted him to the house. He was middle-aged, portly, and nearly bald, sweating heavily, although his county car must have been air-conditioned.

"You the homeowner here?"

I told him about my grandfather.

"You've been hearing noises at night?" he asked.

"Not just noises. Someone's been throwing gravel or something at the house, on the roof. And I saw someone running out there."

"You're here alone?"

"Yes, for the last few days, but I've been here more than two weeks, and this just started two nights ago."

"No one's tried to get in or tampered with a window, nothing like that?"

He was gazing about the foyer, took a step or two into the sitting room and glanced around, came back.

"No. They just throw rocks or gravel onto the roof, first in one place, then another."

"Uh-huh. Let's have a look around outside."

We walked around the house, and he nodded now and again, as if verifying something. "Mighty fine old house," he said. "What? Hundred years old?"

"I guess so."

"Lots of trees and shrubs. You know, there's deer all around these parts, coons, sometimes a coyote."

"I know that. I see deer all the time, and the raccoons come nosing around nearly every night. But they don't throw rocks."

"Now, now," he said, as if soothing a child. "See, these old buildings get set in their ways, just like people. These hot days the wood swells up, cools off, and shrinks back down when it gets good and dark. Old houses like this can make a lot of funny noises. I heard one once that sounded just like someone wailing up a storm. Wood can squeal like that."

"I know what the house sounds like," I snapped. "This is different. It sounds like gravel being thrown on the roof."

"Got a ladder?"

We found a ladder in the garage; he brushed away cobwebs,

leaned it against the garage wall, and climbed up high enough to see the roof. He got down and moved the ladder around to the kitchen wall and did it again. The roof was all angles, with one flat section over the garage, the rest peaked.

"Why don't you have a look," he suggested.

I climbed high enough to see the roof, and there was nothing but fir needles on it. No rocks, no gravel, just needles, especially in the gutter.

"You better get someone out here to clear out those needles before the weather changes in the fall, or you'll have plugged-up downspouts," he said, starting to walk toward his car. "You have a pal around town here, someone who can keep you company a few days?"

I shook my head. I had met the neighbors, people at the credit union, a produce man on the corner. I didn't know anyone else in Eugene.

"Why don't you go check into a nice motel, get some sleep, and think this over," he said. "Once you start hearing old houses at night, it seems like they just get louder and louder. Sometimes a bat gets in that space between the ceiling and the roof and flies around a lot trying to get out again. Or a squirrel gets in and makes a racket. If anyone tries to break in, that alarm system will wake up the dead for a mile around, and it'll sound down at the station. I don't think there's anything for you to worry about. We'll have a patrol car run up Mason Loop during the night. Just get some sleep. Okay?"

I nodded. Okay. Sleep. Rest. Don't worry.

I watched him get in his car and drive away. If he had tried to pat my head, I would have bitten him.

I moved the ladder to another place and looked at the roof again, and even poked around in the fir needles with a stick.

Needles, a few leaves. No rocks, no gravel. There was no space between the garage ceiling and the flat roof. No bats. I tried one more roof section, then put the ladder back in the garage, went inside the house, and made a pot of coffee.

What to do? was the question, and I had no answer. The deputy was right, I should get a motel room and get some sleep and think things over, but then I thought: Was that what they wanted me to do? *They?* I asked myself mockingly. Who they?

Maybe I was just as crazy as all the Landorfs who had gone before me, as crazy as my grandfather with his paranoia about leaving home overnight, or my mother's restlessness that didn't let her stay home for more than a few weeks at a time. But I didn't *feel* crazy. Maybe they didn't, either.

I realized with increasing fury that I was chasing myself in circles again. I slammed my coffee cup down on the table and said, "They're not going to drive me away!" And I heard again that mocking interior voice, *Who they?*

After I cleaned up the splashed coffee, I headed for the couch to take a nap. My head was too fuzzy to think clearly, but if I had to be up for much of the night, I had to get some sleep by day. The house was stifling; every day I opened it to get fresh air, but the temperature kept hovering in the low to mid-nineties. At night I closed it up again and turned on the security system as instructed. Exactly backward. Nighttime temperatures were in the fifties.

I dozed fitfully until the telephone roused me. It was Casey to tell me her flight number and arrival time on Friday. My end of the conversation must have been pitiful, for she stopped talking airily and said, "What's wrong?"

I tried to say, "Nothing," but the word hit the roadblock that sometimes forms between the thought and the deed, and instead

26

I began telling her about the past nights, about the deputy, about my indecision about leaving.

She interrupted. "Baby, let me call you back in a couple of minutes. Won't be long, promise."

I stared at the telephone with dismay after I hung up. Even Casey, I thought miserably. Then she called back to say she had changed her flight.

"Tomorrow, Monday night, nine-forty, if they're on time, which I understand they never are," she said.

"You shouldn't cut your visit short like that."

"Tell you the truth, I'm fed up with being the object in ongoing show-and-tell performances. My old man's determined to parade me in front of everyone he knows. Look at my smart kid! Tomorrow night. Can you hang in there?"

4

I shopped that afternoon for food for two, more fruit, sandwich material, extra bread, whatever I could think of that Casey would like. I even bought Twinkies. I bought batteries for two dead flashlights I had found in the house. And I bought a new flashlight. I killed time, and didn't try to kid myself into believing otherwise.

That night was quiet, but I couldn't sleep. I kept waiting for the noise to start again. Intermittent reinforcement, I thought, remembering Tess in her psychologist's role. Instill fear and reinforce it now and then. Or was it over? Had they tired of the game when they got no positive feedback? I hoped that was the case, but I was still glad that Casey would join me on Monday.

I was at the airport terminal half an hour early, and the waiting seemed endless, but finally her flight arrived. When she appeared at the top of the escalator, I felt weak with relief.

"You look like hell," she said cheerfully when we embraced.

"I have a right," I said.

"Well, I've got loads of stuff. I'll want it when I get to Cal-Tech, but I didn't have any place to send it, so let the airline earn its moolah. You have room in your car for boxes and boxes of stuff?"

"Casey—"

She put her finger on my lips. "Later, baby. Let's snag us a cart. This place does have carts, doesn't it?" She looked dubious. The airport was small compared with anywhere she had been, I guessed, but it did have carts. We took one to the baggage area and waited for the luggage belt to groan to life. While we waited, she talked about her father and mother, about the parade of viewers who had made her feel like a sausage on sale.

When the conveyor belt jerked awake, I left her to haul off her possessions while I got the car and brought it around. Then, the car jammed full, we headed for home.

"When I get rich," she said, "I'll buy them a mansion, room enough so they won't even find each other unless they want to. And they'll never have to lift a finger again. They live above the store, you know."

Her education was financed mostly by grants and scholar-ships, but I knew she felt she was a terrible drain on her parents; they helped as much as they could. My parents, extravagant in most ways, seemed to begrudge every cent they put into my schooling; a waste of my time and their money, they implied. My parents were helping me build character. Her parents were simply loving and generous.

It was clear that Casey didn't want to talk about my dilemma until we reached the house. That was fine by me. It would be helpful if she saw the house and something of the surrounding grounds first. Besides, maybe it was all over.

After we'd put everything away, I took her on a tour of the house. She loved her room, Aunt Lu's old room, and gazed with near reverence at an ancient clawfoot bathtub in one of the bathrooms.

"I'll take long baths every day," she said. "Maybe two a day."

"Right. Let's eat something and I'll tell you what's been going on."

As we ate tuna sandwiches at the kitchen table, I told it all again, this time more coherently than on the phone, I suspected. She nodded now and then without comment until I finished.

"Last night, all quiet on the western front?"

"Yes, and God knows I hope it stays quiet from here on, but if it doesn't, I have to do something."

Although she didn't say it, I could sense that she was as skeptical as the deputy that anything real was going on. She nodded again. "So tonight we just sit and gab and wait?"

"Not exactly. I've been thinking. What if it's the guy down the road who has a flower farm and greenhouses that might be growing more than just daffodils? He could be trying to scare me away. They saw me looking over the hedge at the green-houses, and they might not want a nosy new neighbor."

"You don't want to go out in the middle of the night and confront him," she said emphatically.

"You better believe I don't. What if someone is waiting for me to turn off the security system so they can rush in without setting off alarms? I thought of that, too."

"Right," she said with more emphasis.

I got up and retrieved the new flashlight from the counter and showed it to her. It was huge, heavy with a powerful twelve-volt battery, a spotlight. Casey eyed it. "You think someone's going to step into the limelight and pose?"

"Maybe. Come with me. One more room to look over." I led the way through the kitchen, a big country kitchen with an outside door, one to the dining room, and another at the far end that opened to a short hall out to the garage and the darkroom. I had replaced the bulb in the darkroom and left the door open, but it was stifling and smelled unused and musty. There were no windows. There were two wide shallow sinks on the back, outside wall, with an exhaust fan over them. I motioned Casey toward the sinks, and I lifted the fan away from the wall, leaving a perfect round hole about eight inches in diameter. Earlier that day I had removed the screws that held the fan.

"If he comes, and you're in here with the spotlight, and I'm at the kitchen window, I might get a look at him. See, there's plenty of room to sweep the light from one side of the backyard all the way across. He'll be there. He has to get within range in order to do whatever it is he does to the roof."

Casey looked at the hole, then at the flashlight, and she nodded. "It could work, but I'd be blind in here."

"That doesn't matter. I'll be watching. If it's kids playing dirty tricks, that's one thing. I'll just wait them out until they get bored. If it's the flower boy, I'll tell him I saw him and that if he comes around again, I'll file a formal complaint and there will be a big investigation. I think that would be the end of it."

Casey fitted the fan back into the hole, then removed it again and put the light there, extended it an inch or two, and slowly moved it from one side to the other.

"Start at the right side," I said. "He has to stand over there somewhere to hit the roof over the kitchen."

She swung the flashlight to the side and slowly moved it again from right to left. "Deal," she said then. "Let's have some coffee. It might be a long night." She set the exhaust fan back in place.

I knew it would be hard to see anything after being in the dark for an hour or longer, but it would be worse for him. He would be taken completely by surprise, like a deer in the headlights. He might freeze long enough for me to catch a glimpse, and that was all I needed. I'd know the flower boy instantly: thin, six feet two, long gray hair in a ponytail, big bony nose. . . . I would recognize him.

We made coffee and filled a thermal carafe, then sat in the family room talking. By twelve we turned off the lights, and gradually we grew quieter. I heard Casey yawn, but I was too wound up to feel sleepy. I was terminally tired, but not sleepy. The house began to make its old-house noises, a board creaking, a ceiling beam adjusting to the cool air, just shifting and settling in for the night.

"You ever think about haunts, ghosts, your grandfather's skeletons rattling closet doors?" she asked in the darkness.

"No. And don't you start down that road."

She chuckled. "Not going to, but what a perfect time to tell ghost stories. My old man is a firm believer, and I guess Ma is, too."

"I'm not," I said emphatically, and she laughed again and yawned again.

She probably dozed; I did, not really sleeping, just not wholly awake, drifting in and out of awareness. It started over the bedroom wing.

"Casey!"

"I hear it."

I stood up. "Let's go."

I was the guide, holding her hand, through the family room, the dining room, kitchen, then the darkroom. We felt our way to the sink, and when she said she had the exhaust fan out, the flashlight ready to turn on, I made my way back to the kitchen window. The pattering had moved from the bedroom to the sitting room; it went to the garage, back to the sitting room. I listened hard. It started over my head.

"Now, Casey!"

The light came on, blindingly bright, as I had known it would be. I blinked hard as the light moved, but then I saw him. "Hold it!" I cried.

He was the deer in the headlights for another moment, then he swung around. I heard a noise that sounded like a cannon, and he was gone. Casey yelled something; the light made a sweeping arc and came to rest shining on fir needles high in a tree.

"Casey!" I screamed.

"Get down and stay down!" she called back.

I crouched low and ducked past the window, then ran to the door, collided with the frame, and continued on to the darkroom. Casey was cursing bitterly.

"Are you hurt? Did he hit you?"

She called him names I had never heard her utter before, and I had thought I had heard her entire repertoire. I sank to the floor next to her, and we held each other in the dark.

I had never seen that man in the spotlight before. A stranger stalking me? My fear was doubled, redoubled.

5

After a few minutes, hearing nothing outside, we got up and went through the house, ducking below windows, and turned on lights in every room. Then I called 911 again. This time the dispatcher said she would get someone out as soon as possible, and for us to stay inside, to keep away from the windows. It took fifteen minutes for two deputies to get there.

We told them what happened, but when I began to describe the man I had seen, I realized that they didn't believe a word of it. The man was about five feet ten, 170 or 180 pounds, dressed in black from head to foot, a black cap. . . . Even his hands had been dark, I recalled: dark gloves.

"You saw that much from the window?" the older deputy asked. He was sixty-something, retirement age, overweight, bored, and disbelieving. His partner was about thirty, fair, with pale, lank hair and watery blue eyes.

"He was spotlit," I said, "and I was watching for him."

"And you didn't see anything?" he asked Casey.

"I couldn't," she said. "No windows in that darkroom."

The other one was making notes. He looked up and grinned at Casey, then at me. "You gals have a bit of a spat?"

My cheek was red from hitting the doorframe, and although he couldn't see it, my shoulder had another red blotch. Both would be purple by morning, no doubt. Angrily I said, "I bumped into the door on my way to the darkroom. It was dark in the house and I was running. I thought Casey was shot."

We showed them the setup in the darkroom; I showed them where the man had been standing when I saw him. At that moment, with the house lights on everywhere, the spot was lit, but before, it hadn't been. They looked at fir needles on the roof.

"And he just stood there while you looked him over?"

"Let's turn off the lights, let you see for yourself how dark it was back there," I said, growing angrier by the second. "He was taken by surprise."

"Calm down," the older one said. "Look at it this way. You're city girls, not used to the sound of the countryside at night, wildlife roaming around and such. Up talking late, hear strange noises, everything dark. Were you telling ghost stories, something like that?"

"Did you *boys* ever live in a big city?" Casey drawled. "You know, South Side Chicago, Phoenix, Watts? Guns going off every night? You get so you know what gunfire sounds like. Not strange at all. You know?"

The young one's grin became a grimace; he looked her up and down, then deliberately turned away. The other one said, "Not much more to do here. Why don't you take a little trip to the coast? Stay out there a few days, think about this. See if it doesn't relieve your minds." He was walking toward the door as he spoke, finished.

I was the kid who cried wolf, I thought. It would take a body—probably mine—to convince them that something was going on.

At the door the older one said, "We have your report from a couple of nights ago, and now this. Someone will come by in daylight and see if there's anything out there, or if bullets hit anything."

When they were gone, I looked at Casey, too angry even to speak, and she said, "What you need is a glass of milk and a magic pill, then hop into bed. You're ready to keel right over. God, it's nearly four and I haven't unpacked a thing yet."

"I don't want to go to sleep!"

"But you will. Then we'll talk. Tomorrow. Nope, later today. By the time I get some stuff unpacked and take a bath in that great tub, it will be daylight, and then I'll sleep."

"Casey, those bozos didn't believe—"

"Later, baby. Not a word until later. You talk, it'll be to yourself. I'll go get a pill."

She left me in the foyer, and after a moment I followed. Her room was next to mine. I stood in the doorway and watched her root through a bag that would have done justice to a pharmaceutical rep. I had seen her functioning for three days in a row without sleep, working on a computer problem, running on bennies or something, and then pop a different pill and sleep for twenty-four hours at a time. And she was right; I had to sleep.

When I woke up, it was nearly noon and my head was full of fuzz. I found Casey in one of the other bedrooms setting up her computer. Styrofoam packing material was all over the floor, and a sheet was draped over a chair. I had watched her line a box with the sheet, wrap the monitor in bubble wrap, and position it, cushioning it with plastic peanuts.

"Not a scratch on it," she said with satisfaction. "I spotted your grandfather's computer in his study, but it's such a dinosaur, I decided to get my own up and running. I'll update his before I leave."

"Coffee," I muttered.

I was sipping coffee with my eyes closed when she joined me in the kitchen. Trying to think was like trying to see an image on a television screen full of snow.

Casey remained silent until I emptied my cup and got up to refill it.

"Better?" she asked then.

"No. Have the police been here?"

"Come and gone. I told them I was your maid and you left orders not to be disturbed."

I opened my eyes and glared at her; she grinned. "You're clearing up," she said.

I made toast with whole wheat bread and scrambled an egg, keeping my coffee at hand, drinking it as I moved about the kitchen. Casey made a tuna sandwich on white bread with lots of mayonnaise. I used to shudder at her preferred diet.

"Okay," I said, eating. "Tell. What did they do? Did they find anything?"

"Well, how it goes, you're not really looking, not expecting to find much, and what do you know? That's what you come up with. They said to call if anything else happens, and I said we would certainly do that. Then I went looking." She pulled something from her pocket and handed it to me. "Spent cartridge," she said. "Forty-five-caliber handgun maybe. I'm not a real expert."

"Did you call them back?"

She gave me a pitying look. "And I kept poking around and came up with something else," she said. She pointed to the back door. On newspapers on the floor there was a plastic bag. "Take a look."

I got up and went to examine it. The bag was the kind that held the ice cubes sold in coin machines. Then comprehension hit me.

"He threw ice cubes on the roof!"

"They would probably sound like gravel, and they'd be gone without a trace in no time in this weather. I found the bag off the driveway up near the road. It was still wet inside. I brought it home to show you, but I'll put it back, in case he misses it and comes looking for it. No point in letting him know we're on to him."

I returned to my chair. "He's crazy. He's a psycho who wants to kill me. He doesn't need more reason than that. He wants to."

"Then why hasn't he?" she asked.

I considered it, then nodded. There had been opportunity enough. I came and went throughout the day, sometimes arriving back home after dark; he could well have waited and jumped me before I got inside.

"Let me tell you what I've been thinking," Casey said. "Treat it like a computer problem. You gotta get from A to Z; you know what Z is, but how to reach it is the puzzle. Along the way you begin ruling out things. Like, if he wanted to kill you, he could have done it already. Let's rule that out. You didn't recognize him, so we rule out anything personal. Not a rejected boyfriend, anything like that. Not even a stranger you snubbed. I know how your memory works. If you'd seen him before, you'd know it. Why ice cubes instead of gravel or rocks? So the Keystone Kops wouldn't believe you. No one would believe you."

"But he did shoot at me," I said.

"He didn't even hit the house," she said. "We looked. No bullet holes anywhere. And why didn't he keep shooting if it was his intention to hit you? That shot was a tightening of the screw, if I'm anywhere near right. The cops sure don't believe anyone fired a gun out here."

I nodded, my thoughts racing along with her words. "It has nothing to do with me," I said. "I just happened to get in the way. And he wants me to get back out. There's something in the house that he wants."

"That's how I figured it. I doubt that he has any intention of actually hurting you and bringing in the cops for a real investigation, maybe family coming, your grandfather returning. Problem is, why hasn't he come in and grabbed whatever he's after? Your grandfather was gone for hours every day, and you've been gone hours at a time. And if he has any savvy about wiring, he could get in. I could do it."

I thought about it. I didn't doubt she could do it. She had been taking things apart and putting them back together all her life. I believed she could wire a hot dog and make it bark.

"He might have gotten in to look for something at one time or another, and realized it would take longer. Maybe he'd want time to rip up floorboards, poke holes in walls, something like that."

Casey nodded. "I think that's getting from A to Z. He might need time, and he wouldn't want to be disturbed until he was done."

"We're back to skeletons in the closet," I muttered.

She began to gather up the dishes. "Question is," she said, going to the sink with them, "if there are bones hidden away somewhere, do we want to disturb them?"

"No!" I drew in a breath. "I think we're right, there's something here, but it's been here ever since Grandfather's been here. I don't care what it is. I don't want to know. It's his business, not mine."

"Right. Next question. What are we going to do about the iceman?" She came back to the table and sat down again. "He's still playing the Halloween spook, jumping out of bushes and yelling boo. But if you don't scare and run? Then what?"

After a moment she gave my hand a little squeeze and stood up. "Let's think about it. I'll take that bag back where I found it, and then back to the computer." She went to the door and paused. "Let's stick together for the next few days until we get a handle on this."

I did the dishes, then stood at the sink, gazing out the window at where I had seen the iceman the night before. There had been a plastic pail by him, I remembered. I hadn't mentioned it to the police when I realized how disbelieving they were. I had thought at the time, Insane. He brought his own gravel? His own ice cubes, I thought now. And that explained the dark hands, gloves.

Did he suspect I had seen him? If he did, and if he became desperate, he could still waylay me. I thought of duct tape and being bound in a closet, then shook my head. Not if I had seen him, could identify him. More likely, I would be killed and dragged inside while he went about finding whatever he was after. Not while Casey was there. If he knew someone was there. But maybe he was watching and did know that. She would stay through August, and then go on to CalTech. Then what?

I wandered through the house and found myself eyeing the walls, waist-high hickory paneling in the dining room, knotty-pine paneling in the family room, big cedar-paneled closets with shelves. . . . "Knock it off!" I muttered and forced myself to sit down in the family room and try to think what to do. Under my breath I cursed my grandfather for putting me in this position. I thought about writing to him, telling him I could stay through August and then had to leave. He hadn't called, but I had an address. That would take time, for him to either come home or get someone else to occupy his house. He wouldn't rely on an outsider. Aunt Lu? She probably would do it if no one else would. And she would be in exactly the same situation I was right now, I thought with dismay.

I had to find out who the iceman was, I decided. Maybe if I knew that much, I would know the next step. I suspected that I would tell Grandfather the truth, that someone was forcing me out in order to get in. Even as I thought it, I questioned it. What if he said there wasn't anything there, he didn't know what I was talking about? Then let the iceman have whatever it was he wanted, I thought, answering my own question. If he wrecked the house in his search, so be it.

But I wanted to know who the iceman was. If I wrote to Grandfather, I would have a name to give him.

Sometime later I heard Casey come into the family room and I opened my eyes.

"I thought you were sleeping," she said.

"Thinking. You said you could get through the security system. Could you take a window off the system?"

"Sure. Why?"

"Sit down. I'll tell you what's been going through my mind." When I got to the part about needing to know who the iceman was, she made a rude sound.

"A to Z," I said coldly. "Just listen. If you can get a window off the system, just one, the next time he comes around, I want to go out through it and to the road, find his car and get his license number. If I have that, we can learn whose car it is, and who he is."

She shook her head emphatically. "No way, José. That dude is packing. Remember?"

"I'll wait until he's on the other side of the house, and I'll stay behind trees. He won't even suspect anyone's out there. I thought about turning the system all the way off, but there's a little green light that shows on the outside of the window. He might notice."

"He might not even have a car. Maybe he uses a bike."

I shook my head. "He goes somewhere and buys ice. He has

the ice and the bucket, gloves, who knows what all? He comes by car." I stood up. "I'll show you which window you have to work on. Grandfather's bedroom, the one by the bathroom with the tub you covet."

The bedroom was next to the garage, the only bedroom on that side of the house. It was a corner room with windows on two sides. One side would be lit by the garage light, but the other would be dark, and it was only a few feet from the driveway and then the trees on the other side. While the iceman was throwing ice cubes on the roof over the kitchen in the rear of the house, I would get out the window and in among the trees on the front side.

Casey had a lot of objections. After meeting them all head-on, I finally said that if she wouldn't fix the window, I would turn off the whole system and take my chances that he wouldn't notice.

I showed her the route I would take; I had visualized the entire thing in detail. He would not see or hear a thing.

"We'll both go," she said at last. "You don't know where he parks, how far. You could go one way and never even come across his car. At the road we'll split up, one go left, one right. Wear dark clothes, a scarf for your head."

"We could meet back at the driveway and hide until he leaves and then head back to the house," I said. "Less risky." I feared that if she blundered about through the trees in the dark, she would fall, crash into something, or even run into him. I knew I would be okay, because there was a mental map in my head.

She hated the whole idea; she had hoped I would decide to take off when she did and be done with it. Well, I hated it, too, but I wanted to know who that joker was more than I hated finding out.

6

Casey worked on the window, and I took the screen down and put it in the garage. We went shopping for wire and a black scarf or something to hide my hair. We both had jeans and dark shirts. I bought black sneakers. Casey's were dark gray, but they were all right, we decided. Penlights, to use when one of us reached the car, two small notebooks, pencils . . .

Back at the house, we tested the window. No alarm.

We walked the route we would take to the road, and moved a log and a few rocks; then we did it again. The woods were full of remnants of blowdowns, rocks, and roots, and some of the rocks were dangerously sharp under thick layers of needles or barely hidden, but in either case possible threats. I was careful about the path we would follow. After night fell, we did it one more time without a light, and it was as easy as I had thought it would be. My mental map was just fine. Casey was doubtful.

"I'll hold your hand up to the road," I said. "Then we'll meet again at the end of the driveway and sit under a tree until he leaves. No problem."

There was a sliver of moon, and there was pale ambient light in the sky from the city, so it wasn't totally dark. Of course, under the trees the light failed, but if we kept near the driveway and didn't go wandering, it would be all right.

We would sleep in our clothes, we decided, one of us on the couch in the family room, the other in bed. Whoever heard him first would get the other. Then, as soon as he was out of sight of the window, out we'd go, across the drive, into the trees.

He didn't come that night.

"I think he got scared off," she said the next day, tired and grumpy.

I was just as tired, maybe grumpier. "Cat and mouse," I said. "He's playing with me. God only knows what his next trick will be, but first he'll get me more anxious and more frightened."

After she had her long bath and was dressed in shorts and a tank top, she was in a better frame of mind. "Let's decide what to do about meals," she said.

We made a shopping list for groceries and for cable, connectors, other components for Grandfather's computer. He would think the good fairy had come and waved her magic wand over it, Casey said. I hoped so; I had charged it all to his credit card. She made dinner that night: spicy pork, rice, green beans, sliced tomatoes. And by ten we were both yawning and ready to try to rest until four, when we could really go to sleep. She had the couch this time. When she got her jeans and black top on, she said with a grimace, "One more night in these rags and he'll smell us even if he can't see us."

At two in the morning I heard the pattering on the roof. Casey was already tying her shoes when I got to the family room. I led the way to Grandfather's room and we stood at the window, listening hard. It was like before, first one section of roof, out of hearing range, then another, and another. As soon as I thought he was on the other side of the house, I said, "Now."

I went first. I dropped to the ground, crouched a moment to listen, then raced across the bit of yard to the driveway, across it and to the trees. I watched Casey come after me, a long black shadow among shadows.

We didn't run, but moved with care, keeping a tree or two between us and the driveway until it curved and the house was no longer in a line with it. We stayed at the edge of the woods, afraid he might finish for the night and come up the driveway

with a flashlight. At the road I headed right, toward the strawberry farm, and she turned left.

About a quarter of a mile from the driveway there was a paved
area where the strawberry people parked a tractor, u-pick cus-
tomers could park, and trucks could enter the property to go to
a shed to pick up strawberry flats. I suspected that the iceman
was using that spot, and when I drew near, my suspicion was
confirmed. There was the tractor, with a dark low car next to it.
If the deputy sheriffs actually patrolled Mason Loop, there was
nothing to arouse their suspicions; the car appeared perfectly
normal parked there.

I approached cautiously in case there was an accomplice waiting. But the car was empty. I didn't try the door. No doubt it
was locked, and it might even have an alarm of its own. I did feel
the hood, still hot. Then I dug out my notebook and pencil and,
using my penlight no longer than it took to see the license plate,
I jotted down the number. Done.

"Gotcha, you son of a bitch," I murmured, and turned to
retrace my steps.

We had arranged a signal at the end of the driveway: a small
tree limb propped against a rock. Whoever got back first would
lay it flat. It was unmoved. I put it on the ground and stepped off
the driveway to listen and wait. The woods were quiet. Too
quiet, I thought uneasily. There was always some noise, something rustling, small creatures, tree toads, owls, possibly deer or
raccoons, until a person intruded and all movement stopped.

Also, she should have been back before me. She was to have
gone to a road sign, less than a quarter mile distant, then come
back. I had counted on her getting back first.

It was only about three hundred feet from the house to the
road, but the driveway curved so that the house itself was out of
sight of passersby, and Grandfather had left all the natural

growth free rein. The old noble firs that had not been cut were immense now, with a dense understory of straggly trees fighting for survival. And a lot of rocks.

Then I heard something moving. Not deer, I thought; they knew how to navigate in the dark. After checking the driveway to make certain no one was in sight, I darted across and stepped in among trees on that side. I didn't dare call Casey or show my light, but I could follow her movements as she bumped into branches or stumbled. I was certain it was she; the iceman had no reason to be in the woods there. He was free to use the driveway to come and go. We had not explored this side in the dark and I was not familiar with the ground; I made my way carefully, keeping close to the driveway, listening, tracking her movements as best I could, and we were both heading toward the house. What if she came across the iceman? I hurried, wishing she would just stop and sit down and wait. But she was moving even faster.

Then I heard the snorting peculiar to deer, followed by a scream and the sound of someone thrashing about. A man's guttural cry, another scream, and silence.

"Casey! Where are you? Turn on your light," I yelled, and turned on my penlight. The small beam of light was swallowed by the shadows of the trees, but I saw a flicker, another. As fast as I could, I ran toward it, using my own light in my immediate path. It was useless for more than that.

Finally I saw her, kneeling, holding the light that wavered, as if she had palsy. Sprawled on the ground was the iceman all in black.

I shone my light on her face, which looked zombie-gray in the feeble light; her eyes were enormous. "He's dead," she whispered.

And I thought, Dear God, she killed him!

7

Casey put her hand up to shield her eyes, and I lowered my light to the face of the dead man. The side of his head was visible, one eye wide open, deer in the headlights, frozen. Forever frozen. I nearly dropped the penlight and took a step backward, then another, until I bumped into a tree. Casey was on her feet by then, still shaking as if palsied. Her light danced up, down, here, there.

"We have to get back to the house," she said hoarsely.

I turned and through the trees could see the glow from the front-door light of the house. We were no more than twenty feet from the edge of the woods, the weed-choked yard.

We made our way back to the side of the house and went in by the same window we had used before. I was shaking too hard to key in the code for the electronic lock.

I didn't turn on a light until we reached the kitchen. We both sank down into chairs and drew in deep breaths.

"What happened?" I asked after my shaking became more manageable.

"I was heading back, but I kept looking around, scared, thinking of bears and wildcats. I saw headlights, and I thought it might be the sheriff coming, so I dodged into the woods, but then I thought they might flash a spotlight, just checking, and I went farther back and waited, but no one came and no one came." She was speaking almost too fast to follow the words, but gradually her shaking subsided and her face lost the gray dead look.

"The car must have turned somewhere," she said. "I started back for the road, but I couldn't find it. And I heard something really close, breathing hard, making a weird noise, and I started to run. Whatever it was went crashing by, and all I could think of was bear. Then I stumbled and fell, and I could hear something coming toward me, like it was coming back for me. I just stretched out and covered my head and prayed. God, I prayed!"

She stopped, and I said, "You screamed. I heard you."

"Not then. I was trying to be still so the iceman wouldn't hear me, or the bear wouldn't. I don't know what I was thinking. Then he was running and he tripped over my legs and he crashed down. That's when I screamed, and he made a terrible noise, rattling, yelling. I don't know. I heard you yell, and I turned my light on and saw him. Oh, God!" She covered her face with her hands, shaking hard again.

In a raspy voice she said, "I need a drink. Real bad."

"No!" When the police came, they couldn't smell alcohol. I went to get her a glass of water.

"We have to call the cops," she said then. "They'll arrest me, won't they?" She appeared oblivious of the tears coursing down her cheeks. She ignored the water I placed before her.

"No! It was an accident. You didn't do anything." But my first reaction had been that she had killed him. And they already thought she had hit me. I knew how some of the police officers would see it; I knew how one had seen us. I could imagine what his report had been: lesbian lovers, a violent black woman beating up on her little blond partner. And that deputy would probably think that now she was protecting her property, guarding her turf against a possible white admirer. What he believed, others would accept, at least until proved wrong. They would take it for granted that she had hit a rival with a rock or a club or something. Yes, they would arrest her—and probably me, too—if not tonight, then tomorrow or the next day.

Charges like that wouldn't stick, I told myself. We could clear ourselves eventually. But at what cost? How long would it take?

I had little to lose, but Casey's scholarship? Her parents would impoverish themselves defending her. And even if charges were made and ultimately dropped, there would be the cloud of suspicion. Her brilliant future could vanish without a trace. I had gotten her into this; I was responsible.

I took a sip of her water, then held her hands in mine. She was icy. "Casey, pull yourself together. We have to do something. You have to help me think what we can do."

"Call the cops," she said dully.

"No. Not yet." But what else? What choice did we have? I drew in a breath. "We can get rid of him and his car. If we take him somewhere and leave him, there won't be any reason for them to come here asking questions."

She shook her head. "You're talking crazy! We can't do something like that!"

"Goddamn it, Casey! Listen to me. We have to do something. You're right. They'll arrest you, and even if you get off eventually, you'll go to jail. No CalTech, no future. Think of your mother and father. They'll arrest both of us, a conspiracy or something. We have to get rid of him. And we can if you'll just snap out of it."

She wrenched free of my grasp, picked up the water and took a sip, then shook her head.

"He's dead!" I cried. "We can't help him, or hurt him. But maybe we can save ourselves. A to Z," I said desperately.

"We know what we have to do, but how? What are the middle steps?" I got up and found a box of tissues, put it down on the table. She wiped her eyes and blew her nose, then finished drinking the water, and I took a deep breath in relief. She was thinking.

"We can't drag him through the woods," she said, "and we can't carry him. We have to wrap him in something and drag that. The sheet I used for my monitor. I bought it in a thrift store in Berkeley years ago."

"Can we lift him into the trunk of his car?"

She nodded. And I knew we could. If mothers could carry fifty-pound children around all day, we could lift one man between us. Gradually, discarding many ideas along the way, we filled in the steps from A to Z.

"Not the Arboretum, too close to home," I said when she suggested we take him there and leave him. "The sheriff probably listed us as domestic violence and hysteria. We shouldn't give them cause to reconsider. A city park, someplace with fir trees. City police. No reason for them to compare notes."

At last, at nearly three-thirty we had made all the plans we could and it was time to get his keys and bring his car around. "What if there really is a bear?" she asked in a low voice.

"You heard deer," I said sharply. She had never been in real woods in her life, had never camped, had never seen a deer. "They come around at night, but if a human gets anywhere near, they just freeze and wait for him to leave again. If you get too close, they bolt. They must have scared that guy just about as much as they scared you."

I got yellow utility gloves fom the pantry, and my gardening gloves; we took a good flashlight and went back through the trees to his body. We both came to a stop, and then she dug her fingers into my arm, and we approached him. We had to roll him over to get to his pocket with the keys and his wallet. The bottom side of his head and his face were covered with blood. Fumbling with his wallet to get to his driver's license, I could feel nausea building, and Casey said, "Take deep breaths." I examined the license while she looked for the gun. "I can't find it," she said in a low, hoarse voice. "He must have dropped it."

We left the sheet by him and I ran up the driveway to the road and his car. The neighborhood was dark and still, with pale night-lights here and there, casting no light that far. What I feared most was meeting another car on the road as I drove his car back, but the road remained empty.

"The gloves," I whispered back by the body. "I told the police he was wearing gloves. We have to take them off." I closed my eyes and worked one glove off his limp hand while she got the other one.

We strained to get him wrapped in the sheet, and then to drag the bundle through the trees to the car. We rested before we started to lift his body. I thought we would not be able to do it, but straining, heaving, manhandling him, we got him up over the edge of the trunk and let him roll down. I realized we could not get him out again, and we changed our plan. We would have to leave him there. I remembered to wipe the hood of his car where I had felt it, and we were ready for the next step.

I drove the Accord, and Casey followed in his Mazda, and I was feeling more and more panicky. We had to hurry in order to be back before five, when I was certain the goat people got up to start their milking schedule by five-thirty. I didn't want anyone to see car lights turning in at the driveway at that hour. But I didn't dare speed. If we got stopped— I couldn't finish the thought. At Franklin Boulevard I turned left, went about half a mile to the overpass at I-5, and on the other side drove toward town on Thirtieth. There was no traffic until I was near the intersection with Hilyard. Casey kept a discreet distance behind me all the way.

The one car at the intersection drove on, and I kept going on Thirtieth without seeing anyone else. At Amazon Park I made my turn into the park and turned off my lights. Casey passed me and continued to the far end of the parking lot, then off the pavement onto the grass and under trees. She ran back to my car and got in. She was carrying a plastic bag, the kind ice cubes come in. She tossed it onto the backseat, and I took off. I didn't turn on the headlights for another block.

Neither of us spoke. I drove back by a different route, up Hilyard to Franklin, the route Grandfather took every day, and we arrived at the house at ten minutes before five.

"We did it," she said wearily when we were once more in the kitchen.

"Now you can have your drink."

"Coffee," she said.

There were still things we had to do. Obliterate the trail we had left in the woods, collect any bloody rocks, look for the plastic pail, find the gun . . . It would keep until daylight, less than an hour away by then.

I wrote down the name on his driver's license: Kevin Jasper. He had been thirty-three. I stared at the piece of paper and then burned it.

By seven-thirty we had done what we could, and we had not found a gun anywhere. Later, I thought, exhausted; we had to get a few hours' sleep. I fell across my bed, twitchy with fatigue and sleepless. I would take the rake out and rake weeds, rake needles. We had to find the gun. Had we taken care of everything else? Had we overlooked something? What if they came here? We hadn't even discussed what we would say if they did.

I kept seeing him wrapped in the sheet, like a mummy, and I wanted to scream. We should have called the police, explained. . . . We had panicked instead, and if they accused us now, it would be worse than if we had simply called for help. But the way that young deputy had looked at Casey and me, contemptuous, ready to believe we were lovers who had been fighting . . . I was so tight, I was starting to ache. The way we had dragged him, treated him like a sack of potatoes . . . I opened my fists and tried to relax my neck.

And the thought came unbidden: Had she told me the truth, that he stumbled and fell? The bloodiest rock we had found was jagged, fist-sized. Had she lashed out with it in a panic?

I didn't know, and I knew that I would never know for certain.

8

I was sore all over when I woke up from a few hours of dream-punctuated sleep that had not been restful. I started coffee, then took our clothes from the washer and tossed them into the dryer. Later, after another search for the gun, we would take a drive to one of the many rivers that converged on Eugene, dump the bloody rocks and a bunch of bloody fir needles into the water, and toss his gloves somewhere. And the next day we would go to the coast and leave my black sneakers in a rest area, the plastic pail in a different one, the utility glove and gardening gloves somewhere else.

When Casey came into the kitchen, she asked, "How are you?"

"Sore. You?"

"Sore. Tired."

Our search for the gun was as futile as our previous search had been. I thought, What if he had not had a gun in the first place? What if he had been simply a crazy, a stalker who never intended any real harm, just wanted to frighten me? Perhaps what we had heard and thought was a shot had been something else altogether. A branch snapping? A sudden loud house noise? I had taken Casey's word for it that we had heard gunfire, and her word that he had fallen on the sharp rock, I added miserably.

We watched the noon news: There was a brief account of finding the body of Kevin Jasper, survived by his father, Hollis Jasper, a local attorney, and his mother, Evonne Levinson, who resided in Denver. There were few other details yet. On the evening news they called it murder. "Savagely beaten to death," the newscaster intoned in a hushed voice. He had a few more details to add, some of them right, some wrong.

The late news had more. Jasper had lived with his mother and stepfather in Denver; friends were interviewed and expressed bewilderment and sorrow. His father was shown in a clip or two, drawn and harried, grief-stricken. Jasper had gone to Yale Law School, and in March had started to work for his father in his private practice. He was popular and respected by all.

As soon as the newscast ended, Casey got up and left, then returned with two sleeping pills. "One for you, one for me. We're both punch-drunk."

She did not say it, but we were also terrified. If they came here, I kept thinking, they would charge us both with murder. One look at us would be enough to close the case.

The next morning we got up very early, while it was cool, and took turns pushing the lawn mower over the rough ground, and raking the weeds once more. We had crushed dead and dry weeds when dragging the shrouded body through them; we might have buried his gun under them. We didn't find it.

We drove to the coast and got rid of the rest of the incriminating evidence as we had planned, then we sat on a log and gazed at the ocean. It was almost smooth, the waves low and not crashing at all. The many logs on the beach bespoke of the furious energy of other days when gale winds howled.

"It's shitty, isn't it?" Casey said, breaking a prolonged silence.

I nodded. "He was thirty-three years old." A group of kids came by, wading in the breaking waves. One of them was carrying the plastic bucket I had left half a mile up the beach.

Looking away was little help. The same images were in my head: the mummylike body, the bloody rocks, the lifeless hands, the plastic bucket that still had water in it when we found it. The same thoughts kept coming back with the monotony of the waves: It's my fault. I got us into this.

"Thirty-three," Casey said after a moment. "Loved by all. All sunshine and bright smiles, no shadows in his life. Except he was stalking you, or trying to scare you into a heart attack or something, or get you out of the house in the middle of the night."

I began digging in the sand with a bit of driftwood. "I think you should pack up your stuff, go on down to CalTech," I said, watching sand fall back into the holes as I made them. "As soon as you have an address, I'll send everything."

"You going to hang out here?"

"Yes. I guess I'll start poking around closets, looking for those skeletons, after all." Unless there was something to find, something in the house that he had been after, we had been responsible for the death of someone who might have been harmless.

"I guess I can hang around and help you poke," Casey said. She put her hand on my arm. Her hand was cool. "Is it always this cold on the beach here?"

It was about seventy, twenty degrees cooler than in the valley. I stood up. "I don't want you to stay. If there's something in that closet, it doesn't concern you. My family's skeleton. I keep thinking, Jasper was too young. Grandfather started his house-bound life years before Jasper was even born. But whatever it is, if anything, he must have known about it. And there must be someone else who knows, someone who told him."

"And that someone else might pick up where he left off," she said, getting to her feet. "Baby, we're in this shit together. Real deep. I'll stay awhile."

Reluctantly I nodded. That was exactly where my chaotic thoughts kept leading. If there was something, someone else could be involved. Maybe someone else would try to finish what Jasper had started. Until we knew something, almost anything about what was going on, maybe it was better if we did stay together. Casey could be at risk now, too.

"Let's go," I said. "You're shivering."

When we got back to the car, Casey headed for the driver's side. "I'll drive. You talk. Fill me in on your family. Okay?"

I tossed her the keys, and we got in and started the drive back to Eugene.

I had told Casey a lot about my family over the years we roomed together, but this time I tried to keep some sort of chronology, and I had to stop when I realized there were gaps, unanswered questions. Perhaps I had never asked the right questions.

"What?" Casey asked, keeping her eyes on the winding road over the Coast Range. There was a lot of traffic and the road was almost zigzag in places, and steep.

"I just realized something," I said. "I always thought my grandmother took off when Tess was an infant, but she had to have been older. She was born in 1946, when Grandfather was still going to Tulane. He got his bachelor's from UCLA in 1948." I knew that very well. Tess had dragged out various diplomas from time to time to emphasize how little I was trying. "I don't know when he switched or why," I said. "Anyway, on to Princeton, and a Ph.D. in 1952. They came to Eugene after that. She had to have been six. And I think Grandmother didn't leave for a year or two. Tess was seven or even eight by then."

Once when I asked about our Louisiana relatives, Tess had said she didn't think we had any. She could barely remember her mother, she had said sorrowfully; she had a vague memory of a beautiful woman, that was all. After leaving, her mother had never contacted her.

I had been filled with bitter hatred for the mother who could abandon her daughter that way, and a touch of fear. Tess was gone so much of the time. She had married at eighteen, while a freshman in college, and had continued in school during both pregnancies and afterward. For years she had kept taking classes and collecting degrees, and a nanny looked after my brother and me. While Tess took summer courses in various universities, Ben and I had stayed for weeks or even months at a time with Aunt Lu.

I shook my head to clear it, then said, "The point is that whatever happened in my family, it was before Kevin Jasper was born. The pattern was well in place long before that. It could have been something from Grandfather's army days, or at one of the universities he attended. Or even after he married my grandmother. Maybe he didn't want to get married but had to. My mother was an eight-and-a-half-pound premature baby," I added.

Casey said, "Ah."

"But if it was any of those things, how could it be connected to Kevin Jasper?"

"Was Tess afraid of her father?" Casey asked after a minute or two.

"Of course not. Why do you ask?"

"Well, from outside the circle, it looks like she ran away from home and got married at eighteen and has been running away from home ever since."

I thought about it, then nodded. I wondered if she had talked about it with her therapist. If so, it had not helped; she was still running.

I told Casey about my grandfather's inability to remember faces and names. "It made him seem aloof, detached and uncaring, and I was put off, intimidated even, but never afraid. You know what I mean. I just didn't know how to act with him, so I didn't interact with him any more than I had to. But basically he's a kind man, a gentle man. And he's generous. I doubt he ever gives money a thought. I really believe Shakespeare is the only thing he cares about deeply. Probably nothing else on earth would have made him leave home."

We were winding down the last curve in the Coast Range, and soon the broad, fertile Willamette Valley would stretch out before us with its vast fields of ripening grasses and many orchards. The temperature rose degree by degree with each passing mile.

"I want to stop at Fred Meyer's on the way home," I said. "A big floor fan. See if we can cool down the house before we lock up. And I want graph paper, a twenty-five-foot steel tape, a ruler, pencils. I'll draw a house plan, measure rooms, measure the outside dimensions, see if there's space unaccounted for. Step one."

"While you're scoping out the house," Casey said, "I'll see what all I can dig up about Kevin Jasper."

"Library?"

"Computer. You'd be amazed at what you can find if you know how to look."

If I was amazed at what she could do on a computer, she was equally amazed at what I did on the kitchen table with graph paper, pencil, and ruler.

"You did it from memory?" she said, studying the house plan I had drawn.

The dimensions were not exact yet, but close enough for a start. Every room, every built-in cabinet, every door and window was in its proper place. I had indicated with broken lines where the access doors were to the space above the ceiling and the crawl space under the house. Ben and I had investigated both years before. Spiders, crawly things, dust, maybe mice . . . I did not want to go into either space again, above or below. But I would if necessary, I added to myself.

I did not believe we would find anything in either one; they were too accessible. Put on a dust mask, wear gloves, plan to get filthy and head in, pick up stuff, get out. Too easy. What I was hoping for was a secret room behind a closet; rooms with a too-thick wall between them; a hidden button that would swing part of the fireplace open. . . . All the images were from books or movies. I hated that.

Thursday's newspapers had a picture of Kevin Jasper, and the caption: DID YOU SEE THIS MAN ON MONDAY NIGHT?

His father, Hollis Jasper, was quoted as saying they had dinner together at seven-thirty; he had had a little work to take care of afterward, and had gone into his study. Kevin had been watching television and had said nothing about going out later. In fact, his father had not known he had left the house until the police arrived to give him the tragic news. His son had no enemies, no steady girlfriend. He had not been robbed. There was no earthly reason for anyone to have slain him so brutally.

The newspapers were spread on the kitchen table when Mrs. Hawkins arrived to do her weekly cleaning. I had forgotten all about her. When I introduced Casey, Mrs. Hawkins nodded.

"Good you have company. It can get lonesome out like this." At the kitchen she paused and glanced at the newspapers. "Such a fine-looking young man. At first I thought I knew him, but I didn't. Not with him being a lawyer. You don't want to try to cut those weeds with a lawn mower. I'll send my boy over with a weed whacker. That's what it takes, a heavy-duty weed whacker. Every year I tell Mr. Landorf he can't let those weeds go until the fire season starts, but he waits—"

"What did you mean, you thought you knew him?" I said, motioning to the newspapers.

"Oh, he looks like the telephone man that came last spring. March, I think. The daffodils over at the flower farm were blooming so pretty. Two, three rows all blooming. He said there was trouble on the line and he had to check out the phones here. I stayed with him every minute he was in the house, I can tell you. Mr. Landorf nearly had a fit, but I told him that man was never out of my sight, not even a second. See, I stopped to buy some daffodils and Mr. Landorf acting up like that made me kind of remember it."

"That man? Jasper?" I said.

"No, no. Like I said, at first that's what I thought when I saw that picture, but he was a lawyer, not a telephone repairman. I thought I might do the outside windows today. I haven't touched them since heaven knows when."

He came in March to look over the house, I thought. He must have learned that Grandfather was leaving for England. The story had been reported in the university newspaper. I had been trying to convince myself that he was a pervert, a stalker, that he had targeted me. Or even that he had been a student Grandfather had flunked, one with a serious grudge. But he had gained entrance to the house in March! His father's statement said that Jasper came to Eugene the first of March and started working for him. Had it been his first priority to case my grandfather's house?

I couldn't do my measurements with Mrs. Hawkins around, and I felt suddenly that I had to get out of that house altogether for a time.

I collected Casey. "More sightseeing," I said.

"We sort of knew he must have gotten in one time or another," Casey said in the car when I started to drive.

"I know. But this was right after he got to Eugene. He already knew enough to come out here with his repairman act and have a look around. He was prepared to come here, to hang around Eugene as long as he had to. The article in the school newspaper about Grandfather's lecture series must have seemed like a godsend to him, and he made his plans and came back."

After a moment Casey let out a long breath and said, "Shit."

9

For the next few days I prodded and poked, pried and prowled through closets and the garage. I measured rooms and outside dimensions and drew another house plan, to scale this time with allowances for walls and the stonework of the fireplace. I crawled under the house, and in the space between the ceiling and the roof, then under beds to examine the flooring. I studied paneling inch by inch, searching for any imperfection, a high spot, or a low one, mismatched grain. I moved books and examined shelving, the walls behind shelves. I cleared the mantel and tried to move the two-inch slab of oak itself. I moved towels and blankets and pillows in the linen closet and found real linen bedding, yellowed with age; tablecloths and napkins that had been tucked away for eighty years possibly; hand-embroidered and crocheted doilies and spreads; a cigar box full of old browned toothbrushes with curling bristles that fell out with a touch.

I cursed Yorick for maintaining silence throughout.

Then I tackled the two storage rooms. One was seven feet by twelve, the other eight by nine, both crammed with boxes, a loom, a treadle sewing machine, a broken lamp, a pressure cooker . . . things that hadn't been used in generations, but never discarded. Grandfather never threw anything away.

As I searched, I came across snapshots: in a cigar box on a closet shelf, in cardboard boxes, some loose among the books, others loose here and there. I had looked at them at first, but then started just tossing them all into a box to be sorted later. Now I was emptying cartons, refilling them, not always the same way. Grandfather's college papers and books had been put on top of a pile of rags; there were magazines mixed with old newspapers that cracked and split when I moved them. Broken toys mixed in with plastic spoons and forks and paper plates. Jigsaw puzzles and high-school textbooks . . . I was accumulating a large pile of stuff to be hauled away and dumped. Old toothbrushes! Newspapers from 1960! Boxes of rags and scraps of material!

Calendars, I thought in disgust, dumping another box. And more scraps of fabric. More loose snapshots.

Then I sat back on my heels and considered the box of snapshots I had been gathering. My mother as a child, Aunt Lu and her sons, Ben and me, Grandfather, people I didn't know . . . And not a single picture of my grandmother, I realized.

I picked up the box and carried it out to the dining-room table and dumped it, then started going through the pictures again more carefully. Old cars, a horse, a girl—Aunt Lu?—with a wheelbarrow full of what looked like potatoes . . .

Casey came into the room while I was at it. "Anything?"

I shook my head. Casey had been having a lot more success than I. She was compiling a complete dossier, she said, on Kevin Jasper, and his father as well. She had spent one afternoon at the university library, hours at the public library, and how many hours at the computer I couldn't even guess.

"I just realized," I said, "that there's nothing in this house relating to my grandmother. Not a scrap. Not a picture, or anything else."

"When did you say she took off?"

"I think it was 1954, or about then. Why?"

"Curious. You said she was from New Orleans? Hollis Jasper turned up in Eugene in 1954, and he hailed from New Orleans. Curious."

I thought about what she had told me before: Hollis Jasper had gone to Tulane, on to Yale Law School, to Eugene, where he set himself up in a private practice that seemed to involve things like wills, trusts, civil matters, and not many of them. He was independently wealthy from an inheritance. He got married, had a son, divorced. Tulane, New Orleans, eventually Eugene, just like my grandfather. And my grandmother had come from and returned to New Orleans.

A few minutes later I called Aunt Lu. I had to talk to her; she had been there when my grandmother came and when she left. No one had ever told me any details of that period, and Tess had said she didn't remember a thing about it, she had been too young. But Aunt Lu would know about those days. I would fly up to Seattle, return the same evening. By car it was a five- or six-hour trip, depending on traffic, and I didn't want to leave Casey alone overnight.

Aunt Lu was as effusive and happy to hear from me as I had expected. We chatted a minute or two, then I said, "I told Grandfather I'd organize his books, catalog them, and I decided to clear out a lot of junk along the way. You wouldn't believe the kind of stuff I keep coming across. Old broken toys, used toothbrushes, rags . . . and a lot of snapshots scattered all over the house."

"Rags? What kind of rags?"

"Scraps of fabric, prints, just bits and pieces of this and that."

I heard her draw in a breath. "You found the flour sacks!" Then she said briskly, "Dear, don't throw away a thing yet. I'll come down and visit. Tomorrow—no, make that Friday. I'll drive down on Friday and spend a day or two with you."

I started to ask what was so great about boxes of rags, but I really didn't care. Before she could go on, I said, "Aunt Lu, I can't find a single picture of my grandmother, not a snapshot or anything. Do you have her picture? I'd really like to see what she looked like."

"I'm sure I do. I'll bring my photo album. Remember, don't throw away a scrap of anything." She laughed. "I can't believe they're still there. Friday, dear. Late in the afternoon. I want to miss the morning rush hour."

When Aunt Lu arrived on Friday, she greeted Casey like an old friend, and hugged me fiercely. "You said Casey, and I thought you had a boyfriend here," she said with a little giggle. "I wanted to check him out. I mean, 'Casey, computer genius,' what else was I to think?"

"I'm afraid Casey has your old room, and I have Tess's, so we aired out Randy's room for you. Okay?"

She waved it away. "Fine, fine. Anything. Now, where are those rags you talked about?"

63

I had put all the scraps of fabric into one box, and now I emptied it onto the dining-room table, and we sat there while she fingered the material and talked about it.

"See, before World War One, way back before, cloth was rare. Fine cotton cloth like this, I mean. See how closely woven it is? Two hundred denier? So the flour wouldn't sift through. Big fifty-pound sacks of flour or sugar. And the manufacturers knew that the packaging was as valuable as the contents, and they used cotton prints." She was handling a piece of blue cloth with yellow daisylike flowers, a faint smile on her lips, a distant look on her face. "I remember how my grandmother would rip the seams open, wash the sacks by hand and iron them, and treat them like treasures. Shirts, shirtwaists, little girls' dresses, aprons, bibs and tuckers . . . The women would get together and swap, looking for good matches, for colors that would go together, and every scrap was preserved for quilts. When the shirts or whatever got outgrown, they would rip the seams out and make something else, and eventually add the material to the quilt box."

That night and for the next two days I learned about the tumultuous two years that my grandmother had lived with Grandfather in the Landorf house. It was a discursive, rambling dialogue; she kept veering off the subject I wanted to pursue, I kept edging her back.

Lu had been in San Diego when her father called to say that her mother had been taken ill with meningitis. Lu was six months pregnant, and Johnny was a toddler, but she got on the train for Eugene and arrived home in time to bury her mother. And while there, she was given the devastating news about her husband: His ship had been lost at sea.

She didn't talk about her own grief, but about her father's. "He never got over it," she said, shaking her head. "Benjamin came home when he got out of the army, but he only stayed a couple of weeks. I don't think Dad realized he had been in the war; he kept saying Anna Marie would be back soon, things like that. And Benjamin talked about this wonderful, beautiful, magical girl he had corresponded with, and had met finally. He went back to New Orleans, and a few months later he called to say they were married. Tess was born six months later."

Benjamin came home for his father's funeral; he had been at UCLA by then, but Geneva didn't come with him. It would have been too hard, because of the child, he had explained. They agreed that Lu should stay in the house with her boys; there was never any talk of selling it, dividing the money between them, and he had returned to Los Angeles, then on to Princeton.

"Did he say why he changed schools? Why he left Tulane?" I asked.

She shook her head. "I asked, and he said there were better teachers, something like that. Anyway, he came back in June of 1952, and I got to meet Geneva at last. She was very beautiful, just like he said. You look more like her than like your mother. She had gray eyes like yours, and the same color hair, not honey gold like Tess's, but more flaxen, I think they call it."

Aunt Lu was gazing through time, I suspected, as her eyes became unfocused and an absent look changed her expression. She shook herself and said briskly, "Geneva had a pouty look, and she was not content here. She hated Oregon, hated this house, everything. That first summer Benjamin worked with the carpenters to build the garage and then he outfitted the darkroom and locked himself away for hours at a time, and she roamed through the house like a possessed soul, going through closets, boxes, drawers. I asked her once what she had lost, maybe I could help her find it, but she said nothing. She was bored. She might die of boredom, she said, or go mad. And they fought. Or she did. She wouldn't or couldn't do housework, cook, do laundry, any of the things a household needs, and she made no effort. They both begged me to stay and help out, and I knew it was a mistake, they needed their own space, but then I would look at Tess, her hair dirty and stringy, no breakfast unless I made it, no lunch, just neglected, and I stayed on.

"After Benjamin got his teaching position, things were worse than ever. He didn't have tenure for several years, and they over-worked him terribly, but he loved teaching and studying. Geneva began to drink. Sometimes she would meet him at the door when he got home and start screaming at him, and I could hear them into the night. Every weekday morning the children walked out to the road and caught the school bus, and we'd be home alone until three-thirty. She would start talking early in the day and go on and on about New Orleans, Mardi Gras, the French Quarter, the restaurants, parties, soirees, afternoon teas. And she talked about Bobby Lee, her little brother. It was Bobby Lee this and Bobby Lee that for hours at a time. I never knew before then how homesickness could really be an illness, but I think she became quite ill."

"You didn't like her, did you?" I asked once when she paused, reflecting or remembering.

She shook her head. "I tried to. But I saw her as a selfish, self-centered, spoiled woman. She was a racist. But I suppose that was how she was brought up, and it seemed as natural to her as breathing. She talked about their servants one time, quadroons, or even octoroons, she said; they wouldn't abide anyone too dark in their house, because they stole things. The way she talked, if you didn't know better, you would have thought she was talking about livestock. I told her never to say anything like that to me again, I didn't want to hear about it. I suppose I showed some of the Landorf temper that day. I tried not to, nearly bit my tongue in two more than once, because I felt sorry for her much of the time. She was so unhappy, like the pea princess forced to sleep on a bed of rocks."

"Why did she stay?"

Aunt Lu patted my hand. We were in the family room at the moment, having iced coffee and cookies she had made earlier that day. Casey was in her room doing something on the computer; she always discreetly found something compelling to do when Aunt Lu and I started our family gossip.

"You and your young friend, growing up these days, have no inkling of what it was like in the forties, through the fifties, even later. I remember a woman who was drummed out of our church when I was young. She was a divorcée, a scandalous, wicked woman polluting decent folks. The minister preached about her sin, and I asked my mother what she had done. She wouldn't talk about it. There was a stigma, as visible as the red *A* worn on the breast. Geneva and I grew up in different levels of society, but we shared the same culture. It's absorbed through the skin, the pores, the food you eat, the air you breathe. You don't even know what you're taking in when you're surrounded by your own culture. But then she did leave, remember."

Casey came to the door then and said, "Two questions, Aunt Lu. Do you like spicy food?"

"Yes. Well, I guess I should ask how spicy. Thai food can be a bit much."

"Not Thai. Chicken and rice the way my ma makes it. Just spicy enough."

Aunt Lu nodded. "Next question?"

"Do you drink wine?"

"Well, I don't sneak it around in a little brown paper bag, but I've been known to drink wine with meals."

"All set. I'll start dinner," Casey said with a wave of her hand.

"I like her a lot," Aunt Lu said after Casey wandered off; her face was all crinkly in smile wrinkles. "She called me Aunt Lu."

"I think she noticed that you didn't bat an eye when you met her," I said.

"Because she isn't a man?"

I kept being reminded of why I loved Aunt Lu. I grinned and said, "What about the day Grandmother took off?"

"Let's look at the pictures," she said. "I took a few that day." She pulled a photo album into her lap and opened it, started to leaf through the pages of pictures all carefully labeled and held neatly in place with little corner tabs. "None of the two years she lived here," she said, pausing, then going on to another page. "She said she was turning into an old woman and didn't want any pictures to remind her. Ah, here we are."

She pointed to a snapshot of three young men standing by a station wagon. "Bobby Lee, Holly, and Tadpole," she said. "And this is Geneva and Bobby Lee."

I studied the pictures. Even in the overexposed print, she was very lovely; her hair looked white in the sunlight, not flaxen, and Bobby Lee's hair was just as white. Geneva was laughing. Her hair was long, and she was dressed in a flowing dark skirt and a peasant blouse. Her waist looked to be twenty inches, cinched tight with a wide belt in the style of the fifties. She looked like a girl, not a woman over thirty.

Bobby Lee towered over her, and appeared massive, like a linebacker, but he looked enough like her to be unmistakably her brother. He was grinning broadly, his arm around her shoulders.

"All the time she was here, she wrote to him at least once a week, sometimes more often. He wrote back, not quite as often, but it was a regular correspondence, and that day they just showed up, he and his two friends. It was the first day of summer vacation."

She had promised the children she would take them out for lunch and a movie to celebrate the end of the school year, she said, but Geneva's excitement was contagious, and they wanted to stay home and get in the station wagon, maybe even get a ride in it.

"She kept screaming, 'Why didn't you tell me you were coming? I could have had a heart attack! How's Mama, Papa? You drove all the way across the country? You've grown another six inches!' She kept going on and on, and they all went inside the house and made a big pitcher of lemonade, and they had brought a bottle of rum. Then they went into the family room and closed the door."

She sighed. "The kids were so disappointed. No one had heard their hints about a ride; no one had made a fuss over Tess, and Geneva seemed to have forgotten she even had a daughter. So I took them out for hamburgers and stuffed them and we went on to the movie.

"When we got back, they were still in the family room, whooping with laughter, shrieking, having a party. They sounded drunk. I had just started to string beans when Benjamin got home. I thought he would have a real heart attack when I told him who was there. He turned as white as a ghost and grabbed a chair back, but he didn't say a word and just turned and walked out. I thought he was going to the family room, but he didn't. He went to the darkroom and closed himself up there for a time; then he went to the family room, and the laughing stopped like turning off a faucet, and real screaming and yelling started. No one had ever heard Benjamin roaring that way, but he was yelling for them to get out of his house and stay out, or he'd call the police and have them all arrested.

"I sent the children to their rooms and stayed in the kitchen, but I could hear yelling and doors slamming, footsteps pounding through the hall, Geneva in hysterics.

69

"I could hear some of what they were yelling about, something Benjamin had that they were demanding he hand over. I don't have any idea what it was. Anyway, he yelled that if anything happened to him or his family, then it would turn up and not a day before, and they stormed out and went roaring off in the station wagon."

She stopped, gazing at the picture of the laughing Geneva and her grinning brother.

"Did she leave with them?"

"No. Not that night. I fed the children in the kitchen. Benjamin went to his study and slammed the door and didn't come out for hours. And she went to the bedroom and slammed that door. It's a wonder they didn't knock the house off its foundation that night, all that door slamming." She shook her head. "Now and then she would go to the study, open the door and yell something at him, then *slam,* and back to the bedroom. I made sure the kids all went to bed, and I went on to my own room. I don't think any of us slept much that night. And the next morning she started to throw her belongings into suitcases. She yelled at Tess to pack some clothes, and Benjamin told Tess she wasn't going anywhere. She was crying. Geneva screamed that she would get a lawyer. No one could separate a mother and her child. At that time you really couldn't. Not a court in the land would give custody to the father, I guess. And he said he'd see Tess dead and buried before he let her go with Geneva and Bobby Lee. I'd had enough by then. I told the kids to get jackets and a change of shoes, and we'd go to the coast. And that's what we did. When we got home again, Geneva was gone. He said she had left with Bobby Lee. They were going back to New Orleans. And there wasn't a picture of her, a hairbrush, a slipper, not a trace that she had ever lived in this house."

"Oh, my God," I said, letting out a long breath when she stopped again. "No good-bye or anything?"

She shook her head. "A week or two later a postcard came to Tess, gushing with 'I love you and think of you all the time,' things like that. Benjamin didn't want to give it to her, but I insisted. Tess looked at it, and tore in up and threw it away without a word. I don't think she ever mentioned her mother again."

10

Casey's chicken and rice was wonderful, just spicy enough, as she had said. She warned us that a side dish of salsa might be a bit too much, but Aunt Lu and I both tried it and then added it to our plates. Aunt Lu talked throughout dinner about growing up there in that house.

Benjamin and their father used to go to a neighbor's place, where the strawberry farm was now, and clean the barn, then hitch up the neighbor's old horse and haul a load of manure home to spread on the garden, and that signaled that it was done for that year. She was so relieved then. No more hoeing or weeding or picking tomato worms off plants . . .

"There were things we just left in the ground, rutabagas, carrots, turnips, and we dug them when we needed them. We were never hungry, no matter how hard things were; we ate well. Mom canned and preserved, and we stored what was left."

"Where did you store anything?" I asked, thinking of the old icebox that was in one of the storage rooms.

"In the root cellar. Cabbages, apples, pears, beets, potatoes . . ."

I felt my pulse quicken. "Ben and I never came across a root cellar."

She laughed. "I guess you didn't. It was right next to the

kitchen, where the darkroom is now. Gone, just like the garden. Benjamin had no use for it. See," she said, sipping her wine, obviously contented and full, "Benjamin and Dad dug it themselves, and when they hauled river rocks to build the fireplace, they brought in enough to line the root cellar. After all that digging and hauling, Benjamin hated that cellar with a passion you wouldn't believe."

"Excuse my ignorance," Casey said then, "but what the devil is a root cellar?"

Aunt Lu laughed again. "A glorified hole in the ground. They dug it and put a layer of river sand on the bottom, and Dad got hold of some juniper logs to roof it over, tar paper on top and then more dirt on top of that. It stayed cool all summer and didn't freeze in the winter, perfect for storing produce. They lined the walls with river rocks and made a few shelves with rocks and juniper logs. Things stayed just moist enough to keep well. No water seeped in."

"How did you get in it?" Casey asked. "Sounds like a grave to me."

"There was a top door not covered with dirt. Open it, prop it up, and two or three steps down on rocks, and there you were. It wasn't very high, six feet or less. Mom usually went down and brought up a basket of this or that. Or I did. I hated it, too. Too dark and scary."

I could tell that Casey's interest had taken a sharp turn, just as mine had. She stood up abruptly. "I'll make coffee."

"Not for me," Aunt Lu said. "Spoil the pleasant buzz in my head? No, thank you. Let's have a look at those pictures you found," she said to me.

We spent the rest of the evening looking at pictures and listening to her reminisce, but as soon as she kissed us both good night, Casey and I pored over my house plans.

"Here," I said, pointing to the darkroom. "Monday, after she leaves, we'll find that damn hiding place. Wanna bet?"

"No way. But that's got to be it."

On Sunday we went out and picked blackberries, and that night Aunt Lu made dinner, with blackberry pie for dessert. I had not had anything that good since the last time she made one. She talked about the quilts she planned to make for the grandchildren, and one for me, for finding the pieces, she said.

"There's not enough for that many," I said.

"We'll see. A flower design in the center, against a nice background, maybe. Here, I'll show you what I mean." She looked at my pad of graph paper. "May I?"

"Sure." I pushed it across the table to her.

She sketched a square with a mandala design centered on it. "Something like that. All different, of course."

She could always draw anything, I recalled; that was her Landorf gift. Flowers, paper doll clothes, animals, castles . . . She should have become an artist. I imagined the quilts she intended to make, and I decided she had become an artist.

We loaded her car that night, the quilt pieces, no longer scraps or rags, but quilt pieces now; a few pictures she wanted; a pail of blackberries. She would make jam, she said. She gave me the two pictures of my grandmother.

On Monday morning she left. The moment the car was out of sight Casey and I hurried to the darkroom.

It was stifling, although the weather had cooled magically by then. Still, the closed-up room in midsummer was like an oven. The first thing I did was turn on the exhaust fan; another switch turned on air intakes, two of them, with some kind of baffle system that let air be moved into the room without admitting any light. That made it more bearable, and in a few minutes even comfortable.

Opposite the door was an electric heater, like a small furnace. Then cabinets along that wall, with shelves over them, continued around the corner, and on to two shallow sinks and more built-in cabinets. To the left of the door was a light table. The floor was concrete, like the garage, with a heavy-duty rubber mat down the center. We started with the mat, rolling it up to inspect the floor. Brittle with age, it crumbled as we rolled it. Under it was just more concrete, with minute, hairline cracks, but nothing to indicate an opening was possible. We opened cabinets and examined the bottoms, saw how they were fastened to the walls with nails or screws. They weren't going anywhere. The sinks were fixed by plumbing, immovable. The light table was all that was left.

The table was gray metal, with the light box on top, a translucent plastic cover that had turned yellow and looked brittle, and two shelves, one at the floor level, the other two-thirds of the way up. It could not have weighed much, I thought, trying to lift it. The tubular legs were riveted to a metal base that was bolted to the floor. Immovable.

Casey said in a deflated toneless way, "Good try."

I nodded, turned off fans and the light, and we left the darkroom and closed the door behind us. Good try. I would finish up in the storage rooms that day, and then what?

No longer a hot news item, the death of Kevin Jasper had faded into oblivion. We had no way of knowing what the police investigators were doing, what they had learned, what they suspected. And more and more often the thought that I had been responsible for the death of a crank, possibly a pervert, but also possibly just a harmless nut, rose in my mind with meticulously envisioned details of the night he died. He had not deserved the treatment after death that we had bestowed upon him, treating his body like a piece of trash to be disposed of.

Back in the kitchen I put on coffee, and Casey said, "He must have dumped whatever it was into the grave and then built the garage and darkroom over it all, covered it with concrete, done with it." I was jerked back from the night of Jasper's death to my grandfather.

"I don't think so," I said, getting out coffee mugs. "Sit down; I'll tell you what Aunt Lu told me about that last day or two before Grandmother took off."

We drank coffee and I filled her in with family gossip. "So, rushing around in a rage, she must not have packed everything of hers. No one could in that short a time. I mean, pictures, a little makeup, a sweater, something, or more likely a number of things must have been left. But they were all gone when Aunt Lu got home that day. Grandfather cleared out everything, and he put it all somewhere. I think he had access to his secret hiding place. And what he told Bobby Lee, that if anything happened to him, stuff would turn up and not before that. I just don't believe it's buried under six inches of concrete. He had to get to it somehow."

We looked at the two pictures: Geneva with Bobby Lee; Bobby Lee, Holly, and Tadpole. Both prints were overexposed. "Holly," I said. "Hollis Jasper? Probably. That's when he came; he stayed and Grandmother left."

I scowled at the picture: two big football-player types, a shorter, slightly built man standing between them, all grinning idiotically, telling me nothing.

Casey picked up the picture of my grandmother and Bobby Lee. "You look like her," she said. "She's more Marilyn Monroe, but that's makeup and the way she's dressed. And she knows how to pose and make pretty for the camera. I bet she was a terrible flirt."

"Probably. She was a genuine southern belle. Let's knock off for the rest of the day, take a little jaunt up over McKenzie Pass. I'll show you some Oregon scenery."

"Deal," Casey said promptly. "I'll shut down the computers."

"I'll put together some lunch stuff. Wear good hiking shoes. And bring a sweater or something."

I began to get out tuna fish and lettuce, a tomato; then I paused, seeing in clear detail the light table again. There was something nagging, something elusive that I had seen and paid no attention to, something that now was insisting on attention. The shelves, one about two-thirds of the way up, one at floor level . . . Why a shelf at floor level? I closed my eyes to get a better picture of the tubular legs, and I had it. About a third of the way up there were small holes, as if the bottom shelf could be positioned there instead of as low as it was. The shelves were metal, with about an inch turned down, rounded at the corners to make a snug smooth fit against the legs. And a small knob. The end of a screw or rivet? But why at floor level? The turned-down edge of the lower shelf touched the metal plate beneath the table. Why bolted to the floor, when obviously the table had been made lightweight, as if to make it easy to move around?

I put down the tomato I was holding and looked in the tool drawer for pliers, picked up the spotlight flash, and went back to the darkroom. This time I got on my knees and examined the legs of the table carefully. I tried to move the knob on the front of one leg. It was smooth and did not budge. Then, using the flashlight, I peered under the table and realized that the shelf was held in place by slender metal rods that reached diagonally from the front legs to the rear legs. And the rods could have been threaded, the rear knobs removable to get the rod out, disassemble the table. I reached around the table and felt a rear furled knob.

I used the pliers to loosen the rear knob, then finished unscrewing it with my fingers, and slowly I pulled the rod out and away. It was flattened in the middle where the two rods crossed. In the same way I took the other rod out, and then tilted the shelf and slipped it away from the frame and set it aside. The bottom shelf was held in the same fashion, and came out the same way. When I tilted it to remove it, I caught my breath, then exhaled softly. A hole gaped open in the floor. The metal plate was not solid, was in fact no more than a frame that outlined the opening to the old root cellar.

The light box was held in place with two more rods, and I removed them and then carefully lifted the light box. It weighed very little, but it was difficult to remove. It had its own tubular legs that fitted into the upright tubes of the frame. I had to lift it high enough to clear the standing legs, but then it was free, and there was our doorway.

I shone my light into the hole: an aluminum ladder led down. I went to collect Casey. We were in this together; we would learn my grandfather's secret together.

I found Casey in her room tying her bootlaces. Wordlessly I beckoned. "Hey," she said, "I thought you said to put on boots— What's wrong?"

I motioned for her to come with me and I led the way back to the darkroom, and this time she gasped. "Holy shit! You found it! Did you go down yet?"

"No. I'll go first."

"Wait. The air might be bad. Let's turn on the fans again."

She turned on the fans; I opened the door wider, then closed it all the way and turned the lock. When I glanced at her, she nodded. No interruptions, not now. After waiting a few minutes for the darkroom to be freshened with outside air, I started down the ladder. When I stepped off at the bottom, she handed me the flashlight and came after me.

He had put plywood down on the floor. All that sand, I thought distantly, shining the light all around. The space was about six feet by eight, not quite six feet high. It smelled musty but not wet, not moldy, and the rocks that lined the sidewalls were dry, as were the pale juniper beams overhead. The stone steps were at the far end, the entrance the family had used so long ago, and now the steps served as shelves, with a few boxes on them, and a metal case the size of an overnight bag. Silently we went to the steps.

The first box I opened held Geneva's clothes, stiletto-heeled sandals, a strapless bra, a blouse. . . . I dropped the items back into the box and opened another one—pictures, some framed studio pictures. Their wedding picture? How young they looked, how happy he looked. Another studio picture of her with Tess when she was an infant. The three of them in another photograph. I closed that box, and looked at the case. That was the real secret, not the things he had scoured the house for the day she left. Casey was gazing fixedly at the case, and I opened it. No lock. Of course, any intruder who got this far would not be stopped by a lock.

More pictures on top of something white, a sheet, or some-thing. The top picture was of Bobby Lee and the two young men who had come with him to Oregon, Tadpole and Holly, all smil-ing, and very young. Like teenagers. The shortest one was hold-ing a stein of beer in a semisalute. I moved it aside and saw the next two photographs: Geneva posed with Holly and Bobby Lee, then with Tadpole and Holly.

Casey picked up a manila envelope and shook out several more pictures; she made a choking sound, a deep guttural animal noise. Three men, two of them in white robes with hoods, one—Bobby Lee—in a robe, holding a hood, smiling.

"Klansmen," Casey whispered hoarsely.

Another picture. The three figures, all hooded, and in the background a figure hanging from a tree. I felt nausea rising, rising, and Casey backed away, making strange noises, as if she could not breathe.

My fingers felt nerveless, and I felt almost as if I were removed—observing, not acting—as I shoved the pictures away and lifted the white object and held it up. A robe, and under it the hood.

Casey cried out and stumbled in her rush to get out of the dirt cellar. She scrambled up the ladder and was fumbling at the locked door when I got to her. Her hands were shaking too hard to manage the lock; I reached past her and turned it, and she fled. I followed.

She ran through the house and out the kitchen door, then came to a stop in the backyard, her face raised to the sky as she heaved, gasping for breath.

What if she was having an asthma attack, like her mother? I thought, panicked by her choking, rasping gasps for air. "Casey?" When she did not respond, I reached out and touched her arm, as cold as death. She jerked away as if lightning had struck her.

"Don't touch me! Leave me alone!"

"Casey, please—"

"All those lily-white people . . . running them to ground like animals . . . mutilating . . . butchering . . . hanging them like hogs." She hugged her arms to herself and rocked back and forth, her eyes shut tight.

Helpless, I didn't move, didn't speak, didn't dare touch her again. Abruptly she swung around and faced me, her eyes blazing, her face mottled with red and pale blotches. "You don't know! You can't know! Lily-white, halos, respected, killers! *Murderers!*" Her voice rose and she stopped as suddenly as she had started, then she ran back into the house, and following slowly, I heard her door slam.

I sat on the couch in the family room, thinking nothing coherent, listening to her movements. At four-thirty she came into the room, dressed in jeans, her Berkeley sweatshirt—I had one just like it—and sneakers. Travel clothes.

"I can't stay here," she said in a toneless voice. "I couldn't get a flight out, but there's a seat on the train available. It leaves at five-thirty. I should get there by five."

I stood up wordlessly, nodded.

"I packed up everything," she continued. "I'll take it all on the train. Be done with it."

Done with me, I thought, and nodded again. "We should leave as soon as we get your things in the car."

Silently we loaded the car, and silently I drove to the train station in Eugene. She checked in, bought her ticket; we loaded her boxes onto a wagon and went to stand outside and wait for the train. It was fifteen minutes late. We did not speak while we waited.

Then, when it pulled in, she boarded, and I stood and watched until all the passengers were loaded, those arriving in Eugene dispersed, the train was out of sight, and I was the only one remaining on the loading platform.

PART TWO

11

For the next two nights I was afraid to sleep, and when I did doze off, I repeatedly jerked awake from nightmares. When I thought of Grandfather with his skeletons, and of my own skeleton, I felt as if I had been caught in a mental tornado. I tried not to think of the dreams: carrying a bleeding man on my back through quicksand was an especially terrifying one. I didn't want to eat anything and paid no attention to mealtimes, did no cooking, just picked at whatever was at hand—a piece of bread or an apple, a cracker. . . . Curiously, neither could I think of anything in particular, no matter how much I tried. I told myself again and again to think through the situation, to do something, and then the resolution was gone. I existed in a state of inertia punctuated by fitful sleep and nightmares that left me with scattered evil images.

I knew I had to return to the crypt—that was how I thought of the root cellar—and put everything away, reassemble the light table, hide the hole in the floor. But I made no effort to do anything about it and forgot what I had to do until the thought returned with driving force again, only to vanish once more.

When Mrs. Hawkins came on Thursday, she drew in her breath. "Oh, dear, are you sick?"

"No. No, just a . . . a migraine. It's better today."

I fled to my room and sat on the side of the bed, and thought clearly: I needed a shower, needed to eat something, and needed to stop the blizzard that kept whirling through my mind. My grandfather had participated in a lynching. Or he had not participated but had become aware of it later. Or witnessed it. Or he was one of those hooded men. Geneva—I would never think of her as my grandmother again—had been smiling, standing with the hooded men, smiling. Her brother, Bobby Lee . . . Tess knew something and had been running away from it all her life.

The thoughts swirled faster and faster—questions, possibilities—then stopped with the realization that I had to go back to the crypt and examine everything in that metal case, look through every box. I jumped up, then sat down again. Not while Mrs. Hawkins was there. Had I closed the darkroom door? I couldn't remember. I hurried out to the garage and checked; the door was closed. I looked in the room Casey had used, and found a manila envelope, her notes on Hollis Jasper and his son, Kevin. Hollis—Holly—one of the hooded men. I shuddered.

Later, showered and in clean clothes, I made a sandwich and drank a glass of milk, made coffee, and wished that Mrs. Hawkins would just knock off and leave. She hummed and went about her cleaning chores.

I felt frenzied with nervous energy and couldn't be still, couldn't stop moving. I thought at one point that this must be how Tess was driven all the time, and I wondered how she could bear it. Mrs. Hawkins talked whenever I got within range: "Too bad your friend couldn't stay longer. So nice to have company, out like this. . . . Have you been sorting through all that junk in the spare rooms? My, my. I wanted to a million times, but Mr.

Landorf always said to leave it be, so that's what I did. When you get a load of stuff to haul out, my boy will come over with his truck. Didn't he do a fine job cutting down all those weeds? . . . You want me to strip that other bed, too? You had more company?"

I said Aunt Lu had been there for a visit.

"Oh, I'm sorry I missed her. Lu is such a kick. Was that her pie in the kitchen? You know it got moldy? I threw it out."

But finally she said she was done and left. I turned on the security system, then rushed to the darkroom, switched on fans, and descended into the crypt. I took the big flashlight with me.

There was no place to spread out the pictures and examine them; I put the loose ones back in the envelope to take up to the darkroom, where I could use the counter. Under the robe I found two small metal canisters, like medicine containers. "Film," I said under my breath. "He didn't develop all the film." And there was a shiny something, gleaming silver and olive green. I touched it. Snakeskin? Alligator? I picked it up, a book. On the inside cover was written in beautiful flowing script: *For Benjamin, my love. Christmas 1946. Forever yours, Geneva.* I flipped open a page or two and saw Grandfather's small, precise lettering. A diary! My hand was shaking when I put it with the envelope of snapshots to be taken to the darkroom.

The two cardboard cartons held only Geneva's belongings—some clothes, the framed studio pictures, even some bath salts in a decorative jar with stained-glass violets on it.

A few minutes later, up in the darkroom again, I emptied the manila envelope onto the counter and looked at the pictures he had printed. The hooded men, Bobby Lee with and without his white robe, Bobby Lee and Geneva . . . I caught my breath and swallowed hard. A picture of the hanged black man. He was naked, blood dried on his legs, his hands tied behind his back, lash marks on his chest. I turned that one facedown, sickened, and then stopped breathing again when I uncovered the next photograph: a white woman, blond, also naked, lying on some grass with a harsh light on her. Her eyes were closed; I couldn't tell if she was dead or alive. There was a front view, and another one of her back with crisscrossing welts, blood oozing from some of the lash marks.

I backed away from the counter, closed my eyes, and gulped air, feeling suffocated. Then with a swift motion, I turned those two photographs facedown, and emptied a small envelope of negatives. There were more negatives than prints.

Enough, I cried silently. I was suffocating; the air was bad, not enough fresh air. I felt as if I might pass out or throw up, or both.

Hurriedly I put the negatives and the snapshots back in the two envelopes, but I kept the diary. Down in the crypt again, I replaced everything, hesitated over the two canisters, left them in the case, and closed it.

I reassembled the light table and then, clutching the diary, left the darkroom. In my head the question pounded: Who had taken the pictures? My grandfather? He had not been in any of them, but someone had been there with a camera. Three hooded men and Geneva were all posed in one of the photographs. Whose robe and hood were in the metal case? My hand clutching the diary felt alternately on fire and completely numb.

I sat at my grandfather's desk in his study to read his diary. It seemed fitting, an invasion of his mind and his private space. The first entries were sparse, even pathetic. *January 3. I don't have anything to write about. Geneva says once or twice a week is plenty, and I'll be glad when I'm rich and famous to have this recorded memory to guide me when I write my memoirs. Today it rained. Done for the week.*

More weather reports, an account of his day: classes, homework, take care of Tess, who seemed to cry a lot. Then I read more slowly.

Sunday night. Geneva is hungover, busy with her diary, no doubt all about the party last night, who attended, what people wore, what they said, what they ate, how much they drank. Was she like this when we met? I can't remember. But I was drunk with her beauty, with my good fortune. Survive a war, win the most beautiful girl in the South, attend a university. The three wishes of fairy tales. All granted. Now all I can see is this bungalow where her mother or father, even Bobby Lee, might wander in at any time. Melly, whose name is Melody, and who is fifteen years old and is our housekeeper, won't look at me, or anyone else. What is she so afraid of? Everything smells of mildew and rot.

More weather reports, a reference to apartment hunting. *I'll keep looking, and if she says no the next time, I'll take it anyway. I hate this bungalow!*

I reread that one, puzzled. Then I moved on.

Melody left a newspaper called the Bayou News *in the kitchen today. I think on purpose. It's a local paper of some sort, with a lot of news about the colored community that I've never seen mentioned in other newspapers. I didn't suspect they had their own newspapers. I should have, I guess, but I just never thought of it. When G came in, she had been to the races, she had a fit. She would have slapped Melody if I hadn't caught her hand. And she went running off to complain to her father and mother. I always thought of her father as a dry, dull, rather pompous ass, but I suspect there's more to him than I realized. He called me to his study for a man-to-man talk. The gist of his talk was to intimate that I was a simple country boy who didn't understand the culture I had married into. Suppose, he said, you were surrounded by hostile Indians, vastly outnumbered, and you knew they were just waiting for a chance to start an uprising. You, your loved ones, everything you've worked for could be destroyed in the blink of an eye. You'd take steps to see that it didn't happen. You would see to it that they knew their place and stayed in it. Self-preservation demands that. You'd erect a barrier and you would make damn sure that no one crossed it, from either side. That's all we demand, a respect for that barrier.*

I got up and walked to the kitchen, where I stood indecisively, not hungry, unable to keep reading; a sense of oppression, heavy and relentless, weighed me down. Three wishes, I kept thinking, unscathed by the war, the beautiful bride, a bright future. I could almost smell the mildew and rot in the bungalow. It must have been on her parents' property, their house, their largesse, their generosity to the young couple. I washed my hands, drank a glass of water, and returned to the study to finish reading.

I was naive. I didn't understand the power structure, and didn't know there was anything to grasp beyond what was visible. Robert Lee Fontaine Sr. and a group of others like him are the power. They decide who will run for office, who will be the judges, who will live in the governor's mansion. They are not elected, but their power is undisputed. They run Louisiana; they own Louisiana. Now I see things that were invisible to me before. The separate schools and churches, separate drinking fountains, separate washrooms, even separate parade routes for Mardi Gras. The barrier is strong, its message clear: Thou shalt not pass.

He had stopped writing in the diary for longer and longer periods. The next entry was dated April 17. *Last night G and I had a long talk, or I talked and she cried. For weeks I have been picking up a copy of the* Bayou News *every Wednesday. It is poorly printed on cheap paper, but it covers the colored community, revivals, visiting musicians, neighborhood meetings, that sort of thing. And it gives detailed accounts of lynchings, two this spring. I told her I can't live in such a place, where murder isn't even reported. That as soon as I finish this school year at Tulane, we have to move and never come back. Her argument was the old familiar one, that every place has a few evil people who do evil things, and it has nothing to do with us. I asked her point-blank if the big party, Bobby Lee's eighteenth birthday party, and initiation was to admit him into the Klan, and she said yes, but the Klan didn't do wicked things now. They were for peaceful coexistence, for maintaining a decent Christian society, they were a strong force for keeping order, and so on. I showed her the article that finally made me act. A veteran, William Tully, a former corporal in the United States Army, had been mutilated and hanged, his wife had been beaten, and the Klan was responsible. I didn't say what I suspected, that Bobby Lee was involved. I couldn't let myself go that far. I didn't believe it, but I kept thinking of his initiation, her excitement, his. And his best friends who had been initiated at the same time, Stanhope, Dumarie, Jasper, Tilden, how they had acted, giddy with excitement, as if on dope or something. I didn't believe it, or maybe I just didn't want to believe it.*

My palms were wet, but I was shivering with a chill as I read the next entry.

April 30. G would not pack, or let Melody pack for her, and I started it myself. And I found a robe and hood, film cans, and a driver's license made out to William Tully, a souvenir, I assume. When I showed the license to G, she snatched it from me and ran to the bathroom and burned it. So he's in the Klan, she cried. So is everyone who's anyone. You can't prove he did anything. I don't think she realized yet that I had the film, the case with the robe and hood, everything. I put them in a safe place and told her we were leaving. She could come with Tess and me or stay. Bobby Lee, Tadpole, Holly, and Walter called on me that night, and I told them I would never betray my wife, that we would leave and never come back. I said if anything happened to me or to Tess, those pictures would be in the hands of a newspaper reporter I knew and be spread out for the world to see. God help me, I don't know what is on the film. I don't know if I'll ever see it developed. I'm afraid to see what is on it. God help me. With my silence I become complicit. I don't know what else I can do.

The rest of the diary was blank.

I sat at the desk for a long time, numb, shivering now and again, until gradually the room came into focus once more, and I found myself staring at the equally blank Yorick. "I don't know what to do," I whispered.

Grandfather had run away from it, lost himself in studying, in the magic of Shakespeare; Tess had run away from something, lost herself in whatever she could find, and always had to move on to something else and lose herself over and over. But something had happened that made Grandfather learn enough about photography to develop some of the film, and two years after moving into this house, Geneva had run away. Like a star gone nova, I thought distantly, the family exploded, the family members dispersed, fleeing one another as fast as possible.

It had grown dark while I read the diary and sat gazing at Yorick, or at nothing. And by then I really did have a headache, and I knew I had to eat something, had to move. I should have left the crypt open, I thought dully, in order to replace the diary.

I took it to my room and put it in a drawer. Tomorrow I would rent a safe-deposit box, I decided, and put the diary and an account of my stay here away, where they would be accessible if anything happened to me. I couldn't write anything about Kevin Jasper, the thought swiftly followed. I couldn't implicate Casey in that, endanger her.

I shivered again, but I did not deny that there was danger both from the law and from outside the law. The ripples that started forty-five years ago were still in motion, disturbing the space-time continuum that I lived in. Hollis Jasper was still out there. It was not over yet.

Then, as Grandfather had done, I breathed a prayer: God help me, I don't know what to do.

12

The next day I put the diary in a safe-deposit box. I had not written a word about the ice cubes on the roof or about the iceman. Whenever I started to, I got bogged down because it didn't make any sense unless I told more than I was willing to reveal. Later, I promised myself. That weekend, still driven by nervous energy that would not let me sit still, I cleared some more junk from the storage rooms, just to have something real to do while I tried to think of a way out of the dilemma I had stumbled into.

On Monday morning I was startled by the sound of the doorbell. No one had rung that bell since Mrs. Hawkins had come on Thursday.

A man stood outside, gazing around, grinning slightly. "Phil Cottrell," he said when I opened the door. "Is Dr. Landorf in? He's expecting me."

"Sorry," I said. "He's out of town." I had never heard anyone refer to my grandfather as "doctor," I realized. The man at the door was thirty-something, with dark wavy hair, blue eyes, a small scar on his chin. He was dressed in jeans, a T-shirt, running shoes. A student?

His grin faded. "But he said . . . Can I wait?"

"I'm sorry, Mr. Cottrell, apparently there's been a misunderstanding. He won't be back for a couple of months. He must have forgotten your appointment."

"He was going to read my dissertation, and we were supposed to talk about it."

He spoke with what I thought of as a southern cadence, not a pronounced accent, but a lilt, a rhythm.

I shrugged. "What can I say? He isn't here."

"I know," he said, his grin wider than before. "He's lecturing at Oxford and won't be back until late November. And you're his granddaughter, Marilee Donne. But that's a pretty good cover story, isn't it? You would have accepted it without hesitation, wouldn't you?"

"Who are you? What do you want?" I took a step back, preparing to slam the door.

"FBI," he said. He fished out identification from his jeans pocket. "May I come in and explain?"

I shook my head. "I want to verify this first. I don't have anything to say to the FBI."

"Good for you. Look it up in the phone book, and ask for extension one forty-two, my supervisor. I'll wait. Here, you'll want this, my badge number, full name, and so on." He held out his ID.

I glanced at it, then shook my head and closed the door, locked it, and set the security system. In the kitchen I wrote down the badge number I had seen and his name, not Phil Cottrell, but David Prather. Then I called the FBI, got extension

142, and spoke to someone who said that David Prather was there on official business.

When I hung up, my hands were wet. I wiped them on a dish towel, and stood for another minute with my eyes closed, waiting for the panic to subside.

He was still gazing about, whistling, when I opened the door to let him in.

"What do you want?" I asked in the foyer.

"Maybe we can sit down somewhere? This is a neat old house. Love that fireplace. Is that petrified wood on the mantel? Neato. Wood to burn, wood that's past all harm." He was moving as he talked, a few steps into the sitting room, then out again. "Not there. You expect a crabby old maid to come in with a tea tray any second."

I led the way to the family room and sat down on the couch, and motioned toward a chair which he ignored as he walked about the room, looking at things—the piano, my beginner's book, the old stereo, books on shelves, on tables.

I sat without moving, watching him. He turned toward me and flashed his big grin and said, "Breathe."

"Just tell me what you want."

"Right." He sat on the other end of the couch, and I resisted the impulse to jump up and move to a chair.

"Why didn't you do that history paper and pass the course?" he asked. "That one incomplete grade, no diploma. Tough. And after four years of great work, mucho credits."

I swallowed hard, every muscle in my body tense.

"Relax," he said. "I'm not out to get you. Just wanted your full attention, and I reckon I got it, didn't I? I'll tell you a story and you don't have to say a word. Just listen. Okay?"

I didn't move.

"I'll take that as a yes. Grandfather calls you to guard his cas-

93

tle, and before long, things get weird. Funny business, throwing something invisible at the house, but you heard what you heard, even if no one believed you. Your old school chum comes to visit and you set a trap for the prowler. But still no one believes a word of it, and you take matters into your own hands. Understandable. I commend you for it, actually. You tried to keep it clean, but without cooperation, what else could you do? You and Casada are smarter than he was. He underestimated you bigtime. So you and your pal waylay the guy and bash in his head, then pack him up and cart him away. Done. A good job. No questions asked. I don't think I'd want to make you mad at me, but, hey, it was a dirty job and someone had to do it." He shook his head, and his smile became rueful.

"The problem is that you and Casada, for all the pains you took, are still amateurs and you overlooked a few things. Fir needles, for instance, from a distinctive kind of fir tree. Noble fir needles, crushed Queen Anne's lace, orchard grass, some thistle burs, dirt all embedded in his clothes and the sheet. All traceable, of course, if anyone happened to look in the right place. And, no doubt, traces of blood could be found under the fir trees. People don't realize how hard it is to get rid of the blood. Insects would have been working on it, but still. . . ."

He leaned forward slightly. "You okay? You're not going to pass out or anything, are you? Tell you what, let's go to the kitchen and put on some coffee. I'll put on coffee and you just sit and relax." He stood up. "Come on, let's do it."

He started to walk, motioning for me to come, and I got up numbly and led the way to the kitchen.

I sat at the table while he made coffee. He did not ask for help, nor did I offer any. After he turned on the coffeemaker, he joined me at the table, where he saw the notepad with his name and number. He nodded, then ripped that sheet off the pad and put it in his pocket. "For the duration, the foreseeable future, I'm Phil Cottrell," he said.

"What do you want?" My voice was hoarse, a stranger's voice.

"You must have a thousand questions," he said. "I'll just finish my little story, and then you can fire away. See, the fact is, we'd been keeping an eye on Kevin Jasper, not around the clock, but generally keeping track of his whereabouts, his activities. It doesn't matter why, that's how it was. And we were aware of his father's comings and goings, and your grandfather's, except there weren't any comings and goings on his part. At one time we thought we might approach your grandfather for assistance, but we dropped the idea. Our profiler said no way would he work out. He has a funny memory. You know about that?"

Reluctantly I nodded.

"You do, too, but in an altogether different way. Yours is pretty amazing, how you glanced at my ID and had the name and number. That's pretty good going. Anyway, back to Jasper. It was a bummer, having him turn up looking like a corn dog, but there it was. The locals are trying to tie it in with the drug scene." He shrugged. "That's okay by us. Can't hurt for them to poke into the drug world now and then. But we want more. Frankly, if your grandfather hadn't already left for England, we probably would have invited him to the office to answer a few questions. Anyway, he wasn't around. So someone began looking over police records for the past few months—actually that's pretty routine—and before long the Landorf residence and your name popped up in the sheriff's files. Bingo. Jasper buys the farm, and peace and quiet are restored in the countryside." He stood up. "Is it coffee yet? Smells like it."

He busied himself at the counter, then brought back two mugs with coffee, went back for half-and-half, and sat down again. He knew I took cream; he left his black. My fear was deep, all-pervasive, thinking how they had spied on me, how unaware I had been. But they knew about the incomplete history grade, how I took my coffee, about Casey. . . .

"Okay," he said briskly then. "We began shuffling puzzle pieces, and we came up with the notion that Jasper wanted in the house here; he was looking for something; and to make a real search, he had to drive you away. We want that same something, Ms. Donne."

I shook my head. "I don't know what he wanted. I never met him."

"No, of course not. Old houses have secrets, you know? We want to find the secret in this house."

"You can't just come in here searching for something, not without Grandfather's permission."

"Try some of the coffee. It's pretty good." He sipped his, keeping a level gaze fixed on me. "See, the problem is that we could get a search warrant, go that route, but then it doesn't stay private the way we want to keep it. But we can do it that way if we have to."

I picked up my coffee, put it down untasted.

"You really don't have a lot of choice," he said. "At one time we thought there might be a connection between you and Jasper, but as I said, we know where he's been for many years, and after a little poking around, we learned where you've been. If you met, it had to have been on the astral plane. You're the innocent bystander caught in the middle."

"You don't know that there's anything! You're guessing, jumping to conclusions!"

He shook his head. "So, if there's nothing here, we will find nothing. If there is something, we'll find it. Either way, you're out of it when we're done." Very seriously then he said, "Hope we find it. Because if we don't, others will come looking sooner or later, before your grandfather returns. They might decide it's their only chance, while he's away. Or they might wait for his return and persuade him to cooperate. And he would end up cooperative, Ms. Donne."

I drank some of the coffee, trying to think what to do, and I knew he had spoken the truth: I had little choice. If they told the police their theory about Jasper's death, there would be no problem getting a search warrant. Even if they didn't tell, they probably could get one. But would anyone find the hole in the darkroom floor? No one could know about the old root cellar; all they would see was a concrete floor, a continuation of the garage floor. Grandfather wasn't due back for months, but he was the one who had to decide what to do with the pictures, the case.

"What do you want from me?" I asked dully then.

"In the morning I'll come by and pick you up, take you away for the day, buy you lunch and dinner, and get you back home before dark. And on Wednesday, do it again. When Mrs. Hawkins comes on Thursday, there won't be a sign, not a trace, of anyone's presence, not a thing disturbed, no walls opened up, no floors taken apart. Nothing."

I stood up. I wasn't even to see if they found the crypt. "I can't just leave and let strangers ransack the house."

"We prefer it this way," he said, rising. "Now, if you don't mind, I'd like a quick walk-through, just to get an idea of the layout. Okay?"

Silently I nodded and took him on a house tour, not saying a word as we entered and left room after room. In the first storage room he paused. "You've been looking for something?"

I pointed to a bulging trash bag. "Cleaning. Fifty years of junk." A box was full of broken toys. "Next I plan to catalog the books."

He nodded, then motioned toward the bag and box. "Mind just leaving those for the time being? Let our people have a look." He smiled. "When you don't know exactly what you're looking for, you want to have a crack at everything."

I shrugged, and we moved on.

In the darkroom he eyed the rolled-up mat. "More cleaning?"

"It's so brittle, it crumbled when I walked on it. I'm going to restock the darkroom, learn photography."

"Cleaning, cataloging, beginning piano, beginning photography—you have a busy schedule lined up."

"Are you finished?"

"Yes. I'll be on my way. Eight tomorrow morning. Is that too early? We could have breakfast somewhere."

"It isn't too early."

He led the way back through the house to the foyer. "Eight o'clock," he said at the door. He hesitated a moment. "I'm sorry about all this, Ms. Donne. See you in the morning."

I watched him get into a dark green van and drive away. Then I closed the door and stood with my forehead pressed against it, and all I could think was that I was being blackmailed by the FBI.

Later I sat at the kitchen table and read the material Casey had gathered about Hollis Jasper and his son, Kevin. She had told me most of it as she went along, but I read it thoroughly, knowing I would have to burn it afterward. The only thing I learned was that Hollis Jasper had come into an inheritance of more than a million dollars when he was twenty-five, the year he, Bobby Lee, and Tadpole had come to Oregon and he had stayed and started his law practice. Good old respectable family, Yale . . . nothing. Kevin was even less interesting. Bounced back and forth between Eugene and Denver, on to Yale, a year or two bumming around, seeing the country, a year traveling in Europe, then Eugene. And death. Nothing.

The nights had become cool enough that a fire would not be suspicious, I decided, and I brought in a few pieces of wood and burned the papers and my house plans. When they were all consumed, I stirred the ashes and made a little fire on top of them. I even moved the chair from in front of the door to the family room close to the fireplace. Let them think I sat there shivering.

Anything else? I thought of the spent shell casing in my dresser drawer and retrieved it, then stood holding it. Finally I slipped it into my purse. I would keep it with me, along with a small Swiss Army knife Casey had given me for my birthday when I turned twenty-one. Never go out unarmed, she had said. I blinked hard, wishing she would get in touch, let me know where she was, how she was, admitting to myself that she might never get in touch again.

I packed a few things in a tote bag—a head scarf, extra hooded sweatshirt, sweater, and a couple of books. I looked over the family room and my bedroom, looking for anything I would not want them to find, and then I thought of the light table. Had I left marks, signs that it was movable?

Resignedly I went to the darkroom to check; it seemed glaringly obvious to me that it came apart, that it had been taken apart recently. It was too clean, although dust lay on everything else in the room. I bit my lip, then went back to the kitchen and picked up a small rug outside the door, a mud catcher, but this time of year, a dust catcher. I folded it and carried it back to the darkroom, where I stood close to the light table and shook the rug, choking on the cloud of dust that rose.

"That's enough," I said under my breath. I felt empty, fearful; I had done what I could to keep the crypt hidden, and if they found it in spite of my efforts, so be it. I thought guiltily that I might even be glad if they found it. I could stop worrying. Possibly I could even start sleeping my usual deep, restful sleep. I yearned for sleep without nightmares, and I suspected that that night would not grant me it.

13

The doorbell rang promptly at eight. I opened the door and nodded at David Prather. Three other men were with him, all carrying cases, boxes, even a cooler. No one introduced anyone else, and the three men passed me silently and set their burdens down in the foyer.

"Ready?" Prather asked.

I picked up my purse and the tote bag, and we left. In the van, driving toward town, he said, "What I thought we might do is head out to the coast. I've only been in the state a few months, not long enough to get more than a glimpse of the coast one time. Meander up north, hit the tourist places along the way, stroll on the beach, stop for coffee, seafood, whatever presents itself. Sound good?"

I shrugged. "You're calling the play. Let's get one thing straight. This is not a nice little boy-girl outing. I'm more or less a prisoner, a victim of blackmail, and I don't feel especially friendly. Do what you want."

"Ms. Donne, I'm under orders. I didn't set this up as a get-acquainted day at the beach."

"The gulag guards were following orders, and the Chinese secret police rounding up dissidents, and the Nazi guards at the death camps. Let's leave it at that."

He sighed. "It's going to be a long day."

It did not take more than a few minutes to leave town and

skirt Fern Ridge Reservoir, where some sailboats were already bobbing in the breeze.

Then a cornfield took the high ground on our left, and a pasture with horses the right. "I like that," Prather said. "Every farm with something different. I'm even starting to appreciate corn again. Grew up in Iowa, corn to the left, corn to the right, horizon to horizon, corn and blue sky all summer, corn stubble and gray sky all winter. This is better."

I reached into the tote bag and brought out one of the books I had packed. Proust. I had started it half a dozen times and never got past the first two chapters, always too busy. Proust was for a long ocean voyage, I had decided, but this day trip would do. I opened it and began to read the first chapter. I always had to start over.

"I don't suppose you'd read it out loud," he said.

"Right. I won't."

It was a sham; I wasn't taking in a word, just going through the motions. I was thinking of Harry Carmody, the last in a series of boyfriends, the one I had thought might be forever, until he became too possessive; he even wanted to check out the names in my little red phone book. But I missed him. I missed his body, his lovemaking, I reminded myself. We had been good together, that was what it amounted to. The night before, I had lain awake yearning for Harry, or Doug, or someone, almost anyone, and I had bolted up with the realization that they were counting on my loneliness. They? The FBI profilers. They knew so much about me, they probably knew about the guys in my life, that I had been alone long enough to be hurting.

I could imagine the scenario: get her alone with a good-looking agent, someone charming, not too old, someone she can have fun with, and she'll be in his arms within twenty-four hours. For what purpose? I had demanded of myself, and had no answer. I didn't know what they wanted or why they were taking an interest in a murder committed forty-five years ago, if that's what they were interested in. But what else could it be? I had not slept a great deal after that, and now, trying to read Proust in the moving van, an answer seemed more elusive than ever. What were they after?

What I had decided during the sleepless night was that it was possible that they wanted more than unwilling cooperation from me, that they wanted me to trust this man, to confide in him, to tell him something, and were not certain what that something was. They couldn't just demand it and be done with it. They had me in such a bind that almost anything they demanded would be impossible to resist, however unwilling I might be.

That didn't make a lot of sense—they must know what they were searching for—but since nothing else made any sense at all, I would accept that it was as close to the truth as I was likely to get. And I would trust David Prather exactly as much as I would trust a rattlesnake coiled in the grass.

I stopped pretending with Proust, closed the book, and gazed out the side window at the exuberant forest of the Coast Range. Forest primeval, except where the loggers had left obscene scars of clear-cuts.

"I brought my son out to the coast in June," he said suddenly. "He's ten, his first time out West. He was afraid the trees would fall on him. He never saw so many trees before. So many, and so big." He was silent for a moment, then said, "I tried to show him everything, and as a result we saw very little. A glimpse of the coast, the rain forest, the Cascades and a glacier, the high desert, just a glimpse here and there. He kept his nose in comic books."

Resolutely I kept my face turned toward the side window,

thinking, So much for my pat theory. A seducer doesn't start by talking about his ten-year-old son.

"You stirred up memories," he said. "Sorry. We were like this toward the end, nothing to say to each other; she would sit and stare at the television for hours, never once glance at me, and pretend to be fascinated with pet-food commercials if I broke the silence. We're friendly now, more than we were for the last couple of years we were together." He added, "She loves Iowa."

I felt almost relieved, and vindicated. He had become a lonely divorcé; we had loneliness in common. I continued to gaze out the window. Very soon we wound around the last curve, and the Siuslaw River came into view with many fishing boats, flat-bottomed, two or three people on each, spaced like birds on a telephone wire. I could smell the river, mud flats, fish, and I could smell the ocean.

South of Florence sand dunes rolled along for miles. Ben and I used to love to go there and slip and slide on the dunes, wade, or even swim in the warm pools of fresh water dotted here and there, but the dunes were not what most people wanted to see at the coast. Prather turned north, and drove on the rugged mountain road that followed the shoreline, up and down, with sharp curves, and many lookout spots, rest areas, campgrounds. One stunning view after another appeared and vanished: blue water; blue-green, frothy whitecaps; thunderous waves on cliffs; geysers of spray reaching for the sky, falling back in a rainbow effect.

We stopped frequently; the first time when we left the van and went down to the beach, I turned one way and when he fell into step with me, I stopped and deliberately went the other way, and he kept walking in the opposite direction. That set the pattern we followed, together in the van, separate when we left it.

Together, apart, we made our way northward to Yachats, where we stopped at a small restaurant and had lunch, a silent meal at a window table overlooking the endless blue Pacific Ocean.

At Lincoln City I said I would like to shop in the factory outlet stores, and he pulled in and parked. "Anything in particular?" he asked.

I shook my head. "I may be quite a while."

"I'll wait in the van," he said.

I started at the end store, and took my time examining blue jeans and sweatshirts, on to an Adidas outlet, handbags, outdoor furniture, children's clothing, kitchenware. . . . I hit every one, and by the time I finished, it was after four o'clock. Shopping with a friend or two was fun; shopping alone to kill time was excruciatingly boring. I hoped he was as bored as I was.

When I got back to the van, he was standing outside the door, stretching and yawning. "Sorry," he said. "I was reading the book you left on the seat, afraid it put me to sleep. Let's find coffee, and head back down the coast. By the time we get to Newport, it will be time for some dinner, and then back to Eugene. Okay?"

It was as if he was determined to remain cheerful and pleasant, no matter how I behaved. I had not left the book on the seat. Small matter if he had gone through the tote bag, but it was annoying for him to lie so blatantly. I nodded, ready to sit down and have coffee. My feet were tired and my back ached.

Returning down the coast, we stopped to watch sea lions once, and a kite contest another time, then on to a seafood restaurant in Newport, and after another silent meal, we started for home. I kept thinking of a long soaking bath and bed. I could not calculate how many miles I had walked on the beach, and I had walked every aisle in one store after another. I was exhausted.

In the driveway when he stopped outside the front door of the house, he said, "If they found it, we'll all vanish, and you're home free. If they didn't, I'm afraid we'll have another day together tomorrow. Is there any place you'd like to go, anything you'd like to do?"

"I would like to stay home and get on with cleaning."

"Yeah. I know. Okay, let's call it quits for now."

His crew was gathered in the foyer with their boxes, cases, and the cooler. They nodded and slipped out when we entered.

"Be right back," he said, and followed them. At the van they talked for a moment, then he returned. "Eight o'clock in the morning. Up and over the mountains. Hiking boots maybe. Get some sleep." It pleased me that he looked as tired as I felt.

As soon as the van was out of sight, I locked up and headed toward the darkroom, then stopped and veered off to the kitchen instead. What if they had spy devices in the house, watching or listening to see if I hurried to a secret hiding place? I derided myself for becoming as paranoid as Grandfather, but I went to the kitchen and got a glass of water, thinking. Then I went through the house checking windows and doors, having a look. I could tell which rooms they had been in, although they left few real traces, just a book moved, or a lamp turned a little bit, a magazine not where I had left it. Grandfather's studio, the sitting room, both storage rooms . . . Finally I went to the garage, looked inside the car, and only then opened the door to the darkroom. They had unrolled the rubber mat, rolled it up again. Bits of dust-dry rubber were scattered on the floor, more dust on the light table and counter, in the sink.

After my survey, I turned on the water in the clawfoot tub, and collected my nightshirt and robe. There was a good wall light over the tub; Grandfather apparently liked to soak and read, and Casey had spent hours doing the same, but I didn't bother to turn it on. I just wanted to soak and think.

Another day with what's-his-name, and then what? That was my starting place, and I stalled there for a long time. Would they really let me off the hook? Prather said they would, but I didn't dare believe anything he told me. And why was I so reluctant to hand over the photographs and robe? From all appearances Grandfather was in the clear. Not really, I corrected myself: He had concealed evidence of murder. I had no idea how serious a crime that was, concealing evidence, but if they came across the crypt and found the metal case, my fingerprints were all over things, and I was as guilty of concealing evidence as my grandfather was. Not only what was in the crypt, but concerning the death of Kevin Jasper, too.

I wished I had someone I could talk to, and had to choke back laughter when I realized that Grandfather was the only person in the world I could discuss this with. After I reintroduced myself.

If only I had a little wriggle room, I thought. But they had me; if they said jump, I had little choice. Then I sat up straight in the bathtub. Maybe I did have something. It was hard to believe that they would be putting in so many man-hours on a forty-five-year-old lynching, but maybe there was something else on that film. Something they would put in time and expense to obtain. Something that might give me a little bargaining power.

When I was showing Prather through the house and we entered the darkroom, I had said the first thing that came to mind, that I intended to take up photography. Exactly so, I thought; I had seen a beginner's photography book in Grandfather's study in the past. I would take up photography.

At eight in the morning, the agents returned; as before, the three men entered my house without a word and set down their burdens. Prather and I left.

"Crater Lake," he said in the van. "We can do a little hiking around the lake; then I plan to sit somewhere and read, and at four head back." He was businesslike, not putting on the friendly puppy act of the day before. That was fine with me. I got out the photography book before he started the engine. To my surprise, he put a cassette in the tape deck, and the overture to *Lohengrin* blasted the air. He adjusted the sound and started to drive. The day before, I had pretended to read, to give him the message that I wasn't having any of his palsy-walsy comradeship. That day I was not pretending, but with the opera playing, it was hard to concentrate.

The instructions were for developing black-and-white film, and that was good. The photographs I had seen had all been black-and-white, and although the film in my camera was color, no doubt the lodge at the lake would have film for sale. He would spend the day reading; I would start a new career as a photographer. Another new beginning, I thought ruefully; how Tess would snort with scorn.

I tried to focus on the book, not on the music. I would have to take a lot of snapshots, I decided, get a lot of practice developing film before I dared even to touch the canisters in the crypt. I imagined handing them over to a professional, his reaction when he saw what he had. How long after that would it take for the police to come knocking at my door? But if Grandfather had learned enough to develop some of them, I could certainly finish the job for him. Finally, a job I fully intended to finish. I couldn't even really get started on my first lesson, though; I kept getting swept up by the music, and finally I closed the book, let the scenery ebb and flow in my awareness, and listened.

I had been to Crater Lake two other times, but that day I was as unprepared as I had been previously for the spectacular beauty of the lake, the intensity of the blue water against the tan and ochre cliffs and green trees. We had arrived by way of the north rim, and we drove around the lake slowly, stopping again and again for different views of the constantly changing scene. I finished the roll of color film in my camera, glad that it was color and aware that no camera could capture such exquisite beauty. Bold Steller's jays and chipmunks kept watch, not out of fear but hoping for a handout, a scrap of food, a dropped crust of bread or bun. Too tame to be wild, too wild to be tame. Adaptive. Overhead a hawk soared, caught a thermal, and rode it higher and higher, out of sight.

I dropped my camera back into my daypack when I finished the film.

"Enough?" Prather asked.

"Out of film. I'll buy some more at the lodge."

We walked back to the van, then stood another moment just looking around. The lake on one side, a vast field of dun-colored lava rocks on the other. The rocks were in thin slices, like shingles blown off a roof and scattered over many acres. Nature showing off, I thought. I had been awestruck as a child, thinking of the power of volcanoes that brought the inside of the world to the surface, created lava fields and lakes, black-as-pitch obsidian formations, pumice like cotton candy turned to rock. . . . I was still awestruck.

A group of tourists had followed us from the lookout to the parking area. "It's so pretty!" a woman said. "I had no idea it really looked like the postcards!"

Prather made a noise low in his throat and opened the van door. When we were both seated, he said, "*Pretty* is the last word in my vocabulary to describe this place."

I nodded.

At the lodge, which was crowded, I bought film and he bought a map of the entire park. When we met again after our purchases, he said, "It's nearly noon. Let's have lunch and pick out a trail to follow. Today, Ms. Donne, would you mind if we sort of go on the same trail, together, I mean?" A faint smile crossed his face, disappeared.

"Why not? You know we're up about eight thousand feet. I'm not in shape for a really strenuous hike at this altitude."

"Good," he said, evidently relieved. "Neither am I. Let's consult over a salad and sandwich."

We ate lunch, chose a trail, a three-mile loop along the rim of the lake, past a waterfall, with a side trip to a nature museum, which we would not visit. We hiked, going slower and slower as we climbed, and I took pictures: chipmunks, the small sign warning us not to feed them and cautioning that plague was endemic in the West and that chipmunks spread it. I took pictures of pinecones, the lake, Mystery Island jutting up from the middle of the water, trees, shadows on rocks, and even two or three of Prather when he wasn't looking. Might as well make the record of the day complete, I thought, but as my thighs began to throb, and the sun became hotter, I abandoned my newest pursuit of photography and concentrated on keeping on my feet and breathing. We did not talk, but the hike itself was cause for silence. I needed all the air I could take in just to survive, with none left over for meaningless conversation.

The sun was broiling hot, but the air was cool, a constant flux of hot and cold as we passed in and out of shadows. There was even snow banked in places that the sun failed to reach. Hot and cold.

By the time we returned to the lodge, we were ready to sit down and have a long cool drink. He pointed to a bench in light shade from a high pine tree. "Not too shady," he said. "Just not in the sun. You want to nab it while I get us something? I want a double iced coffee with a scoop of vanilla ice cream. What do you want?"

"That sounds good." He went inside the lodge, and I went to the bench and sank down onto it gratefully.

"Coffee because it's a stimulant," he said when he came back and handed me a tall plastic glass. "Iced because I'm burning up, or freezing. I can't decide which. Ice cream because it's just decadent enough. Cheers."

The coffee was perfect. I was content to just sit still and drink it.

"Dad has a grain elevator," he said in a low voice a short time later. He sounded drowsy. "And Mom is a schoolteacher, fourth grade. Connie, the girl next door, eight miles away from our house, but that's next door in Iowa, is a loan officer in a bank. My brother has a nice farm; he married a nice girl who is a very nice wife, and they have four nice children. Church every Sunday, PTA, softball practice, nice family get-together dinners, potlucks, barbecues out back. All very nice. The world starts and stops right there, no need for anything else. So very, very nice. I said once, Let's save up and go to Italy someday, and Connie said, What for? She'd rather go to Graceland. I like Wagner and Puccini, she likes Elvis."

He became silent, and I didn't move. Too private, too revealing, I wanted no part of his memory-lane stroll.

"I said you stirred things up," he said, as if reading my thoughts. "You did, but your being quiet isn't like she was when she froze me out. I mean, I'd get near and it was like a wall came down, with her on one side, me on the other. Wary—God, was she wary! Alert to my every motion, as if she was afraid I might gather myself together and launch an attack at any time, and she had to have her defenses ready."

He finished his coffee, his gaze on the distant trees, or on nothing. "You're not like that. You've been thrown into the company of someone not of your choice, and you've done a good job of maintaining your privacy, your dignity in a damn tough situation. I keep wishing we had met in a coffee shop, or a bookstore, at someone's party, something like that." Abruptly he stood up. "Sorry. I never talked to anyone about her; I didn't know exactly how I felt about those years. I'm going to go get that book I mentioned."

I watched him stride off toward the van, and I didn't know what I thought. An act? The real Prather coming through? A lonely man who needed someone to talk to as much as I needed that same thing? I didn't know.

He read and I took more pictures, then browsed in the lodge gift shop. At four o'clock he waved to me, motioning toward the van. Time to go home.

We listened to the last act of *Lohengrin* and did not talk on the drive back to Eugene.

"Dinner?" he asked as we drove into town.

I shook my head. "I'd rather just go on home. I'm pretty tired."

"Yeah. Me, too. Okay. Home."

It was the same as the day before; we arrived, his crew left without a word, and I locked up the house. Then I sat in the kitchen, trying to sort out my feelings.

"Cognitive dissonance," I said under my breath, a favorite phrase that Tess used to toss off. But I wanted to talk to Prather, really confide in him, and I feared and distrusted him in equal measures.

14

On Thursday while Mrs. Hawkins did her cleaning, I worked on the darkroom, hauled the mat out to a growing pile of trash, and studied the photography book. I waited for the phone to ring or for Prather to show up with a new demand, disbelieving that they would cut me loose. The phone remained silent, and no one came to the door.

On Friday morning a florist delivery van pulled up to the house and the driver handed me a box, saluted, and left. The box held a dozen roses, gold, edged with pink in bud, ready to open. Peace Roses, a card said. An envelope contained a handwritten note: *I'm truly sorry we met the way we did. In spite of every-thing, I enjoyed being with you, watching your face as you concentrated on snapping your pictures. If I can be of any service to you, please call me. One day I'll get in touch, when all this has been filed away out of sight, out of mind.* His initials, DP, and a telephone number completed the message.

More confused than ever, I put the roses in a vase with water. They were very fragrant.

Giving up on his motives, and my reaction, I went shopping for darkroom supplies and realized almost instantly in the shop that I was out of my depth.

"You might want to take a course," the salesman said when I showed him the book I had brought along. "Things have changed some since that was written. Some pretty good courses out at LCC, or the university." He was solemn, even mournful as he glanced over the book. Almost hesitantly he asked, "Do you have a camera?"

I showed him my Hasselblad, and he brightened. "Top of the line," he said.

I had suspected as much; it was a Christmas present from Geo from years back. Always top of the line, that was his motto.

"Problem is, you can't get in this late," the salesman said gloomily. "Classes fill up pretty fast. You might try private lessons. Carl Townbridge holds classes. He's really good."

He gave me a copy of an announcement about private lessons, limited to eight students, four days a week for three weeks of intensive study. I shook my head at the price: a thousand dollars, plus supplies. The list of supplies was long and included several lenses, two books, a Polaroid camera in addition to a 35-millimeter camera. Another thousand dollars? I was afraid so.

That night I called Tess and told her I wanted to go into art, photography to be specific, and she gasped, lectured about missed opportunities, complained, and eventually said, "Your own studio here in Los Angeles would be nice. Movie stars, fashion models, entertainers, they all need endless supplies of photographs. I need them myself, in fact. Geo and I could steer people to you. Our family has always been artistic. . . ." I understood perfectly well that she was grasping at any hope she glimpsed that I would find something to do and settle down.

As soon as I hung up, I called Carl Townbridge's number.

That night I planned the next month. Lessons would start the following Monday.

As much as I wanted to look at the negatives Grandfather had not printed, I resisted. I didn't want to touch them again until I learned how to handle them without destroying them. And I didn't even consider opening the canisters yet.

Two weeks passed like a dream, half remembered, half experienced, fleeting and very busy. For the first time in my life I was the star of a class, I applied myself so assiduously. If I had worked this hard for the past four years, I thought one night, I would have a diploma by now, a desk with a secretary attached, three telephones. . . .

My darkroom would have made a professional photographer proud; it made me proud. To my surprise I loved taking pictures, developing them, printing, all of it. The teacher, Carl Townbridge, said I had an excellent eye, I was a natural—and that made me proud. Of course, I reminded myself frequently, there was no future in it. I could recognize how good Townbridge was, his work was real art, but I suspected he made his living with the classes he taught four times a year for three weeks at a time, just to give him the rest of the year for his photography, and none of it commercial in any sense. The list of things he did not do was long: babies, weddings, graduations, reunions, anniversaries, birthdays. . . . Certainly not movie stars, rappers, fashion models. At those times I reminded myself that I was not pursuing a career.

On Tuesday of the third week of classes, Townbridge said that on Wednesday and Thursday we would take field trips, one to the coast, one to a nature preserve, and I decided to opt out. I had enough of the basics to start on the negatives and then to tackle the canisters. It had been a short school term. Maybe that was the secret, cram a year's worth of lessons in a two- or three-week period, one subject at a time, intensive study, and be done with it.

On Wednesday, using a magnifying glass, I studied the negatives Grandfather had not printed. Bobby Lee and Geneva. One of Geneva by herself, her hair a perfect halo around her perfect face. Another one of five hooded men before a tree, this one showing them from the top of their hoods down to the ground. Spanish moss dripped from a tree limb, and I gasped and my hand shook as I realized it wasn't all moss. The hanged man was there. I put that negative aside to print.

The next one I examined was of Geneva and four of the hooded men in front of the hanging tree; she was holding a half mask before her face, smiling. I put that negative with the other one that I would print.

The rest of the negatives I left alone, more of the same, or too murky to see, overexposed, underexposed, or just bad. As I worked, I thought about what Aunt Lu had said. When Grand-father arrived home that day and she told him Bobby Lee and friends were there, he had gone off to his darkroom. Of course, I thought; he had to pull the pictures and refresh his memory. He might not have recognized Bobby Lee or his pals otherwise. I couldn't imagine living with a memory like that. And he had printed only those few. I had assumed that he stopped printing them because he had seen enough; now I thought he had stopped when he saw too much.

I returned everything to the crypt, reassembled the light table one more time, and glanced around to make certain I had not missed anything. It was a bother to take the table apart and put it back together, but I had decided never to leave a thing in the darkroom that I would object to having held up to scrutiny. The lock was on the inside, no lock on the outside. I had made it a habit to lock the door every time I entered the darkroom, but no one would find that strange: a darkroom could not have light spilling in unexpectedly. Before I left the room, I spread out some of my own negatives on the light table, and my prints on the counter. I had taken hundreds of pictures by then, developed and printed more than a hundred. If there were still prowlers having an occasional look, let them admire toadstools and chipmunks and shadows on rocks.

On Thursday while Mrs. Hawkins was there, I shopped for the weekend; I wanted to be undisturbed once I started on the film in the canisters. I had asked Townbridge about developing old film, and he had given me some pointers but then added that usually old film was brittle and likely to crack when unrolled, and not worth the trouble. If it had been kept cool and dry, in an airtight container, like those old-fashioned canisters, it might be okay, he had said doubtfully, and I assured him that I was just curious.

My gloved hands appeared unattached, luminous under the red light, like the magic hands in *Beauty and the Beast*. The film was brittle, especially one edge, where some of the holes cracked open as I unwound the roll. After being coiled so tightly for so many years, it was like a spring that had no intention of ever straightening out again. "Easy, easy," I muttered, working it out slowly. Fitting it over the sprockets of the developer was painfully slow work; more holes split open, then they began to hold. And I started.

Pictures of a crowd of happy people? I peered at the negatives, unable to tell what I was looking at. I decided I needed proof sheets and went to work on them, and then studied the proofs. Drunken men holding one another up, laughing. An old woman with a lacy parasol, a champagne glass raised as if in salute; people wearing masks, in grotesque or even lovely costumes; children; old people; spectators at a parade. Then I understood. Mardi Gras pictures, taken from a float. There were a lot of them, but as I went from one to the next, they made sense. I gasped, held my breath, and leaned in closer. A black man with his arm around a blond woman. "William Tully," I whispered. Their faces were too indistinct in the proofs to tell anything more than that he was black and she was blond, and they were standing on something raised, something that put them higher than people in the foreground. No other black person was on any of the other proofs.

I backed away from the light table, thinking: They spotted him at the parade, tracked him down, and killed him. I felt feverish and chilled, sick. I took a deep breath, another, and then I returned to the counter to finish examining the images.

The entire roll seemed to have been taken at the parade. A few were of the people on the float, all masked, gorgeously dressed in French Empire costumes. I was sure that one of the elaborately dressed women with a half mask was Geneva.

The second roll of film was different. Pictures had been taken in bad lighting with no flash attachment, and many of them were too dark to make out. A hall of some sort, men in tuxedos, women in formal wear. Many of them in costumes like those on the float. A party? A ball? A group of costumed men laughing. Then men in white robes, wearing hoods. Four men in robes but without the hoods. The men were not posed for the camera; they were talking to one another apparently—joking? I glanced at the other negatives on the light table; no one in this roll had been posing, or even aware of the camera from all appearances. A hidden camera? A secret photographer? It was hard to tell much from the dark proofs. I returned to the proof of the four men in a convivial group, and stared at the picture until my eyes burned. That one, I thought. I know him.

Panic seized me as the realization hit that I was looking at a picture of Walter Dumarie as a young man. "Oh, my God," I whispered, and it was a real prayer.

Walter Dumarie, a Klansman who might have participated in a lynching, was running for the presidency as a third-party candidate.

I sat down on the high stool, my back against the counter, my thoughts tumbling out of control as I realized the implications of what I had found.

I was sure it was Dumarie. Even in the dark proof he was recognizable; his large head of wavy and curling hair gave him away. His hair was like a Clairol hair-coloring ad: red-gold waves and soft curls, worn just a little long, long enough to catch a breeze and be ruffled, then settle into the waves that had become his trademark. Caricaturists loved him.

Grandfather had mentioned him in his diary, but I had not made the connection. I had never seen him in person, but his face was familiar from television appearances, late-night talk shows, magazine covers. He made the news again and again, and he was extremely photogenic, movie-star handsome, even now in his sixties. As a young man he had been devastatingly good-looking. Those who went to his rallies, reporters, others all agreed that his charm was almost hypnotically compelling. One of the great orators of the century, *Newsweek* had labeled him. A racist, a fascist, he made Attila look like a liberal.

A Klansman, a killer, I thought. I had to print the picture, lighten it, erase any doubt that it was Dumarie, but then what?

I had never been interested in politics. Possibly living with Geo and Tess had cured me of believing in anything; Geo certainly didn't, except the power of money and the market. And while Tess believed in things with wrenching intensity, they never endured very long before she was off on a different course. Serial convictions was how I thought of her passions. But my uninterest did not imply that I was blind or deaf. I knew who was running for president, but I wasn't even registered to vote, convinced as I was that it wouldn't make any difference which one got the prize. As for the minor candidates, except for Dumarie, I didn't even know who they were or what they stood for. Some environmentalist probably, a socialist possibly; it didn't matter.

Even in my state of ignorance, I was aware of some of the issues, and I was aware that Dumarie had captured the imagination of a lot of people with his populist talk about saving America for the rightful owners of the country, the working people, the decent people, the God-fearing people. And I was aware that he had the backing of extremely powerful and wealthy people. There had been ugly stories while I was still at Berkeley about some of the tactics his party had used to quell opposition, nothing ever proved, no charges ever brought, fervent denials all around, but people had vanished or had left politics for good. And Dumarie had come up smiling through it all, unblemished.

I thought of the three rolls of film, one that Grandfather had developed, the two that I had developed. Who knew about them? Only the photographer could know exactly what had been photographed, and after all these years even that was problematic. Geneva and Bobby Lee had known something, and Tadpole and Holly. They had come to Oregon presumably to get the film and the robe and hood, but left without them. Why? And if Dumarie knew about them, why hadn't he sent his troops to collect them years ago?

And equally important, how and why had the FBI become involved after so many years?

Finally I stood up, I was getting nowhere trying to puzzle it out. I began the routine of putting things away. Tomorrow I would print the pictures, but now I had to get away from the darkroom and just think.

By late the following day I had proof that Dumarie had been on the Mardi Gras float, at the party or ball, and with the group of hooded men witnessing the lynching of William Tully. The problem was how to get those pictures to the FBI without implicating Geneva or her brother. I would try to protect them exactly the same way Grandfather had protected them, not out of any feeling of family loyalty, but for his sake. I was desperate to keep him out of it. He never saw those other two rolls of film; he never knew what he had. He knew only that he could not betray his wife, the mother of his child. It must have tormented him to hide the lynching, protect the guilty, but he must have reasoned that if he turned over anything, he would have had to turn it all over. The rock and hard place with a vengeance, and that was the predicament I was in. How to give them some of the negatives and prints without handing over everything.

I could say I found some rolls of film, and developed and printed them for practice. It never occurred to me until I saw the prints that the FBI agents might have been searching for film. They never told me what they were looking for. They wouldn't believe me, but what could they do if I stuck to that story? It was virtually the truth, a lie of omission. I remembered what Prather had said, that Casey and I were amateurs, overlooked a few things, and I felt I was doing it again, overlooking things.

Z to A, I told myself. Where could I say I found them? A place they had missed in their two-day search. I wandered through the house considering hiding places: the piano, no. They would have looked there. Not behind any books. No safe tucked away behind a picture. The FBI, if they had been looking for the robe and hood, would have been looking for a larger space than I needed, but I suspected that they had been thorough.

In my room I stopped roving and gazed at two handmade rag dolls seated at a miniature table with two chairs. I had started to toss them all into the junk heap, then cleaned them instead and set them up. I had played with them as a small child; Tess had played with them, Aunt Lu. . . . They had been her mother's, Aunt Lu had told me. Not in one of them, I thought, considering ripping open a seam, pretending I had come across the film there. Then I remembered another ancient toy, even older than the dolls and furniture. I hurried back to the storage room, looked through the box of discarded and broken toys, and pulled out a log truck, also handmade. Two horses had pulled it at one time; now only one three-legged horse was still attached. But the load of logs on the truck bed was still held in place with a strip of leather. The logs were real wood, perfectly in scale with the truck and horse. I took the log truck to the kitchen table and examined the leather strap. Rotten enough to break if it was dropped? Or thrown down? I tried dropping it, then banged it on the table and the strap broke, the logs tumbled out.

"The boys, my great uncles, must have found the canisters," I said under my breath. "They put them on the truck bed and piled logs on top of them, and probably forgot all about them."

It would do, I decided. They might doubt my story, but I would stick to it. It was after ten, too late to call. Besides, it was

Saturday night. Prather would be out somewhere, and the office closed. It would have to keep until Monday. After forty-five years it could wait another day.

Now that I knew what I had, I was very frightened. I kept reminding myself that if Dumarie had known there was such damning evidence on film, he would have taken whatever measures he had to to get it, and he had done nothing. Holly Jasper and his son might have had their own personal reasons to try to get it, but that business had been even more amateurish than Casey's and mine. And Holly had done nothing since the death of his son, Kevin. Maybe that had been Kevin's idea from the beginning; after all, Holly Jasper had been in the area for almost forty years and had not acted.

Dumarie didn't know a thing about it, I told myself repeatedly. That was the lifeline I clung to.

On Monday morning I called the FBI office. I had decided to keep this matter strictly business, nothing personal, no suspicion that I had even considered calling Prather at his own number. Routine business, I told myself as I dialed. A woman answered, equally businesslike, and I asked for extension 142.

"I'm sorry," she said. "We don't have extension numbers. To whom did you wish to speak?"

My hand holding the phone had gone moist with her words. This was all wrong; a man had answered before, his manner had been brusque.

"I want Mr. Prather's supervisor," I said.

"I'm afraid we don't have a Mr. Prather," she said. "What is the nature of your call? Perhaps I can direct you to someone who can help."

I hung up. I had been frightened, but this was worse than that, much worse than anything I had ever known. I was panic-stricken, terrified. Prather, those other men . . . not FBI. Dumarie's people? That explained why Holly Jasper had not made a move; moves were made on his behalf. And I had to get out. Now. What if they had a tap on the telephone? They would know I had called the FBI, and probably guess that I had found something.

I became frenzied all in a second, raced through the house to my room, and threw some things into an overnight bag. I added the big envelope with the negatives, the prints, and film canisters. I had planned to take them to the FBI office, and I was afraid now to go to the darkroom, dismantle the light table, hide everything, put the table together again. It would take too long. Even as I packed my things, I imagined that those nameless silent men were getting into the van, starting for the house. I ran faster, and I knew I was running for my life.

15

I drove north on I-5 with no destination in mind, just *run, run.* I drove slowly enough that everything on the road had to pass me or be conspicuous. I cursed myself for running before I knew there was a threat. Then I cursed myself for keeping the damning photographs and film in my possession. Between the two maledictions, I praised myself for getting out before I was apprehended. Now what?

I should have gone straight to the FBI office in Eugene, but if they were not involved, I did not want to involve them, not directly. Also, I thought bleakly, Prather had known too much about Kevin Jasper's death—the fir needles, weeds on his clothing and on the sheet. He had learned that from someone. So no FBI, not yet. And no other local law-enforcement agency. Hollis Jasper was a local attorney, he might know people inside the district attorney's office, the investigators, judges. . . .

A newspaper, I thought then. That was what Grandfather had threatened: hand everything over to a newspaper and let them unravel the story. I bit my lip. I had no idea what newspaper to approach, who might be willing to take some action, or who might set a match to everything. Perillo was right, I thought. I, everyone, should pay more attention to local politics, world politics, government—*Bruno Perillo*! My hands tightened on the steering wheel.

He had been a T.A. in a journalism class I took my freshman year. Hardly older than half the students he taught, he had come on like an embittered, fossilized professor. He had given us a pop quiz, which 90 percent of us failed. The quiz had been about local politics, world leaders, committee chairmen in Washington. . . . Several students had protested, and he had lectured us about our ignorance, scorned our professed desire to get into journalism, mocked our zeal for getting good grades without bothering to get an education.

He was an intensely ugly man, swarthy, with coarse black hair that tended to stand out in strange ways, as if in perpetual electric shock; his eyebrows were thick and unruly, growing this way and that. Most annoying, he had a habit of sticking out his forefinger as if stabbing the air, pointing to a student. He pinned me to the board that way and said in a grating, mean voice, "You go into journalism and you'll report on dog shows, cat shows, the county fair. Half of what you write will get edited out, the rest will be no more than an announcement. You'll get bored and quit. Why? Because you're brain-dead as far as curiosity is concerned. You don't have any."

He jabbed at someone else then and continued the diatribe. I knew he wouldn't remember me, but I would never forget him.

It didn't matter that I detested him, I recognized that he was possibly the most honest man I knew. When curiosity was handed out, he got in line twice. At the end of the school year there had been a story about him in the school paper along with a cartoon of Diogenes and his lantern, a balloon with the words: "I found him! Watch out, San Jose, an honest man is on the way." Bruno Perillo had landed a job on a San Jose newspaper.

I began to pay attention to where I was on the long stretch between Eugene and Portland. Nearing Salem, apparently. That would do.

A few minutes later I sat near a pay phone outside a Wendy's, thinking of what to say, how to convince Perillo that I had something, that I wasn't just a crank or a stalker or something. Finally I went to the phone, got the newspaper number from directory assistance, and dialed.

It took a long time to get through to him. Waiting, I wondered if he was still doing county fairs and dog shows. He sounded annoyed when he snapped, "Yeah, Perillo." That was exactly the way I remembered him.

"Bruno Perillo," I said, "I know you, but you have no reason to know me. I was in a class you taught at Berkeley four years ago. I have a story for you, but you have to come to Portland, Oregon, to get it."

"Lady, I have things to do right here. Bring it to the office—"

"Shut up and listen," I said. "I have proof that Walter Dumarie was present at, or participated in, the lynching of a black man in New Orleans in 1947. The black man's name was William Tully. He had been a corporal in the United States Army." I drew in a breath. "Do you want the story or not? If you don't, I'll hand my material over to someone at the Portland newspaper."

"Jesus! Who are you? Where are you? What do you have?"

"I have film, prints, negatives. I'll give you everything, but you have to come up here for it."

"Look, hop on the first plane. We'll pay the fare—"

"Perillo, I have the material with me, and Dumarie's men may know I have it by now. I won't go near an airport. Verify Tully's death, make a hotel reservation, a plane reservation. I'll call you back in an hour and you can tell me what you've decided." Without waiting for any argument, I hung up.

An hour later I was in a sprawling shopping mall in Portland, looking for a public phone. I had bought a briefcase and transferred my envelope of film to it, and locked my overnight bag in the trunk of the car. The mall was crowded, as I had known it would be. That was exactly what I wanted, crowds.

This time when I called, I was put through instantly. Perillo said, "My editor is on the line. He wants to speak to you."

The next voice was high-pitched, and the man spoke fast. "Miss, if you have what you say you have, you're in danger, but you already know that. Bruno's flying up there, seven-thirty arrival time. We made a reservation for Mr. and Mrs. Jack Henderson at the Benson Hotel in downtown Portland. Don't talk to Bruno anyplace that's public, no bar or restaurant, like that. The rest of the day, stay in crowds, see a movie, get your hair done. You might want to change your appearance, you know, cut your hair short if it's long, dye it, something like that. Don't go near any of the places where Dumarie's people might look for you. Bookstores, the university, library, like that. Here's Bruno."

He was gone, and I had not said a word.

"Okay, you're on," Bruno said. "When I get to town, I'll

check in and dump my gear, then head for the bar. Will you recognize me?"

"Yes."

"Okay. Just mosey up to me and say hi, long time no see. We'll go up to the room and talk. Got that?"

I nodded. "I'll see you in the bar." I hung up.

Even the longest day finally does end, and that was one of the longest I had ever endured. When I entered the Benson bar at 7:45 my hair was short, beautifully styled, and dark brown. I was wearing a beige silk dress with a lightweight jacket; my nails had been manicured; I had bought and applied understated and expensive makeup. I had changed my appearance so much that I didn't recognize the woman who gazed back at me from a mirror.

I was too early, but I wanted to be in place when Bruno arrived, look him over, make certain he was alone. I had never suspected I could become this paranoid, but I was taking every precaution and was as nervous as a cat on a vet's examination table.

When Bruno arrived, he still looked like a T.A., rumpled, tired, bad hair and all, like someone who had put in a long day and wanted nothing more than a drink, dinner, and bed. He glanced around the bar, took a stool, and ordered. I waited until the bartender put a draft beer down for him, and he had taken a long drink, then I walked over to him, clutching my new briefcase.

"Hi. Long time, no see."

He looked me over, his gaze lingering for a moment on the briefcase, then took another long drink and stood up. "Let's go."

We walked through the lobby to the elevators without

another word; it pleased me to look so elegant and cool when he was so travel-worn and wrinkled, and in need of a shave. His hair was as coarse and unruly as I remembered, and his eyebrows even wilder and thicker. He pushed the button for five. No one in the lobby or in the elevator paid any attention to us.

He opened the door to his room, a suite actually; the room we entered had a king-size bed, and an open door led to a second room. He turned the lock in the door and put on the chain, then looked me over again and said flatly, "I never saw you before in my life."

"You never *saw* any of the people in your class. We were warm bodies you were permitted to bully and harass long enough to finish your degree."

"You going to tell me your name, anything else?"

I shook my head. "This is what you came for." I handed him the briefcase. I turned to leave, and he grabbed my wrist hard and jerked me around.

"Not so fast. Let's see what you brought me."

I glared at him, at his hand holding me, but, oblivious, he pulled me to the adjoining room, where there was a smaller bed, and a sofa and two upholstered chairs around a coffee table.

He pushed me down into one of the chairs and dumped the contents of the envelope onto the coffee table. He shuffled the prints around a bit, then looked at me and said angrily, "Okay. I give. What's the story?"

"They were in order until you messed with them," I said. I put them back in order; the float pictures first, then the ball, then the lynching scene.

He studied the prints, spending a long time gazing at the hanged man and the woman on the ground, then he said furiously, "You said you had proof. All I see here is that a man was hanged, a woman beaten, and that Dumarie was at a party."

"Are you brain-dead or something?" I asked, a pointless reference since he didn't remember a thing about his days as a teaching assistant. "Someone took pictures from a Mardi Gras float of the spectators and some of the others on the float. One of the pictures shows a black man and a blond woman watching. The only black man, I might add. Dig up a picture of William Tully and compare the two. And notice those shoes." I pointed to a man's ornate shoes with silver tassels. The photo was of a couple tossing out beads or something; a man's lower legs and feet happened to have been in the same frame. The man was not visible, only ankles clad in white hose and the shoes.

"Here, a party, no idea when, but some of the costumes are the same, so I assume it followed the parade. See, the shoes again. This time on the feet of Dumarie." He picked it up and studied it, put it down without a word.

The third set was of the lynching scene. I pointed once more, this time to a group of hooded men with the hanged man in the background. "They were there, they saw it, or participated in it. And there are the same shoes."

At first glance the row of hooded, robed men showed no distinguishing characteristics; the figures appeared as identical as reiterating shapes in funhouse mirrors, but their shoes were visible, and they were different, from one pair to the next. Among them were the white hose, and the fancy French Empire–style shoes with the silver tassels.

Bruno Perillo stared at the lynching print, then at the other two that showed the same shoes, and finally looked up with a bleak expression. "Okay. Same shoes, and I can see why you thought you had proof, but it's not enough. Mardi Gras, dress-up parties, who knows how many men wore shoes pretty much like those?"

"Look at them!" I cried. "Look at the left shoe. Does

129

Dumarie have a bad leg, one shorter than the other? One shoe is built up at least an inch! In all those pictures, it's the same built-up shoe. How many other men do you suppose had special-order shoes with the left shoe built up an inch higher than the right?"

He compared the prints again, then ran his hand over his face, and said in a hoarse whisper, "Holy shit! It's the same fucking shoe!"

I started to get up, and almost absently he reached across the table and shoved me back into the chair. "Not yet," he said. With his other hand he picked up the telephone from an end table and dialed. He held up my purse. "Car keys, money, credit cards? I'll hold on to it for a while."

There was little need. All day fear, adrenaline, panic, had been like a steel rod holding me upright, and now I felt as if the rod had vanished; I was limp with relief. It was out of my hands. Someone else would do something about William Tully and Walter Dumarie.

Bruno began to talk. "If the boy has a bad leg, left leg shorter than the right, we've got him. I never heard anything like that about it." He listened, grunted several times, said "yeah" several times, said, "room 522," then hung up.

"Have you eaten?" he asked. "He said for us to hang out for a while, he'll call back. Let's order some chow from room service."

"I don't want anything to eat. Give me my purse. I gave you what I said I would; now I want to leave."

"No way. Not yet. Look, I'll order for two, just in case you change your mind. You like fish? Steak? Pasta?"

I shook my head.

Holding my purse, he got up and crossed the room, came back with the hotel guide and opened it to the room-service menu. "Ah, halibut. Grilled. Red potatoes . . . That'll do. And a bottle of chardonnay."

He called in the order for two, with a large pot of coffee, asked if it came in a thermal carafe, and when done, he gazed at me for several seconds. "I'd remember you if you'd been in my class."

When I didn't respond, he said, "Okay, I'll tell you a story. See, William Tully was a draftee, put in four years, the last one in Germany after the war ended. He met Ilse Gerhard. Her mother was English, her dad a soldier in the German army, trained to shoot and kill Englishmen. Mother took the kid home to England when war broke out, and when it ended, Ilse went back to look for her father, never found him, and ended up as a translator for the Americans. She and Tully met, hit it off, and got married. His father was a congressman from New Jersey: he pulled some strings, and she got into the States with Tully when he mustered out, and later they decided to see what the Mardi Gras excitement was all about."

He stood up and started to roam around the room, still holding my purse. "Maybe he thought, because of his dad's connections, that he was immune to the dangers faced by a black man and a white woman in the South. Anyway, you know more than I do about what happened down there. The next day when folks came and cut him down, they took her to the hospital, and she developed a high fever, encephalitis, and two weeks later she died. Two birds, one stone. Tully's father raised hell, but no charges were brought, no one was even seriously questioned, case shelved for lack of evidence. And to this day it hasn't been taken down and dusted off."

He stopped moving and regarded me with a thoughtful look. "And Jane Doe turns up with the whole package, signed, sealed, delivered. How far do you think Dumarie would go to get his hands on that stuff? Burn it, bury it, and anyone who knows about it? I'm very much afraid, Ms. Doe, that we have to keep you under wraps until all that stuff is in a very safe place, not just a hotel room in Portland."

I jumped up. "That's ridiculous! I can't stay here."

"There's no choice," he said. "If they're looking for you, believe me, they'll find you. And if they find you, you'll tell them whatever they want to hear. It's that simple. Not just your sweet ass at risk, but mine, too. And the prize goes to the winner, doesn't it? They'll end up with everything, two more missing persons to clutter up the police files, and the case closed for all time. I really don't see any alternative. Do you?"

After a moment I sat down again. He was right. If they caught me, they would find out everything. I had no illusions about my bravery. There was no reason for Prather and his crew to go back to Grandfather's house, not after having three men spend two days searching it, but they might have someone watching it for my return. If they were looking for me, it was because they thought I had what they wanted. That explained this suite, I thought then. Bruno and his editor had known from the start that I couldn't be turned loose yet.

Bruno nodded his approval when I sank down into the chair again. "I don't think I'll wait for room service and the bottle of wine," he said. "Let's see what's in the minibar. I usually don't go near one, but this is on the expense account, so what the hell."

He opened it and took a beer for himself; when he asked if I wanted hard stuff, wine, or beer, I said wine. Even prisoners get to name their poison, I thought dismally.

"You know Dumarie?" he asked, returning to the table. He began to put the prints back in the envelope.

"No. I've never even seen him in person, just on the news a few times. Magazine pictures."

"Yeah. He doesn't look like that picture, but you spotted him. Strange."

"Not really. A few years ago, six or seven years probably, there was a feature about him in *People*. It had pictures of him when he was younger."

Bruno was scowling. "Not many people would have put that together with that photograph. I say that's strange. You were a freshman four years ago. I taught only two freshman classes."

"And you were a lousy teacher. You hated us."

"I hated teaching, and the classes were filled with rich little boys and girls playing let's go to school."

No doubt I had been on a tighter budget than his, I thought, but I shrugged and let it go. "Are you still doing stories about dog shows and county fairs?"

"Sometimes. And whale watching and county commissioner meetings. See, the difference is, I won't keep doing that. And the kids I had to teach, for the most part, would never get beyond it. Did you land a job?"

I shook my head.

"Why didn't you take that stuff to the local cops, or the FBI?" he said, pointing to the envelope.

I hesitated, then said, "I wanted to make certain that someone would do something about it. Will you write the story?"

"There isn't a story yet. We have some pictures we can't account for, a mysterious lady we don't know, maybe a setup from start to finish." He grinned and spread his hands as if to demonstrate that they were empty.

He had a crooked smile that seemed to signify more skepticism than amusement. I remembered that nasty smile quite well.

"What will it take?" I asked. I had put my wine down after one sip. I had had a glass of wine in the bar, and no food since . . . I had to think about it. I might have eaten breakfast, but that seemed another day, another week even. Now I wished room service would bring some food.

"Verification, confirmation. Is that black man Tully? Is that his wife? Are they the same people who were watching the parade?"

"She's the same woman," I said. "It's harder to tell about him."

"How can you tell it's her?"

"It's the same face in both pictures," I said. "Anyone can tell that."

"I couldn't. Describe her."

"You do like your impromptu tests, don't you? Her eyebrows are straight across, no arch. Her chin is pointed a little. Her cheekbones look almost flat. And the hair is exactly the same, the same hairline, same part at the cowlick. . . ."

He dug though the envelope and pulled out the pictures and studied them, then replaced them, and now his gaze on me was more penetrating and interested. He held the hotel menu in front of his own face. "Describe me."

I did so, down to a small gold cap on a lower left tooth.

He put the menu down, raised his can of beer in a salute, and said, "You aced it, Sherlock. You don't miss a thing, do you?" He grinned that same crooked grin, then said, "You've got this great eye for details and you have great recall, but you're bone ignorant. Not a bad combination, if you can be taught." He held up his hand to forestall my furious response. "Lighten up. Everyone's ignorant until they learn a few things. See, from what little you've already told me, by the end of the day tomorrow I would have been able to learn who you are, what your grades were, what your old man does, everything on the school records. And there's always a lot in the record books. I flunked you, apparently, and you're still sore about that. So I must have thought you were a deadbeat back then, and you must not have given me cause to change my mind, back then. Now you have."

"You didn't flunk me."

"Ah, you failed one of my famous quizzes. Most kids did. If I had flunked you all the way, I guess you'd have shown up with a gun on your hip, not just a chip on your shoulder." This time his grin was mirthful.

Our food arrived then, and we were both silent until the waiter was gone again. During this time I was thinking furiously. He was right, of course. He could find out who I was, but there was no reason for him to take it past Donne all the way to my grandfather and grandmother and the name Landorf. I had to tell him something, and while we waited, I tried to sort out what details to admit to, what to leave out.

I thought with dismay of the tangled web I had been weaving and would continue to weave, and how firmly I was caught up in it, with no way out.

16

"Got it all together yet, Sherlock?" Perillo asked when we sat down to eat.

With my first bite of salad I realized that I was ravenous. I didn't even bother to ask him what he meant; I suspected he knew I had been concocting a story for him. Then, between bites of grilled halibut, browned potatoes, salad, and asparagus, I told him the story I was still trying to put together. Eating gave me reason to stop frequently to create the next scene, the next chapter.

"I'm Lee Donne," I said. "My father is George Thomas Donne. You may have heard of him. Many people have."

His eyes widened slightly, and he nodded. "Oh, my yes, I've heard of him."

"My mother has three doctorates, and I didn't graduate. I have an incomplete in history. My folks are miffed." As far as possible, I was going to stick to the truth; it was just easier that way. "Okay, you've got the picture. I didn't want to go home, and I don't have any money of my own. Some people I know planned to be away from their house for about six months, and they asked me to house-sit for them. I grabbed the chance. I was studying photography, they had a darkroom, and I could do my history paper, get the grade and the diploma, and dump the black-sheep bodysuit. It sounded perfect."

I had begun to stray from the straight and narrow, then I took a giant step off the path. "My friends bought the house fairly recently, and it still has a lot of junk the previous owners left behind. They didn't have time to go through it and discard things. I said I would do it for them. So they took off. There is an elaborate security system that they had installed after a break-in attempt, I should add. But I didn't give that a thought. My parents have a security system. A lot of people do."

I was slowing down, and during a pause I finished the halibut. He had already eaten most of his dinner, listening intently, not interrupting.

"A couple of weeks ago some men came to the door," I said then. "They said they were FBI agents and asked if they could enter and search the house. Of course, I said they couldn't. The one who was in charge said I should call the office, verify that this was official business. He said that they could get a search warrant if necessary, but they really wanted my cooperation. They didn't want any publicity, and a warrant would probably cause some. I looked up the number in the phone book and called the FBI office and got the extension the guy said I should ask for. His supervisor, he said. A man answered and confirmed that it was official business. They promised that the house would not be upset, nothing moved or destroyed, no walls broken, anything like that. I let them in."

Perillo's look was incredulous. "What were they searching for? Did they tell you?"

"No. They said it was something that might have been in the house for many years. I assumed they had a tip or something. Anyway, I let them in. I thought they were legitimate federal agents on legitimate business." I drank my wine and he refilled my glass.

"They spent two days and then went away. They didn't say if they found anything. I thought it was over with that, and I went back to clearing out junk and sorting things I thought might prove to be valuable."

The intensity of his gaze was unnerving, and his stillness. It was as if he had stopped breathing altogether. I took another sip of wine; my mouth was almost too dry to continue.

I described some of the broken toys, some of the other junk in the storage rooms, and the old log truck in detail. Then I said, "When I tossed the log truck into the box of junk, the strap broke and the logs tumbled out, and I saw the film canisters. I imagined a little boy coming across them at some point in the past and putting them with the logs, and I decided to develop the film, for practice. As I said, I was studying photography, but I had only developed my own film up till then. So I developed them."

"Some of those prints are not recent," he said flatly. "You didn't develop all of them."

I looked at my plate, as if searching for another bite of fish.

God, I thought in dismay, they could tell that? I took a bite of potato, then said, "You're right. When I saw what I had, I went back to the junk box and looked at the truck again and I found an envelope taped to the truck bed. It had the prints of the hanged man, the ones already developed and printed."

"You knew that's what the feds were looking for. Why didn't you hand them over?"

"I was going to this morning," I said. "The man who came had ID with his name, David Prather, and he gave me his private number and said I should call him directly if anything came up. But I called the office instead. I didn't want to talk to Prather, or have anything more to do with him. A switchboard operator or receptionist or someone said there was no such extension, and no David Prather there." I drank more wine. "I sort of fell apart. I thought they must have intercepted my call, they might have a tap on the phone, they would know I had tried to call Prather's supervisor. I left in a panic."

"And here we are," he said when I stopped. He moved his plate back and reached for the coffee. "Would you recognize Prather again, the men with him?"

I nodded.

"More to the point, would they recognize you now?"

"Prather probably would if he got a good look. Not the other three. Prather kept me in sight while they searched, and we talked."

"Sherlock, you picked up a live stick of dynamite, and it's smoldering away. If they are Dumarie's people, they have resources, like the Pinkertons, only more private even than that bunch. And if they had a tap on that phone, they'll have the bloodhounds out in force by now." He glanced at the table; nothing edible was left on it. "Let's order up some dessert."

He ordered pie, and I had coffee. What I really wanted was more wine, enough to get drunk and pass out and sleep until this was all over and I could go home and commiserate with Yorick. Alas, I thought. Indeed, alas, alas. I was so tired, my eyelids felt too heavy to stay open.

Then Perillo jolted me wide awake. "How did you find out Tully's name?"

Something else I had not thought of; I had no ready answer. I stared at him and shook my head and felt incredibly stupid.

"Okay. Okay. We both understand that you might have skipped a few details. We'll let it go at that, and you can come up with an answer."

But I couldn't. I was too tired to have to keep thinking up lies, lies, and damned lies. I was not used to so much lying, or so much wine; my brain had gone to sleep, and the rest of me wanted to go there, too.

"We have to wait for a phone call," Perillo said. "It might take a while, and as soon as that's done, you can tuck it in for the night. Do you have anything to wear? Clothes in the car, anything?"

"A suitcase in my car. In the hotel parking garage."

"Good. After my editor calls, I'll collect it for you. What's your history paper supposed to be about?"

I blinked at the change of subject. "Any ten-year period that changed the course of American history. I don't have a period picked out. Maybe the Civil War years and after. I don't know."

"And don't much care," he said.

That was the truth. It seemed so irrelevant, all those treaties and tariffs, wars and peace negotiations, all repeated endlessly.

"It's because they teach it as something abstract," Perillo said. "If they made you understand that history is about people and what's done to them and with them—"

The phone rang and he snatched it up. "Perillo." He listened, then nodded to me. It was his editor.

I poured more coffee and yawned. His end of the conversation was unintelligible: He said "yeah" a lot and grunted a lot and said, "That's right."

When he hung up, he regarded me with what might have been a fond expression. At least he was not scowling at me, and his cynical grin was not in play.

"We're in," he said. "Dumarie had a congenital birth defect, his left leg an inch shorter than the right. Willy is flying in tomorrow. I'll collect your suitcase, and you can get some sleep. Sound like a plan?"

I was chilled all the way through. Knowing it was Dumarie as long as no one else had quite believed it was one thing, having it confirmed was different, even though it shouldn't have been.

"Hey, Sherlock, don't go to pieces now. You've done everything exactly right so far. I called you an amateur before, but everything you've done to date has been as professional as an old-timer. Buck up. Okay?"

"I'm all right," I said. My lips were stiff.

"I know you are, but I want to make damn sure you know it, too," he said. Then he grinned and I was all right, just very tired. "I'll go get that suitcase now. What's your license-plate number, what kind of car am I looking for? Where's your parking ticket?"

I pointed to my purse on the sofa. He went to it and dumped the contents out on the coffee table, then whistled softly. "Where's the equipment that goes with this?" he asked. He was holding the shell casing. I had forgotten I had dropped in into the purse in what now seemed like another lifetime.

"A souvenir," I said.

"Uh-huh." He put it down and picked up the car keys. I told

him the make, the color, and the license-plate number, and he went out to get my bag.

Tiredly I thought, To hell with it. Overnight, in the morning, sometime I would come up with the missing chapters of my narrative. I went to the bathroom and washed my face, removed all the expensive makeup. The face looking back at me was still unfamiliar. It was the face of a terrified woman.

I was onstage in an amphitheater with a huge audience invisible behind sun-bright lights. Onstage with me was a mummy and a skull, nothing else. I cleared my throat, ready to recite some poetry, but the audience was talking, their voices rising and falling, and I didn't have a microphone. *Please*, I said, my voice no louder than the sigh of a breeze in the loud noise of the audience. Voices rose in shouts, then subsided. I pulled the stage curtains around my head, covering my ears, and tried to get their attention again, to no avail. The mummy was rolling around, the shrouded body writhing, and the skull swiveled to watch me as I ran around the stage looking for a microphone, or a pillow to put over my head, cover my ears. . . .

Then I was struggling to free myself; I had become the mummy swathed in confining sheets, suffocating with a pillow on my face. I was wet with sweat as I twisted free of the bedding and tossed the pillow to the floor. The voices were still rising and falling, and I woke up the rest of the way.

It was nine o'clock, the room bright with daylight, and men were arguing in the adjoining room. Dumarie! They found me! I jumped up and ran to the door to the other room and locked it, and almost instantly someone pounded on the door.

"Hey, Sherlock, it's okay. Willy's here. Get some clothes on and come on out. We're eating breakfast."

I didn't even move away from the door until my heart returned to normal, and then I headed for the shower. Half an hour later I unlocked the door and went into the other room. I had not heard a sound from them in the interval.

"Good morning," Bruno said. "Sherlock, meet my boss, Tom Williston, and that hunk is Jeremy Whosit."

Tom Williston was as round as a cherry and almost as red, five feet six, two hundred pounds; he looked like a sunburned cherub with a fringe of red hair. And Jeremy *was* a hunk, over six feet tall, wide enough to fill a doorway, with blond hair and pretty blue eyes. He smiled a slow, sweet smile and waved in my direction. "Wyzinski's the name," he said amiably.

"Lee Donne," I said, and went to the table set for breakfast. There seemed little left to eat, but a carafe had coffee in it. I poured a cup and sat down.

"There's toast," Bruno said. "We'll order whatever you want."

"Just coffee."

Williston sat opposite me, studying me closely. He said to Bruno, "She's younger than you said."

"Twenty-four, twenty-five," Bruno said. "I told you that."

"She looks younger."

"Hey, you two, stop that. Don't talk through me. What difference does it make how old I am? I gave you the material, and I want to leave here and go somewhere else. Like real soon."

"Not so fast, Ms. Donne," Williston said. "Don't turn around to see. Just tell me what Jeremy's wearing, describe him."

I gave Bruno an icy stare, and he shrugged. He was in full scowl mode that morning.

"Brown slacks, polyester, tan sport shirt, Hush Puppy shoes, straight blond hair, sky blue eyes, big nose, flat ears, lopsided jaw, thick lips . . ."

I stopped and drank the coffee and poured more.

Williston nodded. "Good, good. Very good. See, we don't have a story yet. We have to identify some of those other people, locate the site of the party, find out whose house it was in, make certain Dumarie was there that night on record—many details to see to—and details like that take time. And we don't have the authority the police would have to just go in and start asking questions. While that is going on, we will also gather material about William and Ilse Tully. He was decorated, I believe, a war hero. This is a very big story, Ms. Donne, and big stories don't get whipped out overnight. And until we go to press, not a word can leak about what we're up to. I'm afraid that our opposition already has a crew searching for you, and that takes careful handling also. Today Jeremy will take your car and put it in a safe place, then he and I will return to California and put those pictures in a safe place.

"You and Bruno will have to drive out of the state, I think. Even though you have changed your appearance a great deal, a trained eye might spot you at the airport, which is not quite like O'Hare or Kennedy or even San Francisco. You would attract attention in a small terminal like Portland. So you will drive out as Mr. and Mrs. Jack Henderson. I believe they stop cars at the state border, checking for fruit and such, but it won't be the same as their scrutiny at an airport. I doubt that they will employ the same kind of talent, not expecting you to be with a man already, and leaving in a leisurely manner. A little more red in your hair, a few freckles. We'll play up the youthful appearance, a child bride even. That would be good."

I was staring at him, aghast. I put my coffee cup down hard. "You're out of your mind!" I cried. "I'm not your girl Friday to order around. I want my car keys and my purse, and I'm out of here. I can take care of myself."

"You'll go to a friend and put her in exactly the same danger you're in," Williston said. "I understand you're unemployed. I could start you at a thousand a week, a six-month contract while you're on probation, to see how it works out. It's higher than usual, but you have an unusual talent that may prove very helpful. Your first assignment is to get out of the state of Oregon and down to our office, where I'll ask you to examine a lot of photographs—mug shots, if you will."

I stared at him, then at Bruno, whose face was a deep, dark red. "I can't just leave like that," I said. "I'm supposed to be somewhere. My parents know that; they'll call. Friends will call. My gran— The owners of the house might call. They'll report me missing, and the police will be out looking for me. And I have a job cataloging books. I can't just disappear."

"I'll send a couple of people to the house to catalog the books. They'll cover for you. If anyone calls you, they'll report it and you can call back. No one would expect you to be on hand every minute. And it certainly would not seem strange for you to bring in friends to keep you company. That part isn't a problem."

"I still say she should go to Kingman's and hole up," Bruno said. He turned toward me. "It's a real nice bed-and-breakfast on the Russian River. You could take pictures, do your history paper, relax. No one would find you there."

"I could take her there myself," Jeremy said.

"Jeremy, shut up," Williston snapped without looking around at him. "And you, too, Bruno." He lifted the carafe, put it down, and without glancing around said, "Jeremy, get on the phone, more coffee, more juice. Toast. You really should eat something, Ms. Donne."

Jeremy crossed the room to the phone by the bed and made the call.

"Why are you willing to put in so much money on this?" I

asked. "You and I both know Dumarie isn't going to come any-where near being elected. He's a rich man throwing his weight around, that's all."

"I'm afraid that's a naive view," Williston said. "He knows he won't win, and he doesn't want to, actually. He's building an organization, a power base. Once the election is over, they'll squash the president like a beetle underfoot, and next time around it's Dumarie's show. He'll have the states wrapped up like Christmas presents, no real opposition from any quarter. He's sixty-three and vigorous. His father is still alive and vigor-ous, and he's ninety, and there's a son in the wings waiting for his turn. He's a millionaire many times over, and his backers are millionaires. They know what they're buying, and they're will-ing to pay the price."

He leaned forward, his face redder than ever, an almost fanat-ical gleam in his eyes. "And you and Bruno and I will stop him in his tracks, Ms. Donne."

I drew back, feeling that if I touched him, I would be burned. "Not me," I whispered. "You have what you need in that enve-lope. You don't need me."

"But I do," he said, relaxing once more in his chair. "See, we have to get that house pinned down, and identify those other people, and you have an eye for things like that. I wouldn't have spotted Dumarie in that old snapshot with such bad lighting, and his youth. I wouldn't have given him a second glance. And even after I knew about the shoe, it wasn't obvious to me the way it was to you. You've got a wicked eye, Ms. Donne."

"Tell her the rest," Bruno said sharply.

"Right. See, our paper is going to do a special Mardi Gras fea-ture next spring. We'll send a young green reporter and his pho-tographer down there to get it for us. Anyone looks into their credentials, that's what they'll see. A kid who still does the county-fair stories getting his big chance at a feature, and another kid right out of photography school as his sidekick. Not quite ready for the big time, but trying hard, really hard, to make this a good feature. You and Bruno are perfect."

"You're crazy! I won't go to New Orleans!"

"How many people do you suppose that setup took, when they searched the house? You saw four men, and there had to be a telephone truck somewhere, someone up a pole fixing a line, someone in the truck playing FBI supervisor. And that's just in a backwater state like Oregon. How many men do you suppose will be out there with photographs of Lee Donne, going from motel to motel, one coast town after another, one city after another? You can't hide from them, Lee Donne. They'll be watching your parents' place, your friends', everyone you know. They'll be watching for your car. You won't be able to use a credit card, because they can trace purchases. So we won't try to hide you. We'll flaunt you instead. The purloined letter. You'll hide behind a camera, that's all. The last place on earth they would expect to find you is New Orleans."

He smiled. "I have a makeup man on the way up here to work on the freckles and reddish hair. He'll know the right sort of clothes for you, things like that."

There was a tap on the door; the waiter had brought more breakfast. "Why don't you just step into the other room until he leaves," Williston said.

In the adjoining room I sat down heavily on the side of the bed. I thought about Prather and the crew he had brought to Grandfather's house, and about Hollis Jasper, who had been in the state for so many years. Preparing the ground, getting to know the right people? If Williston sent people to Grandfather's house, they would soon learn whose house it was. I bit my lip. Hollis Jasper must know, I thought, that Casey and I were involved in his son's death, and he had not done a thing about it. He had not told the police, had not come around making accusations, nothing. Under orders? Probably. But if he was that callous about his own son, what did it mean where I was concerned? If I had found the film, if I had seen what was on it, I knew too much to live.

All right, I decided, I would have to go to San Jose; it was true that I couldn't hide by myself, not from people like Prather and his gang. And once in San Jose, I would take off for CalTech and lose myself in a sea of students.

Then, with panic rising again, I thought of Casey. I had to talk to her, warn her. And I couldn't go anywhere near her. They might be watching her already, waiting for me to show up. I picked the pillow up from the floor and sat on the side of the bed holding it tight, rocking back and forth until Bruno knocked on the door, opened it and took a step into the room, far enough to see me, and stopped moving. Then he said, "Hey, Sherlock, hang in there."

17

Williston was buttering a piece of toast when I approached the table again. He glanced at me, motioned toward the opposite chair, and said, "Sit down and eat. I'll lay it out for you, for the next two days anyway. You and Bruno are married, see, Mr. and Mrs. Henderson. Donna, that's a nice name for you. Jack and Donna. Where you from, Jack?"

Without hesitation Bruno said, "Akron, Ohio."

"That's good. So you're having a bit of a vacation, flew in to Portland, and you're heading down the coast to San Francisco. You're a little pregnant, a redhead, with freckles. No one's going to give you a second look."

I stopped walking; I was shaking again, but with fury now. "You listen to me, Willy! I don't work for you. Stop telling me what to do, what I have to do tomorrow. Maybe we can make a deal, maybe not. But there are things I want, and I want them in writing before we talk contract, and I want a contract before work orders!"

He chuckled and took a bite of the toast. "You'll do, Sherlock. What deal?"

"You don't know the house, and I won't tell you unless we have a deal. If I don't show up, or someone doesn't show up in that house, the police will be called. And there was someone there with me; she knows about this. Not all of it, but enough. Prather knows about her, and no doubt they'll be watching her, thinking I'll head there. I have to warn her. You have to help me find her and let me go talk to her. And you have to agree that the house owner will never come into anything you uncover. In writing."

"Not in writing," he said. "Or something like, On this day you and I before witnesses came to a certain understanding regarding your employment . . . and so on. No details in writing. Tell her my word's good, Bruno."

"It is, Sherlock. If he says he'll do it, he will."

"Why should I trust you, any of you? You and Jeremy work for him—of course you'd say that."

"You called me in the first place because you trusted me," Bruno said. "I'm still me."

His gaze held mine until I turned away and sat down. Silently Williston poured coffee.

"Okay," I said. "Just your word. The owner of the house never gets named, never comes into this in any way. Right?"

"Right," Williston said. "Now eat."

Bruno nodded at me, then went to stand by the window, gaz-

148

ing out. Again I skirted the truth and told some of what had happened. "Grandfather moved into the house in 1952, but some of that stuff has been there since the turn of the century, or even longer. And the pictures are from years before he got there. I want him kept out of this."

"You didn't recognize the guy throwing stuff at the house?" Williston asked when I finished my truncated story, which had stopped with the end of the ice cube toss, with not a word yet about Jasper's death.

I shook my head. "Not then. His picture was in the paper a few days after the noise stopped. The article said he had been murdered. His name was Kevin Jasper. His father's an attorney in Eugene."

Williston's eyes narrowed and he leaned back in his chair.

Bruno whistled softly, came to the table, and sat down, regarding me steadily. "That's the leverage the phony FBI guys used to get in to make a search," he said. "Threatened to tell the cops you and your friend were involved in his death. They knew about him, what he had been up to."

Not questions, statements of fact. I nodded. "They could still do that, and it would ruin Casey's life. Mine, too."

Williston shook his head. "They don't want cops. It was a useful ploy at the time; now forget it." He looked at the toast on my plate and said, "That's why you're so skinny. You don't eat. What about your friend, Casey? Why don't you know where she is?"

To my relief and surprise, no one asked if Casey and I had been involved in Jasper's death. Jeremy was gazing at me with a seraphic look of approval, and Bruno was scowling at the coffee carafe. Williston was spreading jam on another piece of toast.

"She's in the graduate program at CalTech. She had planned to stay with me only a week or so, but she got spooked by

Jasper's death and left early. She didn't have an address yet. If she calls and I'm not there, she'll call back a time or two, but then she'll yell for help."

"Okay, okay," Williston said. "We'll find her, and you can have a talk with her. We'll set it up. Good enough?"

I picked up the remaining piece of toast and buttered it. Good enough. I told him Casey's full name, then said, "When you get in touch with her, tell her that Marilee has to talk to Angela, at the risk of having her throat cut. She might be too suspicious to meet anyone unless she knows the message came from me."

Williston shrugged. "Whatever it takes."

The rest of the day was a blur of activity. Jeremy took my car to the airport and left it in long-term parking and returned in a car rented in the name of Jack Henderson. Williston spent an hour or longer on the telephone. A young Vietnamese man arrived, smiled shyly and took my measurements, turned my head this way and that, studying my face, nodded and left. He would be back in an hour, he said softly on the way out. Jeremy left with the envelope of pictures in the briefcase, and two hours later Williston left to meet an incoming flight and give the key and instructions to a couple who would move into Grandfather's house that night and start cataloging books the next day. My old school buddies, he said, Alison Sturgis and Buck Wiston.

The Vietnamese makeup artist did my hair first: a perm, over my protests, and a touch of red, he said softly. Just a touch. He bleached out the day-old dye and redyed it. I ended up with carroty curls. He dyed my eyebrows, too. And he gave me freckles, on my cheeks, nose, and both arms. They wouldn't wash off, he reassured me, but would fade out gradually, the way real freckles did in the winter. He sewed foam padding into a corsetlike garment, added a lining, and handed it to me along with the most hideous polyester pants and maternity top I had ever seen. "Mrs. Jack Henderson's choice," he said. "Try them on."

The finishing touches were white tennis shoes, the kind I thought of as granny shoes, and white anklets, some thrift-store beads, and a pair of sunglasses with sequined rims. I looked like the kind of frumpish woman I would go to great lengths to avoid.

"Perfect, perfect," the makeup artist said, as if in awe of his handiwork. "Perfect."

When Bruno saw me, he laughed. "Hey, cutie, how about a little kiss?"

If he had been within reach, I would have belted him.

The next morning Jack and Donna Henderson started their trek, headed for the coast and points south. I had feared that it might be a trip as silent as the ones I had taken with Prather, but Bruno was talkative and he was funny. He told stories about events he had covered for the newspaper.

"So the dog got the blue ribbon, and when the judge put it around his neck, the mutt raised a leg and let out a stream you wouldn't believe."

"You told our class we'd be stuck doing dog shows and county fairs until we got bored and moved on to something else. Why haven't you moved on?"

"I am moving on," he said. "A few trials during the past year—that's a step up. This one trial, a girl, seventeen, got pinched for shoplifting and since it was her first offense—first time she got caught, at least—she got off on probation. I happened to follow her and her lawyer out to the corridor, and he was groping his pockets, looking for a pen. She had to sign something. Almost absently she pulled his pen from her purse and handed it to him. I didn't add that bit to the story."

"How did you manage to land this story? There must be other reporters with a lot more experience at this kind of thing."

"You'd better believe it. See, I told Willy that I had a contact who could get the goods on Dumarie, but if I didn't get to cover it myself, I'd take my contact out the door and find another home."

I thought about it, then nodded. "That's how the game is played? Coercion? Blackmail of one sort or another? That's why he didn't bat an eye when I said I had to have a deal?"

"Yep. You went up a notch or two in his eyes then and there. That's how we play it." After a moment he said, "But he has a backup team he'll send in if we drop the ball, Sherlock. And he has the evidence. Keep that in mind." He was scowling fiercely again.

"Why are you so angry? Is it me? Because you're stuck with me?"

He was silent so long, I thought he would ignore the question. Then he said, "Let's get this straight. I'm in this because it's exactly where I want to be, the big chance, the story of a lifetime shaping up, possibly. You're here because you stumbled onto something and Willy saw a use for you. I wanted to tuck you away out of sight where you'd be safe and comfortable. He doesn't want that. So we make the best of it."

"He's using me. That's a laugh. You used me and my material, for openers. What's the difference?"

"I used you to get my foot in the door. I didn't intend to drag you through with me."

"You're afraid I'll blow it," I said heatedly. "And I might. I know I'm ignorant of the ways of the news world. It wouldn't occur to me to use people for what I can get out of them and then tuck them away out of sight, out of mind." I turned toward the side window. "Oh, I just wish I had run when that madman threw his first ice cube. I'd be out of it."

"Knock it off, Sherlock. If they didn't find the stuff during their two-day search, they wouldn't have found it if you had taken a powder. Their next step, Willy and I agree, would have been to grab your grandfather and make him tell them where it was. They were trying the easy way first, but do you really think they would have stopped there?"

We shopped in a supermarket and bought a Styrofoam cooler chest, sandwiches, fruit, and juice. He picked up beer for himself and wine for me. For the motel, he said. No alcohol in public. The baby, you know. We had a picnic on the beach that afternoon and took a walk, Mr. and Mrs. Jack Henderson enjoying their brief vacation. The first time or two that I left the car, I was apprehensive and reluctant, but no one paid any attention to me that I could tell. Now and then someone, usually a woman, glanced at me and quickly averted her gaze, as if embarrassed.

After one of our walks, and the climb back up to the car, he said, "What do you do for exercise?" I was huffing from the climb.

"No time for frivolities like that," I said. "I don't own a car, and I walked to classes, then to the bookstore where I worked, the library, grocery. That was about it. I intend to start a regular program any day now."

"You worked in a bookstore? Why?"

"What do you mean, why? Why do people flip hamburgers, or clean other people's houses, or fry doughnuts?"

Then I understood. "Oh, you mean my parents? Geo."

"You call him Geo?"

"Yes," I snapped. "And my mother is Tess. Anything wrong with that?"

"Not a thing. They kept you on a shoe string? What about your brother?"

"That's different. Ben's a genius. When he was ten, he told them he intended to go to medical school, and then into brain research. He's doing his internship." It sounded worse than I had meant it, and I added, "They, Geo and Tess, both think that you appreciate what you earn more than what's just handed to you."

He was silent for a minute, then said, "You've probably seen my dad in old movies. You wouldn't recognize him. Makeup and all that. He was a fencing master and teacher, and sometimes he was the stand-in for an actor who might have cut off his own leg if he'd been given a sword to play with."

"You said 'was.' Did he give it up?"

"Well, today it's all big guns and bang, bang, you're dead. He's into growing grapes now. Anyway, for a long time he groomed my brother and me to be actors, and now and then Rog actually got a part, but I never did. And one day Dad took me aside and said, 'Son, your heart isn't in it. Give it up.' The happiest day of my life. I told him I wanted to go into journalism, and he said, 'Go.' Rog has been getting quite a bit of work in television commercials, and I guess he's going to make it. But I was a throwback to the first Perillo who dropped out of the tree. Ugly as sin and no talent. Thank God!"

I looked at him; he was grinning. I wanted to say, Not all that ugly, but it wouldn't have been true. I said, "If you don't stop scowling all the time, you'll be as wrinkled as a prune before you're thirty, and that won't help matters."

He laughed.

We made our way down the spectacular Oregon coast throughout the day, stopping often to gaze at the water and cliffs, to walk; we bought fruit at a roadside stand, and stopped for the night a few miles north of the California border. Bruno called Willy.

"Alison and Buck are in the house fielding calls," he reported when he hung up. "They've located your friend Casada and will make contact tomorrow. We're to stay on 101 and call in around three or four." He yawned and stretched. "Let's go eat and hit the hay early."

Think of it as camping with your brother, I told myself after dinner, and he must have told himself something comparable, for we didn't even bring up the matter of sleeping in the same room. We just did it.

At nine the next morning we were stopped at the border. It was cool and too foggy for me to hide behind the awful sunglasses. I felt vulnerable and exposed when the inspector looked me over, then asked if we had any fresh produce or plant matter.

"Not really," Bruno said. "Lunch stuff . . . some peaches and plums maybe."

"Sorry, sir. You're not allowed to take any fresh fruit into the state. You can leave it here with me, or go over to that area and dispose of it there. Most folks eat what they can and just leave the rest on the table. Kids hang out looking for stuff. It won't go to waste."

"I paid six bucks for that bag of peaches," Bruno said.

The inspector shrugged and pointed. "Sorry. Rest area's right over there."

"What are they looking for?" I asked when he started to pull over to the rest area.

"Hell, I don't know. Mediterranean fruit bats, plum curlicues, peach fuzz . . ."

There were several other cars and a motorcycle parked in the rest area. A family having a late breakfast, or a second breakfast, some teenagers, a man with binoculars who had been looking at the high trees, then turned them toward us . . .

"While I'm getting the bag of stuff, you get out and walk around the car, look in the cooler and get the tomato," Bruno said when he stopped.

I got out and started around the car, and though I didn't stop or even hesitate, my heart went *klunk*. The man with the binoculars had been with Prather at Grandfather's house. I walked around Bruno and leaned over the cooler on the backseat. "He's one of them," I whispered.

"Right. Straighten up, hold on to Baby, and then waddle off to the rest room," he said in a low voice. "Flush the john two, three times. You have morning sickness." Then in a loud, carrying voice he said, "You had to have peaches. Nothing but peaches. Well, say good-bye to them. They stay here."

I straightened up, held Baby, and headed for the rest rooms, not quite running, but almost. I took my time in the stall, waiting for my heart to steady down again. When I walked out, back toward the car, Bruno met me halfway carrying a water bottle. He held it out.

"Swish some around in your mouth and spit it out. Then get back in the car. We're leaving."

Beyond him, the man with binoculars was studying the trees

again. And in a minute we were back at the checkpoint. The inspector glanced inside the cooler and waved us through. Bruno was whistling softly as he shifted gears and headed south, watching the rearview mirror alternately with the road ahead.

After a minute or two he said, "He looked you over, then went back to birdwatching. You done good, Sherlock."

I nearly wet my pants, I wanted to say, but didn't. "Yeah. Right. You wanted him to get a good look at me, didn't you?"

"Yep. I want that dude to stay there all day watching for birds. I hope it rains."

Within ten minutes a hard rain began. It was a slow drive through mountain country, then heavier and heavier traffic as we drew near San Francisco and bumper-to-bumper traffic through the city. He stopped that afternoon to call Willy.

"Okay. It's set," he said, driving again after the call. "Jeremy will pick up your friend and deliver her to a restaurant a few miles south of San Jose. I'll deliver you there, and you two can have dinner and chat. I'll pick you up again at eight-thirty, and Jeremy will take her home. Good enough?"

"Perfect."

Casey shrieked when she saw me. "Holy shit! I heard about fast workers, but you've beaten all records. What happened to you?"

"I turned into Donna Henderson," I said.

"Looks like in about three months it'll be Ma Donna," she said.

Then, in a dimly lit booth with a bottle of wine on the table and our order dispatched to the kitchen, I began to tell her everything that had happened.

The waiter came with food; we ate, and I talked for the next hour.

"You're not serious," Casey said when I finished. "You're not going down there!"

"What else can I do? I can't hide out for the rest of my life. That scumbag was at the border watching for me. They'll be watching for me everywhere. Even if they know I handed all that stuff over to a newspaper, do you think they'll forgive and forget? I don't. They'll kill me, Casey. That's the bottom line."

"You handed them a story on a platter; what more do they want from you?"

My argument, I recalled, and now I had to take Willy's side in rebuttal. "They need it confirmed, people identified, the party room, whose house it was in, a complete story about Tully, where he stayed in New Orleans, who found him, I don't know what all. But I can get some of it for them."

"Jesus," she muttered. "Sweet Jesus."

The waiter came and removed dishes, returned with coffee. We told him to leave the wine, and we both filled our glasses again. A woman and a man passed our booth on their way out; she paused at the table and leaned in toward me. "Don't you care about that precious life you're carrying? You're poisoning your innocent child with that alcohol." She looked mean enough to lash out and hit me.

"Get lost, bitch," Casey said.

"Sluts like you should be confined," the woman said, and marched out.

Miserably I shifted the foam baby. "I'm burning up. I have a rash. I itch. Killers are looking for me. And she wants to put me in prison. Here's to us, kid." I drank wine.

Bruno slipped into the booth beside me as we were having coffee. I introduced Casey.

"Your driver's waiting," he told her.

"Tell him to take off. I'm going with her," Casey said, pointing to me.

"Casey—" I started.

Bruno interrupted me. "It doesn't matter. I'm taking you to a hotel and then I'm going home. You're still Donna Henderson for one more night, but my masquerade's over. Some people in these parts might recognize me and wonder. I'll pick you up at eight in the morning. She can spend the night."

"Not just tonight," Casey said, leaning back in her seat, a tight smile on her face. "I mean I'm going with her. All the way. Driver, guide, the kid who can get the lowdown on Tully. You two can't, but I can. All the way."

"Thanks, Casey," I said, "but that's really crazy talk. You'll go back to school and do what you're supposed to do."

Casey laughed. "Baby, it took about ten minutes for me and my adviser to realize that I could teach him. He cut me loose. Independent study for a year, two assignments, doctorate. Like that. And I reckon the man behind him"—she motioned toward Bruno—"is gonna buy me a nice new laptop so I can do my work, help carry your gear, get the story on Tully, watch your back, and drive you around Nawlins."

Bruno shook his head. "I doubt it's going to happen just like that."

"You wanna bet?" she said. Then she came forward and said, "I walked out on her once; I turned tail and ran. Not again."

PART THREE

18

The smell of mildew hit me the minute I walked into the terminal at the New Orleans airport. Mildew, mold, dead things . . . Bruno sneezed, then sneezed again louder. Welcome to New Orleans.

Today and for the next week or so, I would be Kristi Reilly, fresh out of photography school at UCLA. I had a sweatshirt, a couple of T-shirts, and the tan that's a requisite for graduates of UCLA to prove it. My makeup friend had broiled me to a turn in a tanning salon until I was one shade darker than the freckles that were now invisible, and he had changed my hair again, to a rich deep auburn, with a nice wave, no curls. At first I had balked at tinted contact lenses, then tried them for a few days, and finally accepted them grudgingly. My eyes were now bright blue, bluer than Tess's. And I had proper Valley Girl clothes, neat pantsuits, silk shirts, designer jeans, and sixty-dollar T-shirts for slumming. Kristi was a poor little rich girl determined to make her way in the world.

A crowd had deplaned, and more crowds swarmed in the terminal; the air was oppressive, hot and humid even if it was late September. I struggled with two camera bags, a carry-on, and my purse, and tried to keep up with Bruno, who paid no attention at all to me.

"Hey, lady, carry your bags? Take you to town? Half-price." A big bony hand reached for the carry-on. I would have recognized that hand as Casey's anywhere on earth.

Casey had on baggy jeans and a shapeless faded sweatshirt cut off at the elbows, high-top tennis shoes laced halfway up, no socks, a baseball cap on sideways, and narrow aviator's sunglasses with yellow lenses. A perfect high-school dropout of the male persuasion.

"Hey, Perillo, wait up," I called. "I have a porter."

He turned around and snapped, "Not on the expense account."

"I'll pay, damn it. Come on, kid. You're hired."

We were on a low-budget, low-priority feature story, and from here on out we would stay in character whenever we were in public.

We made our way through the mob out to the parking lot, where Casey pointed to a ten-year-old Oldsmobile with big rust spots on the back door panel.

"It's better under the hood than on the outside," she muttered as she unlocked it.

A minute or two later, as she drove toward town, she filled in her past few days. She had flown to Mobile, Alabama, as Angela Casada, bought a car, and immediately sold it to Lionel Green, who had been on his way to New Orleans. Lionel had a room in a sleaze joint and had spotted a likely motel for us, and here we all were, she finished. On the seat beside her she had a beat-up duffel bag, which held her laptop. Willy had said in an offhand way that it could be that Dumarie's crew used a computer, and he had heard stories about hackers getting into computers, not that he believed any good could come from such things or that he would suggest anyone do anything illegal.

We had learned a lot during the past week, for instance, that they spelled *crew* funny here: *krewe*, with a *k* and an extra *e*. We knew that Dumarie was a member of the Hesperia Krewe and that there was not just one big parade during Mardi Gras, but a number of them, stretched out over weeks, some taking place in the evening, some starting as early as ten o'clock in the morning. Dumarie's plantation was called Mystic Gardens and was off-limits to the public, but other plantation mansions were open. Some had become museums, and some were still residences and had limited tours, like the British noble houses. And we believed that the ball pictures had been taken in one of the plantation mansions, not in a restaurant or a hired hall.

"Here's the drill," Bruno said. "In the morning Sherlock and I will go down to the newspaper and introduce ourselves. Willy set it up that the features editor will show me around, let me use the morgue, and we'll get parade-route maps. Then you two drive along a couple of them and take pictures. When you come to the one we want, take as many pictures as you can—point-by-point verification that it's the right route. The skyline's changed, and the signs, but some things must be pretty much the same. Do the best you can."

"And switch to black-and-white film at the appropriate time, and wipe my feet before I go in, and keep my nose clean, and don't forget eight glasses of water a day," I muttered. "We've been all over this, Perillo. Remember?"

"Okay. Okay." He scowled, his default expression, and jabbed his finger at me. "Keep in mind that this isn't a game. They're playing for keeps, and so are we. Don't get smart or fancy."

"You stick that finger out like that again and I'll bite it off," I snapped.

He looked at his finger and hastily pulled his hand back. Then he asked Casey, "Is there a decent restaurant near our motel?"

"You kidding? You can't throw a stick without hitting a restaurant, and as far as I can tell, they're all good. Real good."

"We'll check in and go have a bite to eat and call it a day. A long day," Bruno said.

It was eleven o'clock. I hoped we would find a restaurant open; I was so hungry, I didn't much care how good the food was.

"What about you?" Bruno asked Casey. "What's your setup?"

"Oh, I'll mosey around a little. My granddaddy talked so much about the old Zulu Parade, I'm checking it out. When I go back to Chicago, if ever, we can compare notes. The parade didn't get too far, way I hear it. Bars sponsored the floats, old trucks, a wagon pulled by a horse, like that, and of course they had to make an appearance at the sponsors' bars, and sometimes a greatly diminished parade continued. Hard to break away, you know. Great music everywhere. It's big-time now, just like the rest of the parades, but it must have been a kick back then. Tully would have taken it in."

"Is the place you're staying okay?" I asked. I hated it that we would be in a decent motel, and God only knew where she slept.

"Sure. Clean, fair bed, television. I turn on the television, put in earplugs, and go to work." She patted the duffel bag. "I've had worse digs."

We were in the city proper by then, and it looked like any other city at night, lots of bright lights, neon signs, traffic-jammed streets. What was different was the air: It smelled of the ocean and swamps, of fish and decaying vegetation and mildew. It smelled of death.

My room was okay if I ignored the pervasive odor of mold, and if I was careful about opening the door. It appeared that a swarm of tree frogs had taken up residence just outside. Dinner was not just good, it was extraordinary, in a restaurant that had eight tables and a sleepy waiter who recommended the jambalaya or the stuffed crabs.

At the newspaper office the next morning we met Brandon Arnold, who flirted outrageously with me and within minutes had offered lunch, to act as tour guide around the Quarter, dinner, a stroll on the levee. . . . His hand kept floating as if apart from him, as if it ached to pat my fanny. Bruno asked for the route maps, handed them to me, and told me to beat it, to be back at the motel by five, and to keep all receipts.

As I hurried away, I could hear them laughing, good old boys teasing the cute little photographer.

Then in the backseat of the Olds, with Casey at the wheel, I went to work photographing New Orleans. We wound about this way and that; I got pictures of the Streetcar Named Desire, parks, and the Garden District, where Casey sighed and said, "Maybe something like that for Ma and Pop someday." From what we could see of them, the houses were huge, with columns, balconies, and gardens, all tucked behind mammoth live oak trees, magnolia bushes that were as big as trees, oleander and wisteria vines.

"Nah," she added. "Not here. I got some manners taught me last night. See, in this bar, this dude asks what I'm doing down here, and I tell him checking it out, driving this green-as-grass lady photographer around right now, but I'll be looking for work after she's gone. Like that. And he says really serious, Watch your step with a woman, kid. Don't get chummy, eat with her, nothing like that. Know what I mean? Someone might decide to run a truck into that old heap of yours. Happens."

I told her to turn left at the next corner; she nodded and said, "Anyway, I brought up the old Zulu parades, how my grand-daddy came down to watch after the war, and that led to talk about the parades and other things. Like eventually I heard about this old guy who's kept a scrapbook of news stories about lynchings from year 1940 to now."

"Casey! Why didn't you tell Bruno?"

"For what purpose? No one's going to show him that scrap-book. But I might get a look at it. We'll see."

I switched film then; we had come to the parade route that the Hesperia Krewe had taken; it would be in black-and-white from here on out. "Slow down as much as you can without tying up traffic," I said. "If I say stop, find the first place you can pull off."

"Gotcha."

There, I thought then, that steeple. "Stop." She stopped at the curb, I shot several pictures, and she pulled back into the street. I had her stop again within a few feet, and then I said, "It isn't going to work this way. I have to get out and walk along here."

"You haven't done that before," she said in a low voice. "Someone might wonder what's so wonderful about this street."

"Is anyone paying a bit of attention? Just pull over and let me out."

I recognized a balcony with a fleur-de-lis pattern in the wrought-iron railing and balustrades. That night in 1947 it had been jammed full of people, some in costume, some in masks;

now it had some potted geraniums and a trailing vine in a planter. Same balcony.

I walked a block, then rode the next two blocks, seeing little of interest; too many changes, or no pictures had been taken of this section. I recognized nothing. Suddenly I caught my breath.

"Casey, you have to park again and let me out. This time, cross the street and look in those windows. Don't look at me, I want you for scale."

Across the street was an antiques store, with some garden furniture in front on a raised platform of some sort. That was where William Tully and Ilse had stood that night in 1947. It had been a hardware store then, with a wall of people in front, but the light and dark brickwork had not changed, nor had the scrolled iron columns at the door. We had found the building.

It was eerie, seeing in my mind the photographs I had studied, scenes filled with frivolous, partygoing, laughing people, and now the same locations, with only the few passersby intent on their own business or with no one in the frame, which was even weirder. The 1947 photograph was superimposed on the current scene, then eclipsed the current scene, flip-flopping back and forth like a strobe light shining on the past, then present, past, present.

After I took a lot of shots of the antiques store, we moved on and I photographed two or three more sites, but I had gotten what I was after: the place where William Tully's murderers had spotted him with his arm around a white woman.

"Great!" Bruno said when we met at five back at the motel. "Tomorrow the parks. Same thing, two or three parks, and then the Jean Lafitte Park. And hope you can find the same spot. And Wednesday, the mansions. I have a list of the ones that are open to the public, and we'll go to them first, then find a way to get inside the others. Making progress, Sherlock." He grinned widely. "Arnold thinks you're real cute, and if we happen to be in a certain bar around ten, he'll probably be there, too. And it would be nice to buy us a drink, talk shop, and so on."

"Anything for me?" Casey asked. She had been leaning against the Olds, listening, picking her fingernails, looking bored.

"Eight-thirty in the morning," Bruno said. "Nothing tonight."

She nodded and got behind the wheel. "See you later, alligator."

I turned toward my room, but Bruno said, "Buy you a Coke or something. That little café down the street. Come on."

It was a crowded bar with tables on the sidewalk, all filled, and other people milling about. A waiter asked if we wanted to go inside to order, and Bruno shook his head. "We'll wait here for the first empty table," he said. "That okay?" He passed a ten-dollar bill to the waiter, who nodded.

"Yes, sir. I believe that gentleman is finishing up. I'll keep an eye out." He indicated a table at the far end of the sidewalk, where a man was draining a martini glass.

"We could have figured that out by ourselves," I said.

"Watch."

The man wiped his lips on a napkin, folded a newspaper, and stood up. Instantly several people moved in the direction of his table, and the waiter appeared as if my magic and put a RESERVED sign in place, shook his head at the others, and motioned to Bruno.

Then, after we were served beer for Bruno, wine for me, and a plate of canapés to share, he said, "I have several things for us to follow up on. We have to go after the plantation mansions, but if that ball was held in Dumarie's place, we're sunk. No one can get in there. Every year the krewe elects a king for the parade, and most often he holds the ball in his house or rents a hall. Sometimes, if the king doesn't have a suitable ballroom, someone else's mansion is used. I couldn't find out where it was held in

1947, not yet anyway. We have to find it ourselves. The king that year was Conrad Tilden, and he didn't own a plantation mansion, just a house on River Road. They're mansions, too, apparently, but not of sufficient size to hold several thousand people and that's how big those balls ended up."

He drank half his beer and ate a shrimp, his brooding gaze on the crowd of people waiting for a table, a denser crowd now than it had been when we arrived. "Take your time with that wine," he said. "We're in no hurry to move on."

He rubbed his eyes. "Hours staring at microfiche newspapers," he said. "Puts your eyes out. So, that ball. It can be all things to all men, apparently. A debutante party for girls who are coming out, whatever that means. And it honored five young men who were graduating from an academy, a boys' prep school, and the Mardi Gras party all rolled up in one." He poked through the canapés looking for another shrimp, but he had already eaten them all. "The boys," he said. "Walter Dumarie, Dwight Tilden, Thadeus Stanhope, Hollis Jasper, and Robert Lee Fontaine Jr.

"We know it was a private residence," he said. "That big ballroom with the smaller room where the guys felt free to put on their sheets. Tilden is out, no mansion big enough, and Dwight Tilden died in a boating accident years ago. Dumarie, out. Can't get in. Stanhope, maybe. A Mrs. Stanhope is living on the property in a small house; other Stanhopes live in the mansion. One Stanhope son is off campaigning with Dumarie; another son is around. The Jasper place, maybe. It's a working plantation, with some Jaspers living in the mansion, not Hollis, who is in Eugene, Oregon. Fontaine, maybe. When the old man died, his heirs sold the plantation to a conglomerate of some sort, which turned it into a museum. The heirs are still around, but they have no interest in the mansion these days. Robert Lee is Dumarie's right-hand man, with him at all times. No problem getting into that plantation."

When he said the names of the five boys, I automatically translated the three whose names I knew: Holly, Tadpole, and Bobby Lee, and my heart went thud in a disconcerting way. Bruno was paying no attention to me, but my hand was shaking, and I put down my wineglass and clasped my hands in my lap until the shaking stopped.

"We don't even know that the ball was in one of those mansions," I said after a moment.

"I think it was, though. In honor of the five graduates. I read quite a bit about them. They were called the Five Rascalteers when they were pretty young. Inseparable, according to the articles. Then as teens they were called the Five Racketeers. Still inseparable." He leaned in closer, searching for something on the canapé tray, and he added, "I think they had their own private celebration that night, when they were initiated into the Klan. That explains the sheets anyway. Before that night they were just kids; then they got their graduation outfits."

He held up his glass for a refill; I drank my wine and held up my glass, too.

"One other little tidbit I gleaned," he said. "It seems that Stanhope is a big wheel in real estate here, and he owns a share in the newspaper where our pal Brandon Arnold puts in his forty hours each week."

"Oh, God! Does that mean he's in Dumarie's camp?"

"I think, Sherlock, that we should assume that everyone we talk to is in that camp. Cheers." He drained his glass and leaned back in his chair as the waiter approached with fresh drinks.

We took the streetcar to the French Quarter, along with a thousand students from Tulane. My UCLA sweatshirt stood out like a flag among all the Tulane shirts. Bruno had told me to wear my slumming clothes, and I could have passed for one of the students without any trouble at all. When we arrived at Bourbon Street, the French Quarter took me by surprise. Not knowing what to expect, I was not ready for the world's biggest state fair midway, the gaudiest carnival, the honky-tonk, the blare of music from all sides, the wall-to-wall tourists, panhandlers, street musicians, jugglers, fortune-tellers, hucksters, stores and booths offering flowers, peep shows, girly shows, boy shows, Tarot readings, palmists, liquor, wine, hot dogs, ice cream, juice bars.... Every store, every booth had its own variety of music turned up full volume: blues, hard rock, country and western, more rock....

Bruno was muttering under his breath as we were carried along by the tide of people like sticks tossed in a river flood. He kept a tight grip on my arm. Three blocks, he had said, from the streetcar to Josie's Bar, where he expected to run into Brandon Arnold. All around us the crowd surged, the people ranging from frenzied mania to apathetic exhaustion, simply carried along, as we were.

The crowd surged into the street, stopping a cab; the driver showed not a sign of impatience or surprise.

"He advised me to take the streetcar," Bruno said. "Now I get it."

By the time we reached Josie's Bar, I was jittery from the nervous energy of too many people and too much noise.

The bar was as crowded as the street, and a jazz quartet was playing, although no one seemed to be listening.

"Up there," Bruno said, still holding my arm in a death grip. He propelled me toward some stairs, where we had to work our way through people who seemed stuck in their tracks, laughing, talking, drinking.

"Ah, Brandon, fancy meeting you here," Bruno said as we approached a table where Brandon Arnold and another man were seated.

"How about that?" Brandon said, grinning. "Bill, meet Bruno Perillo and his photographer, Kristi Reilly. Bill Stanhope, folks. Sit down. Sit down. Maybe those monkeys will get off the stage any minute now and the real show will begin."

Stanhope had stood up with the introduction, and he shook my hand, held it too long, then shook with Bruno. "Sounds like an interesting project you're doing," he said. "But hasn't Mardi Gras been covered to death already?"

He was Bruno's height, five ten, and heavy, about sixty, with steel gray hair and rimless glasses. He was very deeply tanned. A waiter came for our order.

"Our project is a little different," Bruno said earnestly. "Actually Mardi Gras hasn't had very big coverage on the West Coast, though. But what I thought we'd do is show the transformative effect of a huge event like Mardi Gras on a city. I understand over five million people show up for the party, and I want to get pictures of the city before they get here, and put them side by side with the parades and parties and stuff."

Stanhope was listening to Bruno, but his gaze was still fixed on me in a speculative way.

"It really should be a video," I said. "Still photographs won't get the full effect, you know, streets nearly empty and quiet. Like in the Garden District today, a woman with a baby carriage, a man walking his dog, very quiet, silent even, then morph into a parade scene with a blast of jazz and stuff. A video would work better. And the parks. People sleep in the parks during Mardi Gras, and I want pictures of the same places when they're quiet, restful. Oh, the dreamy ballrooms! A thousand people in costumes, dancing, the orchestra music, then in a blink it's empty, maybe just one little cleaning lady in sight, or maybe just a piece of paper fluttering in a breeze, and deathly still. Back and forth. It's exciting, isn't it?"

Stanhope laughed. "You make it sound very exciting. I expect you'll go far, but how on earth did you manage to land such a plum of a job at your age in the first place?"

"Oh that. See, Daddy knows Mr. Williston from school or something, and he thought being a features photographer would be good experience and Mr. Williston said he thought so, too. And here I am."

"Yeah," Bruno said sourly. "Here we are. Down, Sherlock. Enough."

"Sherlock?" Stanhope said. "What's that about?"

"She can spot a Gucci bag a block away at midnight without a light."

The waiter brought our drinks and Bruno waited until the man left again, then added, "Problem is, she didn't notice that the guy carrying it was about sixteen and running like hell."

"One mistake and he's on my case for the rest of my life," I said in as hurt a voice as I could manage.

He had said to play it by ear. They had had plenty of opportunity to check him out, but I was still an unknown. And to remember that they would be aware that the bloodhounds had lost the trail of Lee Donne.

Stanhope was smiling at me when he asked, "Did you study with Stu Frazier?"

I shook my head. "I couldn't get in his classes. By the time I realized video was the way to go, the wave of the future, sort of, you know, he was filled. I had Paul Dorney. He's really good, too, you know, just not into video."

That was the clincher, Bruno and I agreed when we left Josie's Bar half an hour later to fight our way through the mob back to the streetcar. "How did you happen to know those names?" he asked, obviously pleased with me. He was smiling.

"If my mother knows anyone, she talks about him and I get to sort of know him, too. She mentioned them a few times. She teaches at UCLA now and then."

"Well, you get a gold star for your performance tonight. Good going."

I was as pleased as he was, but five minutes after we arrived back at the motel, I was knocking on his door.

"Someone searched my room," I said when he opened the door.

"Mine, too. That's what this little get-together was all about, I guess. To make sure we'd be out of the way for a while. We don't have anything to hide, just doing our job. Don't let it spook you."

Right, I thought, back in my room with the door locked, the chain on: don't get spooked. But I looked under the bed, and in the closet before I went in to brush my teeth.

19

The grasshopper was at least five inches long, iridescent green, with ruby streaks on its side, and gold. I focused, zoomed in for a closer shot, then held my breath when it stirred and raised its head from the leaf it was munching; after a look around, it returned to its dinner. Good, I thought, one shot with it chomping away, then get it to look at me. I wished I had a ruler near it, for scale; no one would believe how big it was. I shot again, and moved a step to the left; I heard the crunch of footsteps behind me and focused on the grasshopper; it raised its head, as I had hoped it would at the newcomer's steps, and I shot again, then again. With a flash of red-and-gold wings, the creature whirred up and away. I watched it out of sight, then turned to see a police officer observing me.

"Photographer?"

I bit back my snappy response and nodded. "That monster is as big as a sparrow. Your roaches are rat-size; the oak trees survived the last thousand years to all appearances. It's all pretty incredible."

"Yeah, I guess it is," he said. "I've been walking through this park going on five years now and I see something new most every week."

That morning Casey and I had hit three parks, then lunch of deli sandwiches, which she had eaten in the car, heeding the advice to keep her distance from the white lady photographer. After one more city park following lunch, finally I was in the Jean Lafitte Park and Nature Preserve. There were thousands of oak trees that all looked like the one I was searching for, all bearing dense cascades of Spanish moss, some tree trunks as big around as the Olds was long. Casey was back at a picnic table near the car, tired from doing a double shift each day. She was with me most of the day, cruised bars and talked to people until eleven or later, then went to work on the computer. She had gotten into the New Liberty Party database, and had downloaded two disks of information that she had put in the mail to Willy on her way to pick me up. It looked like organizational stuff, she had said, but she was not doing much reading, just finding material and copying it.

I started to walk along the path again, and the officer fell into step beside me.

"I heard there was a mammoth banyan tree in here somewhere," I said. "But I haven't come across it. You know the tree I mean?"

"Sure. It's down by the boat launch. This path goes right to it.

Used to be a road. Folks would drive down to the canal and put in rowboats, canoes, but they closed it off and put in an access road over there a ways, to keep folks from parking under the tree. Come on, I'll show you."

We walked along with others on the path; he spoke to an old couple, told a boy on a bike that there was no riding allowed, and talked to me, all easygoing, pleasant. Then I stopped and stared.

"That's it," I said.

"Yep, first glimpse of it. Better view on down a ways."

There, behind another of the giant oak trees, I could make out the spreading banyan that was in the background of the photographs of the hanged man. In the photographs it had looked at first like a fence or a stockade of some sort. Willy had suggested a banyan, a tree I had never seen before, and there it was. I didn't want to continue down the path; I needed to walk here until I found the right spot to start taking my own pictures, but I had to get rid of the overly helpful officer first.

A minute or two later we rounded the last curve in the path and the gigantic banyan tree came into full view.

"Wow!" I said softly. "It's a Dr. Seuss creation. You wouldn't have a treehouse up there, but a whole village, a tree village."

The officer chuckled. "Never thought of that, but reckon you could."

The air roots had touched ground, dug in, and become trunks with their own canopies, all joined, and new air roots formed. The tree would fill a city block. The tree that ate New Orleans, I thought, focusing my camera.

I began snapping pictures, and after watching me for a time, the officer said, "I'll be on my way. You can find your way back okay, can't you?"

"No problem. And many thanks. I really appreciate your help."

He waved and moved on, following the path toward the boat-launch area. I waited until he was out of sight, then began to back up, taking pictures as I went until I finished the roll of color film and replaced it with a roll of black-and-white. I headed back up the path, back to the oak tree.

In my mind the other picture rose with sharp details: the oak tree with the heavy drapes of moss and the dead man, and dimly behind it the spreading banyan tree, barely visible, spectral. Today the hanging moss was like ghosts, unmoving in the wind-less afternoon, but how it would writhe and toss when the wind rose. I was shivering as I took a few steps, stopped, took a few more steps. The light had been headlights, I thought, as I looked for the right spot. A truck, cars, a lot of bright light on the imme-diate scene, scattered and dim on the banyan in the background. I stopped again; the image in my head had synchronized with the scene before my eyes. One could have been superimposed over the other. Forty years, fifty years meant nothing here; those two trees were what they had been and what they would continue to be for centuries to come. I began to snap pictures.

Then, using the viewfinder, I scanned from the oak trunk out-ward slowly. The hooded men on one side, the hanged man on the other . . . The men had been in full view, pointed hoods to shoes; I backed up step by step. They had been under a branch two feet in diameter, with another branch growing from it. . . . There. Not a second branch, but a callus where it had been cut off and the tree had healed the wound.

I finished the roll of film, then left without a backward look. I felt sick and angry, and more than a little afraid.

I had shots of where Tully had been standing during the

parade, and we could put Dumarie in the float that had passed there. Technicians were analyzing shadows to get the exact time of day the parade had passed, and Bruno was getting the parade-route information. Now I could put Dumarie under the oak tree where Tully had been hanged. Investigators were getting the evidence they needed about the special shoes. The ballroom was next. If we could find it and get pictures, show that the same people who had been on the float had been at that ball, and then under that tree, demonstrate that Dumarie had been at all three places, it would complete the story. Tomorrow, the next day, the next, we would search for the ballroom.

Anyone looking over the snapshots I had taken would not see anything suspicious, I reminded myself: the parade routes, parks, trees, all innocent. Without the others to compare them with, they meant nothing. A second thought followed swiftly: the photographer knew. And he could have been any one of them, or someone we had never heard of. My fear was intensified, and I wished we were done there, out of New Orleans, back where we belonged.

At dinner Bruno said, "I have a ton of stuff, all kinds of publicity pictures, the parades, balls, castles, mansions. The chamber of commerce is delighted with our project, and various krewe members leaned over backward to help. Tomorrow, we'll hit six or eight mansions, and if we don't spot the right one, I'm going to ask Stanhope if he can get us into Dumarie's place."

He had crawfish étouffée, which he eyed suspiciously, then ate heartily. I had crab gumbo. It was another neighborhood restaurant, small, not crowded, with excellent food. They did eat well in New Orleans, I had to admit.

"They raise these critters on farms," Bruno said, spearing a crawfish. "And they have catfish farms and alligator farms. I can imagine the cowboys rounding up the alligators. Giddap!"

A minute later I had to push my plate away. They ate well, and copiously. "Perillo, why now? Those pictures, I mean. Why not ten years ago, or twenty, even longer ago than that? Why make a grab for them now?"

He looked at my plate. "You're not going to finish that?"

"Can't."

"Mind if I have a go at it?"

We traded plates, his scraped clean, and then he said, "Willy and I talked about that. Why now? What makes sense is that the guy with the camera fessed up what shots he had taken right after Dumarie threw his hat in the ring back in January. They knew about some of the pictures, remember. They posed for some of them. But maybe the camera bug said the film was in the secret bat caves where they keep Klan memorabilia, or something to that effect, and no one gave it another thought. But when Dumarie began running hard, the stuff became a definite liability. So they had to go after it." He shrugged. "Speculation, you understand. We don't know any more than you do about the real reason, but that works."

After considering it, I nodded. It did make sense. Possibly Geneva had argued that Benjamin would never betray her, just as he had promised, but they might not believe he would feel the same about Dumarie when he realized he was running for president. I knew that Grandfather would not recognize Dumarie, and probably wouldn't remember his name, but how many others would have known that for certain? I doubted that Grandfather even knew that Dumarie was in the contest; he was as apolitical as I had always been.

———

As we were walking back to the motel, the Olds pulled up and rattled to a stop and Casey called, "Hey, want a ride?"

"What's up?" Bruno asked, getting in the front seat as I crawled into the backseat.

"Let's move first, just in case," Casey said. "Watch out for that bag, it's not a footrest." Then, in light traffic on a side street she said, "Seems that I was wrong about the guy with the scrapbook, thinking he wouldn't show it to honkies, I mean. He'll show it to anyone who'll take the time to look. He wants the whole fucking world to have a look. And *they* know he has it and shows it, and *they* couldn't care less. Keeps the message alive. Every time anyone looks, it's like a warning: Remember. Be careful, or it could happen again. Like that. You guys ready for it?"

"Can we photocopy it?" Bruno asked.

"Nope. He won't let it out of his hands and, besides, it's falling apart. It's been looked at a lot over the years."

"Could I get pictures?" I asked, leaning forward. "I have a close-up lens, and I'd need a good light. Halogen light would work. Is there a store open around here?"

Then, with my portable tripod with telescoping legs, a halogen lamp, my camera, and six rolls of film, we went to Reverend Sealey's house. The streets were narrow and dark, the houses small, huddled together, many of them already dark, with no one on the front stoops, on the porches, and few people on the streets. The house we entered was a box divided into four small rooms and a bath. A tall woman admitted us and stood aside as we entered, and the room immediately became crowded. An old man in a wheelchair nodded to us.

"Reverend, this is the lady photographer I told you about,"

Casey said. "Kristi Reilly. And the reporter, Bruno Perillo. Reverend Sealey."

"And my daughter, Cybil," the old man said. His hands were twisted into grotesque shapes by arthritis, his knuckles swollen, angry-looking. His white hair was so thin, it barely covered his scalp, and his face was pitted with old scars. Cybil did not say a word, simply nodded at the introduction. She was about fifty, straight and strong-looking, much darker than the old man, with frizzy gray hair caught up in a bun held in place with pearlescent combs.

The room had two upholstered chairs, a rocking chair, and a wooden chair, a small television set, several end tables with magazines and some paperback books. A large worn Bible was on a table by the arm of the wheelchair. One wall had six shelves on glass blocks, with more books, a basket of dried flowers, family pictures, a few knickknacks. . . . It was all very clean, obviously cared for. The end tables were lustrous with furniture polish. The odor of fried onions and fish was in the air.

"You want to see the book," Reverend Sealey said.

"Yes, sir. That's what we came for," Bruno said.

The reverend looked at me and my camera bag, then at Casey and her duffel bag, and said, "Looks like you aim to move in with us."

"I brought my camera," I said then. "If you would permit it, I would like to photograph the pages of your scrapbook."

"Why? What will you do with the pictures?"

"We'll make sure they get seen," Bruno said. "I intend to write about New Orleans, not just the glitzy parts, the parties and parades, but about the people who live here, who worked to make it what it is. And the people who died here. You and your scrapbook are part of that story."

"Get the book, Cybil," the old man said.

We looked at it on the kitchen table, but when I started to set up my tripod and light, Bruno said, "Maybe we can talk in the other room while she goes to work." We couldn't all fit into the kitchen, and I was relieved when Reverend Sealey wheeled himself back and away from the door.

"I'll stay and help you," Cybil said.

Probably she wanted to make sure I didn't do any more damage to the scrapbook than time had done already. It was falling apart, as Casey had said, and the pages were yellowed and brittle, the newsprint barely legible in many places. But I would get something, I knew. Maybe just the boldface print, but something. I mounted the camera and turned on the light; Cybil held the scrapbook open, and I started.

It was going to be a long and arduous job, I realized. Each page was a new challenge, with newspaper folded in places, or a heavy crease obscuring words, or a smudge that hid the words. The reverend's voice carried into the kitchen.

"I was just a little boy," he said, "six years old, when they came and took my pa. They made Ma bring me and made us watch. And when they were done, one of them slapped me, see this scar. His ring did that. He said, 'Remember this, boy.' I remember. Oh, Lord, yes, I remember."

I looked at Cybil, whose expression was hard and distant, a face carved in stone. How many times, I wondered, had she heard this story?

"No, no. I began the book later, when I was fourteen or fifteen. See, something happened to Ma that night. It was like she began to fold up, fold into herself, diminish and shrink. I lived with my grandma for a time, then back home, then back with Grandma, up in the bayou. She took me fishing up in the bayou. And Ma kept shrinking until she wasn't hardly there at all, and then she wasn't there, and that's when I started the book."

Cybil turned the page and I focused on the new story, but my eyes were bleary and I had to stop and wipe them before I could continue.

"Grandma always said the happiest day of her life was when she heard me preach for the first time. She claimed credit, whipped me if I missed a day of school, threatened to skin me alive if I didn't make grades. She was strict, and then we'd go fishing. She could catch fish when there weren't any."

I had come to the story of William Tully, and I tried not to show more interest than before, but something was communicated to Cybil. She gave me a hard look.

"He's just like the others," she said. "In the wrong place at the wrong time. That was his crime."

It was nearly midnight when I finished; my back was stiff and aching, and my eyes felt on fire. I hated the contact lenses. "Done," I said wearily, and Cybil closed the scrapbook.

"You'll want a glass of water," she said. "And it's way past bedtime for my father. Is that all?"

"Yes. And thanks, Cybil. Thank you very much."

She brought me a glass of water, then said, "It won't do any good. What's the use? It's history, let it be. That's what they say. Don't rake the coals again. But it doesn't end. Folks don't get strung up on the corner these days, they just disappear. Alligator food. What's the use? You stop one, there's three more waiting to take his place."

"But if you don't stop the one, then there's four of them," I said.

She shrugged and walked back into the other room. "It's time for company to leave," she said to her father. "You'll pay for this tomorrow."

"Often it's worth the price," he said. "But it is time. Will you send me a copy of whatever you write? I'll add it to the book."

"How many times have you heard folks say they're going to do something about all this?" she asked bitterly.

"From these folks, only this once," he said.

No one said a word going back to the motel. When Casey pulled up to the door of my room, Bruno said, "You want to knock off tomorrow, relax?"

"No. I want to finish and get the hell out of here."

Casey said, "Amen."

"Right. Nine o'clock, Lionel. See you at breakfast, Sherlock."

That night I dreamed I was riding a horse in an alligator-infested swamp. The alligators were monstrous; they bit off the legs of my horse and I was sinking, sinking down into the swamp where they awaited me. I woke up fighting the covers, drenched with sweat. All I could think was, God, I want to go home.

20

"This one features rosewood from Brazil, teak from Sumatra, ivory from India, marble from Italy, mahogany from the Philippines," I read from a brochure. We were on our way to the fourth plantation mansion, each one grander than the last. On both sides of the mile-long driveway to the building dense stands of bamboo screened experimental rice fields. The bamboo trunks were green with gold bands, and they gleamed as if shellacked.

"Holy shit!" Casey exclaimed when the mansion came into sight. It could have been lifted stone by stone from a castle fortress compound in Provence. Turrets, battlements, even a drawbridge over a stretch of water that looked like a moat at first glance but proved to be an artificial stream complete with black swans.

"One hundred and two rooms." I finished reading and put the brochure down and picked up my camera. Such ostentatious wealth was getting on my nerves, grating, making me angry.

At the first mansion Casey had taken her computer from the duffel bag and carried it and my two camera bags, and tagged along with us, keeping a respectful distance in the rear; the computer would melt in the hot car, she had muttered. No one gave her a second look, just another kid hustling a buck. I had stopped paying attention to whoever came to greet us and escort us through the mansions. One man had been as surly and brusque as I felt; another wanted to give us coffee and beignets; this one wanted to talk about the new rice, the wave of the future. I ignored him and took pictures. One look at the magnificent ballroom was all I needed. I shook my head at Bruno, and he began easing us toward the entrance, the manager of the farm thrusting literature at him, urging him to write up a story about the importance of experimental rice and what it meant to millions of undernourished people throughout the world.

The money spent on one of the crystal chandeliers in the ballroom would have fed a million people for a year, I was thinking as we returned to the car. There were twenty chandeliers in the ballroom.

"Okay, gang," Bruno said in the car. "Onward to Jasper House. And that's going to be tricky. Just play along with it."

The Jaspers were no longer krewe members, he had learned, and he did not have a brochure about the house; the chamber of commerce man he had talked to said to forget that one. They hadn't had a ball in nearly fifty years, just a working farm now, working people.

His agenda was to promote Mardi Gras and New Orleans;

our agenda was to inspect the ballrooms of the young men who, we believed, had been initiated into the Klan back in 1947, and that list included Hollis Jasper. We did not want to make it obvious that we were singling out Hesperia mansions, or those particular ones, but neither did we want to skip any of them. We had decided to hit three random mansions, then one Hesperia Krewe member's plantation until we got to them all. On to Jasper House.

It was not a castle, but rather a picture-book southern mansion. Massive oak trees lined the driveway to a portico paved with white limestone. A wide veranda was supported by pillars that rose to a third floor and continued around both sides.

"Just a little old farmhouse," Bruno murmured as he rang the bell. "Probably no more than forty or fifty rooms."

A young woman opened the door; she was dressed in jeans and a T-shirt, sandals, her wheat-colored hair in a ponytail.

"Yes?" she said. "Can I help you?"

"Bruno Perillo, from the *San Jose Herald,* and my photographer, Kristi Reilly. We're doing a feature story about New Orleans, some of the fine old houses, Mardi Gras, the works. May we come in?"

She looked us over, frowning slightly, then said apologetically, "Would you mind waiting a second while I check?"

"I have ID and a letter of introduction," Bruno said, but she was already closing the door.

"Maybe we can sneak in through the servants' entrance," I murmured. "Pretend we're termite inspectors." Bruno gave me a mean look.

The door opened again, this time with an older woman standing in our way. She was obviously the young woman's mother, and no doubt her hair had been as light as her daughter's at one time; it was darker now, untouched by gray. They shared the same features—wide, firm lips and a nose a touch too long, brown eyes; she was not really pretty, but good-looking with many smile lines and telltale crow's-feet about her eyes. She was wearing jeans, a tank top with a man's shirt over it, and running shoes that were worn and dirty.

"I'm Beverly Jasper," she said. "I'm afraid there's been a mistake. We're not part of Mardi Gras. There's nothing here for you or your story." She spoke pleasantly but firmly, and seemed ready to close the door exactly as the younger woman had done.

"Your house is on our list," Bruno said. "One of the oldest residences around, one of the finest, where some of the grandest balls used to be held. See, we're comparing the present Mardi Gras scene with how things used to be, how they are the rest of the year. Could we just get a couple of pictures of the house?" He was holding out his ID and the letter of introduction the chamber of commerce had provided, a "To Whom It May Concern" letter verifying his credentials.

She glanced at the letter indifferently, looked at his ID, and then smiled slightly and opened the door wider. "A comparison might prove interesting," she said, motioning us to come in. "I doubt that anyone from the chamber sent you to us, and more likely they pretended they never heard of us."

We entered a spacious foyer with two matching curved staircases and many doors, most of them closed. The stairs led to a balcony, where I could see double doors, also closed. The ballroom, I thought, imagining the costumed partygoers mounting the stairs, laughing, with the orchestra music swelling and ebbing as the double doors opened and closed.

I held up my camera and said, "May I?"

She nodded. "Be my guest. Over there we converted rooms to

offices, and upstairs . . . But come along, I'll show you the ballroom." She was clearly amused as she turned and led the way toward the stairs.

"We dismantled a lot, I'm afraid," she said, going up. "Chandeliers, various light fixtures, some tile work. And we've made a few changes to the ballroom." We reached the double doors and she opened one of them.

I caught my breath in surprise. There were folding screens dividing the space into sections, and fifteen or twenty children who stopped what they were doing as we entered. Desks, blackboards, a piano . . .

"You turned it into a school," I said.

"Kindergarten through sixth grade. Preschool in another room."

The children were black, brown, and white. The young woman who had opened the door the first time was at a desk. Two other women were in the room, one sitting on the floor with children gathered around her.

Hastily I looked at the architecture, the walls, windows, the ceiling stripped of fancy chandeliers and fitted with utilitarian fluorescent lights. Bruno was watching me; I shook my head. Wrong ballroom.

We backed out, and our hostess closed the door quietly.

"Mrs. Jasper, would you tell us your story?" Bruno asked. He sounded almost humble.

She hesitated a moment, then she nodded. "Yes. Come along. We'll have coffee."

We went back down the stairs, and she motioned for us to follow as she started toward the rear of the great foyer.

"I'll wait in the car," Casey said.

"Why? Don't you like coffee? We have soft drinks, or juice if you'd prefer. Come on. This way."

She took us to a small room furnished with rattan chairs and lounges with green-and-white-striped cotton-covered cushions. Beyond the windows was a playground, swings, a jungle gym, monkey bars, an enormous sandbox.

"When the little ones get up from their naps, they'll have a snack and then go out there to play," she said. "Excuse me. Please, make yourselves comfortable. I won't be a minute." She looked at Casey. "Coffee, juice?"

"Coffee's fine," Casey said.

Mrs. Jasper was gone less than a minute. She smiled ruefully and sat down when she returned. "They chased me out of the kitchen. I'd just be in the way while they're preparing the children's snacks. Someone will bring coffee eventually, I hope." She looked at Bruno. "You can take notes, if you'd like. I'm not telling anything that isn't well known around here, but you're not likely to hear all of it. You know the game telephone? How things get scrambled from person to person?"

Bruno nodded and got out his notebook.

"There have always been Jaspers here," she said slowly, as if gathering her thoughts, arranging them. "They built this plantation on cotton and the backs of slaves, and they became extremely wealthy. That part's an old story, of course. Then Luke Jasper, my husband's father, began to get strange ideas. He wanted to pay his workers a decent wage, for one thing, and he wanted to start a school for the workers' children and build a hospital. Not altogether a liberal, but headed that way. And his father called him irresponsible, dissolute, a wastrel, and cut him out of the will. He was not to be trusted with the family fortune, you see; he might spend it on the wrong kind of people. Instead, the fortune was to go to the three grandsons when they became of age, which in this case meant twenty-five years old, and college educated. That was in the will, too, that they had to go to

191

college. The Jaspers always believed in education, for the right people. The three grandsons were Hollis, the eldest, Morley, and my husband, Darien."

She stopped speaking when a young black woman entered with a tray. "Sorry about running you off," she said to Mrs. Jasper. "Here's the coffee, and we thought you and your company might like some of those cookies we made. They're still warm." Her friendly smile included all of us. She set the tray down and left again.

Then, eating fragrant warm cookies and sipping coffee, we heard the rest of the story.

"Well, Luke died, and it seemed that Holly was exactly what his grandfather had in mind as a legitimate heir. He was part of the Dumarie gang, became a krewe member, did all the right things. Both grandparents died while he was off at Yale, and when he came home, it was as if he had swallowed a magic potion or something; he seemed more like his father than his grandfather. He and his brothers talked about running the plantation the way their father would have wanted it. He got his law degree the year Darien and I got married, 1952, but after a few months he began to complain that he couldn't practice law here, and he had no intention of becoming a farmer. Then he turned twenty-five, and we all learned what the will really meant."

She refilled her coffee cup, motioned for us to help ourselves, and leaned back in her chair, gazing out the window. The children had come out to play. She smiled, then resumed speaking.

"The will left the money to Holly, because, their grandfather stated, he was the responsible one of the three. And he left the farm to all three brothers. Everyone was stunned. There was a trust fund for Darien to finish school, but nothing else in the way of cash. Holly said not to worry, they would split everything just as they had planned, and he put some money in a joint account for operating expenses. Then he went off with Bobby Lee Fontaine and Tadpole—Thadeus Stanhope—and never came back."

She was gazing fixedly at Bruno, no longer smiling. "His brothers didn't want him to go. They were afraid Bobby Lee and Tadpole would get to him, that he'd revert back to the old ways, with life just one big party after another. But he wanted to see some of the country out west, one last jaunt before settling down to turn this place into a model farm. The three young men left together; only Bobby Lee and his sister, Geneva, came back." She shrugged.

"What do you mean? What about Tadpole?" Bruno asked.

"He was captivated by San Francisco. They had remained in Eugene, Oregon, for several days getting Holly settled in. He had decided to start his own law practice there. The others went on to San Francisco, but by then Geneva was anxious to get home and didn't want to linger on the West Coast, so she and Bobby Lee drove on and Tadpole stayed. He sent a few post-cards home, I believe, and then dropped out of sight. There was an investigation, of course, but he was just another missing person, a restless young man cutting ties, striking out on his own. The rumor here was that his family was deep in debt and he had little to come back to.

"Meanwhile, back here on the farm, there was enough money in the account to get through the year, and pay taxes, but not enough to keep things up the way they had been. Morley wrote to Holly and never got an answer. The next year Holly trans-ferred money to the bank for taxes, nothing else, just that. The following year a letter came from a lawyer saying that Holly was relinquishing his share of the property, a legal document of some sort, and he was no longer a part owner and no longer responsible for any debts the plantation accrued. No more tax money, no more operating expenses. No more anything."

She drew in a long breath. "So. There we were, Morley and his wife, Darien and I with a huge plantation on our hands and no money to run it with. We decided to give up cotton altogether and start a truck farm, fresh vegetables and herbs for the restaurants of New Orleans, and we made it work. We couldn't get a mortgage or even a loan; my father helped out. And we worked. My God, did we work. We swore we would pay decent wages, and we would turn the old slave quarters into habitable houses and provide day care and educate the workers' children. They used to run wild when their parents were working. And we've done all those things." She smiled. "Today we can't grow enough to meet the demand of the best restaurants in the city. No matter what we charge, they are willing to pay it."

"That's the story," Bruno said softly when she stopped. "Why did Holly say he couldn't practice law here?"

"He said the cards were stacked against him, that the Jasper name was anathema to the powers that be. When we tried to get a mortgage, we realized the truth of that."

We spent another hour on the plantation and I shot three rolls of film: the greenhouses, the ballroom school, the preschool rooms, the children at play, and Mrs. Jasper.

"Not like this," she protested with a quick glance at her clothes when I asked permission to get her photograph.

"Exactly like that," I said.

When we were ready to leave, she said quietly. "It's a story, but for whom? I said at the start, everyone around here knows it already, and who else cares?"

Driving back to town, Casey said, "A guy told me about the bayous the other night. He said you go along in a boat and there's nothing but black water, filled with cottonmouths and alligators, and the sun don't shine, the jungly growth is so thick, and then you come to a hummock, a high spot with firm ground and sunshine and birds singing. We came to a hummock today."

Bruno made a note.

21

"That's it for today," Bruno said in the car, heading back toward the city. "It's after four, too late to hit the Fontaine mansion. It'll keep. Dumarie's having a televised press conference at eight tonight local time. I want to catch it."

On both sides of the road the land had yielded to swamps. Wherever the land sank a few inches, the water seeped or ran in; marshes, swamps, bayous formed. I had read that if you dug a posthole, you'd have a well before you could get the post in. Even the dead were buried aboveground here. But people loved this wet country. The night before, I had listened to Reverend Sealey talking to Bruno while I took photographs: "Sent my boys away, up north, where they could make a man's living and raise a family. Abe, the youngest, couldn't stand it. He came back. Lives up in the bayou where my grandma used to live. He's content there."

"He doesn't have two dimes he can rub together," Cybil had said in a loud voice.

"Doesn't want to rub dimes together. He wants to fish and net shrimp and run his crab traps and be left alone. Doesn't take a dime to do that."

"Sherlock, I asked if you want to go with me to hear Dumarie."

I jerked back to the present. "Go where?"

"Morrison's Bar. Good working-class bar. I want to see how the locals react to Dumarie. We can go get a bite to eat after he's done."

Casey had already said she was going to eat and then stay in her room and work on the computer, and get to bed early. I had no desire to hear Dumarie in a noisy white bar, but it would be better than having dinner alone. I had learned that although desegregation was the law of the land, segregation ruled. I nodded.

"Good. Take a nap or something, I'll come by at seven-thirty."

The bar was too crowded for us to get in at first, then a cluster of five or six people left with looks of disgust on their faces, and Bruno pushed through several others milling about and forced his way inside, pulling me along.

The television was on loud, and on the screen, behind a wide bare desk, sat Walter Dumarie. He was a good-looking man, with a mop of enviable, white-gold gleaming waves. He was very tanned, his face unlined, and either he had had a face-lift or he had found a way to ward off sags and the jowls that so often mark men in their sixties. He was talking as we found a place to stand. The clink of glasses was the only sound in the bar.

"... so if you have a bunch of boys over six feet tall and you have a few who are about five feet seven or five feet eight, would it be fair to any of them to start the short boys halfway down the track and call it a fair race? You know it wouldn't. Let them compete with their own kind. Let them all toe the mark exactly the same way. If they can't cut it with the tall boys, let them run against others like themselves. And let the winners achieve honest victories according to the ability of the competitors, not some arbitrary preset rule that tries to even the playing field."

The bar erupted into whistles and clapping, drowning out the next question. Dumarie smiled benignly at the questioner, and the bar fell into an eerie silence again.

"What I meant, and what the audience understood I meant at the time, has been twisted out of recognition. See, if the Creator had wanted his creatures to be green, we'd all be green. But he didn't want that. He created separate and distinct races. What his purposes were is not given to us to know. We just have to accept a divine plan beyond our comprehension. For millennia his plan endured, but we have lost faith, lost our ability to accept what we cannot understand, and we are endangering our humanity. Every race has its very own distinct virtues, no one denies that, but when you start mixing the races, you dilute those virtues until in the end you have left only the worst of both. Take the horse and the donkey, both fine animals, and if each is bred with its own kind, their virtues remain intact. But if you breed one to the other, you lose the fine qualities of the horse and the fine qualities of the donkey and end up with an animal that is neither one nor the other, and has none of the virtues of either parent. The mule is a mongrel, sterile and doomed. Mixing the races is contrary to God's plan and can lead only to the destruction of the entire human race."

He kept smiling and smiling, like a kind and patient father explaining the world to a child, meaning no harm, wanting only what was good and right. The bar had burst into applause again, and I felt queasy and too hot.

The next question had to do with immigration, I assumed. As before, the bar noise drowned out the questioner.

"Right. See, the Mexican people are good, decent, hardworking folks who have problems with their own economy. But why should a struggling farmer in Iowa, a poor crab netter in Louisiana, or a bone-weary steelworker in Illinois sweat and labor and watch his tax money go to solve another country's domestic problems? Is that fair or just? We have enough of our own problems to deal with, don't we? And why should the American people allow those in trouble to swarm into this country and bring about the same conditions they are fleeing?"

He was going on, but I was suffocating. I tugged on Bruno's arm and whispered that I would wait for him outside, and I made my escape. The days had been quite warm and very humid, the nights rather cool and humid; and after the overheated bar, I was chilled out on the sidewalk. Not only from the lowered temperature, I realized, but also from watching Dumarie.

He was dangerous, I thought, surprised. I had never heard him speak and had read very little of his various position statements, and I had been expecting him to rant, to be more like the televangelists, to be a master of the often-mocked southern style of overheated oratory. But he didn't come on as a hatemonger; he appeared reasonable, soft-spoken, charming, handsome, and so very patient. He was taking serious, complex problems, making them sound simple, and offering simple solutions that were easily grasped. The bar burst into loud shouts and applause again, and I moved farther away from the door and then began to walk, to the corner, back, again.

Twenty minutes later Bruno joined me. "Chicken," he said. "You missed some of the best parts. Now I understand God's plan for women, and, Sherlock, you ain't measuring up."

"Jesus! Give me a break. I've walked this block until I know every crack in the sidewalk. There's a fancy restaurant down on the corner, big expensive cars unloading fancy people. I want to eat there."

"No tie," he said, pointing to his neck.

"Thumbtack a ten-dollar bill to your chin. Some of them didn't have ties, either. Come on. I'm freezing and starving."

Walking to the corner, Bruno said, "There were some dissenters in there, but they were keeping a low profile."

"That man's scary," I said.

"Where have you been for the past three or four years? I know he's scary. This the joint?"

We entered the restaurant where the maître d' was much too well bred to frown on Bruno's windbreaker or my UCLA sweatshirt. Tourists, what can you expect?

That night in bed I thought about what Bruno had said about Dumarie—where had I been the past three or four years? Running away from what I didn't want to see, I admitted. That's what the Landorfs do; they run from things unpleasant, things frightening, things out of their control. The image of Casey came to mind, Casey running out into the backyard, tears streaming, gasping for breath with her face lifted to the sky: "You don't know! You can't know!"

It was a long time before I could fall asleep.

"'The Fontaine House Museum,'" Bruno said, reading the brochure, "'boasts an eclectic collection which depicts the first settlements of Louisiana, through the Louisiana Purchase, the Arcadians, cajun cooking, life in the bayous, the building of the levees, and the development from the first cotton plantation to the most modern present-day cotton plantations.' That's a handful for one little old house in the country." He put the brochure in his briefcase. "Also, it's twenty-two miles from downtown New Orleans. That must have been quite a trip back and forth in the good old days. Did you know that some of these roads used to be made with cypress logs? They called them corduroy roads."

"Wanna bet that in the old pictures the darkies will all be wearing smiley faces?" Casey muttered.

"You don't have to go in," I said.

"Baby, I wouldn't miss it for all the tea in China."

I alternated between dread and anticipation. This was where Geneva, my grandmother, had grown up. On this property was the bungalow she and my grandfather had lived in with their child, my mother. In my head, like a mantra, I kept saying, *Don't let it be this one.*

Every day he traveled this road, I thought, back and forth to Tulane, and she spent her time in the comfort and luxury of her family home while their servant Melody tended the child and the bungalow. Was he, even then, turning a blind eye to everything around him, losing himself in commuting, in school, studies, Shakespeare? When had he started running from the reality of his marriage with the beautiful southern belle?

When the mansion came into view, Bruno whistled softly and Casey muttered a curse. From the brochure I had learned that this building was T-shaped, with a huge central section and two long wings, each ending in a tower. The towers were four stories high, red and white brick, octagonal, with ten-foot-high French doors on four walls on the ground floor of the east tower. The doors opened to terraces and two acres of gardens. The balls sometimes had lasted until sunrise.

A large parking lot had three other cars.

"Okay, gang," Bruno said. "Once more into the breach."

"I long for a nice four-bedroom ranch house," I said.

"This ain't it, Sherlock. Let's do it."

A small area with a desk holding only a bell had been walled off from the entrance foyer. A middle-aged woman came from somewhere when Bruno rang the bell. Admission was five dollars, she said, and she had self-guided tour aides—headsets, handheld cassette players, one dollar each—and the map of the museum was free. She beamed at us as she offered her wares.

We took the map and entered the foyer. "Just the east tower," I said. "I've had my fill of how the other half lived and lives."

"I want to see the replicas of the Mississippi River paddle boats," Bruno said, studying the map. "West tower. I'll catch up with you."

He headed one way, and Casey and I turned the other way to enter a gallery with tall windows on the outside wall, mirrors on the opposite wall. "They copied it from Versailles," I said in a low voice. I had seen a video of Versailles; this was almost exactly the same, if not quite as large. "The folks had banquets here, fed a hundred at a time." Now there were display cases along the mirrored wall. We did not slow down to examine the contents.

"That's a lot of fried catfish," Casey said. She was being the good porter Lionel, two or three steps behind me all the way.

Doors in the mirrored wall led to other rooms, to another hall, the kitchen. At the end of the gallery giant folding doors were open; we entered the ballroom.

It was two stories high, and from the chandeliers dangled handmade Venetian glass reflectors in many pastel colors, tapered and scalloped like seashells: a dozen small chandeliers circled a mammoth one dangling with the same kind of delicate and beautiful glass. The French doors were closed, uncovered by curtains or drapes, and between them cotton wall hangings filled the space, twelve feet wide, seamless, and lovely.

"Sheets," Casey murmured. "That's all they are. Oversize sheets."

They had left this room, except for the wall hangings, exactly as it had always been, with a raised platform for an orchestra, and room for five hundred couples to waltz to the strains of Strauss. According to the brochure, the ballroom was rented out for Mardi Gras dances years in advance.

The photographs I had seen had been dim, poorly lit, and filled with costumed people, but there had been some details. White woodwork had shone through the dimness. I narrowed my eyes and studied the woodwork over the high French doors. It was deeply carved, scrolled, with a seashell motif at the outer corners: The seashells of the woodwork and those of the chandeliers were the same. I felt very distant, unreal, as I studied the woodwork through my viewfinder.

"This is it," I said, and hardly recognized my own voice. Mechanically I began moving around the room, searching for a match with the pictures in my head. It was difficult: the wall hangings were a distraction, and flooded with light, as it was now, and empty, the room looked altogether different. But it was the room. My worst fear, what I had dreaded most, I had found, and was not surprised to find. I felt as if I had known from the start that the running had to stop there. I had to face it, and in time Geneva, Bobby Lee, even Grandfather had to face it.

Then I stopped moving around and began shooting. I was standing where the photographer had stood so many years ago and snapped pictures of Dumarie and three others in a laughing conversation. Casey must have gone to tell Bruno, for when I looked up, he was standing near the great folded doors watching me. I nodded at him. He didn't ask if I was sure. He simply nodded. I motioned for him to join me.

"I need you to walk out on the floor and keep going until I say stop. I want a full-person view with that woodwork above his head."

I was snapping his picture when another couple entered the ballroom and came to a stop, as if reluctant to get in the way.

"Would you mind standing by my friend?" I asked. "I'm trying to show the scale of this room."

"It's enormous," the woman said. "Can't you just imagine yourself in the arms of Rhett Butler, waltzing away the hours? Isn't it the most romantic room you ever saw!" They went to stand by Bruno, and I took another half dozen snapshots.

I was thinking: that night the music must have stopped, people were standing around talking, waiting to resume dancing, and the photographer had taken advantage of the pause to get the pictures of Dumarie and others. Secretly, I added; they had not been posing for the camera. How can you hide a camera?

I thanked the couple, but Bruno asked for their names, and explained that we were doing a feature article for a newspaper, and after that the woman seemed to want to tag along with us, perhaps hoping to get her picture in the newspaper more than once. Bruno told them they really should see the paddle-wheel boats; one was big enough to board, and they wandered off.

"Had to get their names," he said apologetically. "If we use their picture, we'll need a release. Lesson umpteen."

"Okay. Now, another room where the other pictures were taken. Smaller, much smaller, I'd guess."

"So we do a museum tour," he said, pulling out the guide map.

We saw cotton gins and looms, horse-drawn plows and reapers, pictures of fields of cotton with tufts that looked like snow, kitchen utensils from 1800. . . . Then in what the brochure called a bedroom suite—bedroom, sitting room, dressing room, and bath—one of six such apartments within the mansion, I said, "Something like this, I think. There was a chest along a wall, and a table." Paneled walls, I remembered. Pale paneling—knotty pine, possibly—and a picture on the wall, a seascape. Of course, the personal things would be gone, but the paneling should still be there. And the paneling had dark and light spots. Unless the spots had washed off, or been painted over, I would recognize the paneling.

We found it in the fourth suite. There was no way to tell whose apartment it had been; it was cluttered with display cases of folk art made of cotton—dolls, stuffed animals, cotton flowers. . . .

It took a long time. I studied the paneling board by board, moved around the room, and studied it again, then again. Table here, chest against that wall, picture . . . I moved again. Then I was standing in an open doorway to an adjoining room, thinking, bedroom, sitting room. . . . Someone had stood there. I had it.

"Perillo, move closer to that display case. Back up a step or two. . . . Left a couple of inches."

"Not much farther," he complained. "If you didn't notice, there's a display case."

"Shut up and stand still." I began to snap pictures, then lowered the camera. Children's voices?

"Come on, Sherlock. Kiddie hour's starting or something," Bruno said.

I snapped more pictures. Done, I thought, and lowered the camera again. We could put Dumarie in this room with the sheets and the hoods.

"Let's get the hell out of here," Bruno said.

"Not a minute too soon for me."

On our way to the front entrance we passed about a gazillion children, all talking at once. And outside was a school bus. Field trip, I thought. See where the money came from. Learn something about the history of your state, kids.

In the car, leaving the grounds, Bruno said, "Sherlock, you're something else. You really are something else."

"Can I go home now?"

"Not on your life. We have a date with Bill Stanhope at two. He's willing to give us a personal tour of his little old shack, and even throw in a drink. So, lunch, and then press on."

I groaned. My eyes hurt, and I was tired of grand houses, tired of taking pictures. I was getting a headache. We had what we had come for, and I wanted to go home. Or at the very least take out the damn contact lenses.

22

"Listen, Perillo," I said as we entered Stanhope's property. "I've had it. Really had it. I have a headache and I'm in no mood to be jolly and take a tour. I'll get pictures of the ballroom, and then I'll go sit on a bench under a tree or something and wait for you."

He shrugged. "Okay. It might take a little while. I want to turn the conversation to Dumarie, get the lowdown on his local troops, if I can."

"Will you look at that!" Casey said, slowing down almost to a stop in a long driveway that curved and twisted like a snake.

Ahead, in the distance, not clearly discernible, was a topiary zoo. I could see an elephant and a horse, with other animals behind them, living green statues on a carpet of emerald velvet.

The mansion was on a rise with marble stairs leading to the entrance. "The house of twenty-seven gables," I muttered. It looked like a building that had had many additions, all with peaked roofs and gables, with small balconies that appeared to be placed randomly on the upper two floors.

Bill Stanhope met us at the top of the stairs. "Welcome," he said. "My home. Not as grandiose as Fontaine House or Mystic Gardens, but we like it. Come in. Come in."

He was voluble as he ushered us into the foyer and began pointing out the native materials: cypress, bricks made on the plantation, oak paneling. . . .

"Where to start," he said musingly. "I believe you said you were getting photographs of ballrooms primarily. Is that right?" He smiled a snake-oil-salesman smile.

"Yes, sir. That's my assignment. Ballrooms and outside shots of the mansions and some of the grounds. I saw the topiary zoo. I really want to get to it."

"Well, I can understand that. Amazing, aren't they? And they get better closer up. So, the ballroom first. It's relatively new. By 'new' in these parts you mean within fifty or so years. The family started to do some remodeling back in the thirties, but the war came along, and supplies and workers vanished. So we waited, and tackled it again in the early fifties. At first our thought was to refurbish the old ballroom, but it was a tad small, so we changed our minds. That became our rec room with a swimming pool and exercise equipment, and we built a whole new ballroom. This way." He looked at me, smiling. "Perhaps you would like to see the rec room before you depart for the menagerie."

Before I could say no, that would not be necessary, Bruno said, "Sure. We might even use something like that as part of the story. The contrast between the old and the new."

Oh, I thought, of course. That had been the ballroom in 1947: He wanted me to look it over, but I didn't know why I should. I knew we already had the right one. I shrugged. "He's the boss."

Stanhope took us through a wide corridor with artwork on both walls. "We encourage local artists by showing their work, a regular gallery, with an opening-night party, the whole thing. Change it every two months. It's considered an honor to be chosen. And here we are."

The ballroom was as stunning as they all were: I took pictures, expressing my awe, and we moved on, through another long corridor with more art, and into a room that looked like the YMCA. I took pictures of it, too.

"Okay, Sherlock," Bruno said then. "I'll tell Willy you did your job like a good little soldier. Go on out and play with the animals."

With Casey in tow, I left them, and heard Bruno say in a voice meant to carry to me, "Damn baby-sitter, that's what I've turned into." Stanhope laughed.

The animals were amazing: a six-foot-tall green pig, a four-foot rabbit with two small ones, a cow. . . . Twisting paths led in and out of the display, with benches and white marble pedestals holding large blue reflecting balls spaced throughout. I took a lot of pictures as we wandered, sometimes laughing out loud at the zoo. We had entered the park at the rear, gradually made our way to the far side, and started back on a zigzag course that eventually would take us to the elephant we had glimpsed from the driveway.

Then I stopped moving as I heard a woman's garrulous voice: "I told you they are over there, not here."

"Haven't come across them yet," a man's soft voice said in a soothing tone. "I'll keep looking until I do, ma'am."

"You won't find them over here. I saw them over there, nasty things, swarming all around."

I stepped around a giraffe and saw her, an old white-haired

woman, stout, dressed in a long gray silk dress with long sleeves. She was leaning on a bench, pointing a cane. Nearby, a black man held a long sharp tool of some sort. He stuck it into the grass, pulled it out.

"Not any here."

"Idiot! How many times do I have to tell you? Over there by the rhinoceros." She stopped berating him when she saw me. "Who the hell are you?"

"Kristi Reilly," I said meekly. "A photographer. My partner and I are doing a story about the fine old houses in these parts."

"Who's that with you?"

"That's Lionel. He's helping me carry my things."

"You can't be too careful," she said, eyeing Casey suspiciously. "Turn this garden into an amusement park and attract all sorts of people. They come in and dump their trash." To the black man, she said, "Find those goddamned ants! And not over here." She beckoned to me. "Give my your arm, girl. I'll show you the oldest house in the parish. My house."

Helplessly, I glanced at the black man, whose face held no expression whatsoever. Then I went to the old woman, and she clutched my arm. She tottered a little when we started to walk, and I wondered what the cane was for, since she didn't seem to use it for balance.

She walked on the grass, and when I suggested we might use the path, she cackled an eerie laugh. "I never use the path. They booby-trap it. A log one time, wet leaves once. They think I'll fall and break my hip, and if you break your hip when you're eighty-five years old, you die. They know that, and I know that. No path. Don't worry about snakes. If I see one, I'll hit it." She brandished her cane menacingly.

"This used to be a beautiful garden, and Billy turned it into an abomination. They sneak in to see it, and if you run them off, they sneak back in and dump buckets of fire ants or booby-trap the path. I know what they're up to. I watch for them when they think I'm sleeping."

I hadn't given a thought to snakes, but fire ants? I looked at the velvety grass with alarm.

"Not here. Not here. Over there by the rhinoceros. That old fool couldn't find an anthill if he was pegged down on it."

We made slow progress until we came within sight of a white building that looked like a house that real people lived in. One floor, russet trim, with a wide porch and open windows.

"That's the first Stanhope house," the old woman said, waving her cane at it. "I was born there. They wanted to tear it down when they built the big house, and Mama said leave it be, and now it's my house. I don't go to the big house anymore. Air-conditioning. It spreads disease, the reason people have things we never heard of before. Boys with hair down to their asses, girls with their belly buttons showing. Pictures of naked people. Obscene statues. They swim naked," she said in a harsh whisper.

"Oh, you're Mrs. Stanhope?"

"Yes, I am, and this, all of this, is mine, but Billy thinks he has a right to do what he wants when he wants, acts like he owns it all. If I see his trashy company and speak up, he orders me— orders me!—to go back to my own house! It's all mine, all of it!"

When we got near the porch, she stopped walking and yelled, "Lettie, come out here!"

A young black woman hurried from the house. She was dressed as a nurse, down to spotless white shoes.

"Get behind me," Mrs. Stanhope said. She did not loosen her grasp of my arm. "I make her stand behind me," she said. "She can catch me. But I don't fall. Do I, Lettie? Do I fall?"

"No, ma'am. You're as steady as a twenty-year-old."

Tottering no more than she had done on the smooth lawn, she

mounted the single step to the porch, where she turned and said to Casey, "You stay out here."

Still holding my arm, she crossed the porch and drew me inside with her. "My house. Isn't it pretty?"

It was bright and clean, with bare, gleaming, wide-plank floors; pictures of irises and roses were on the wall of the foyer. Mrs. Stanhope led me into a comfortable living room, with upholstered furnishings covered with flowered material. A red-brick fireplace took up one wall, and more pictures of flowers were on the walls. A crystal bowl held roses on an end table. There were framed pictures everywhere, studio portraits and candid shots on every table, every flat surface.

She sank down onto the sofa and said, "Lettie, don't just stand there like a post. Bring us something to drink. The usual. Sit down, sit down," she said to me. "Those floors are cypress. It doesn't rot or wear out, ever. Those floors will last a thousand years. The whole house is built out of cypress, and they wanted to tear it down! Mama said leave it be. I was only two years old. It's going to be here when that big house is a pile of rubble.

"That's Mama," she said, using her cane as a pointer. A studio picture of a woman in Victorian dress was centered on the mantel, crowded by other family pictures.

"Your mother was very beautiful," I said.

"She was pretty as a picture. There's my boys." She pointed again, this time to four children lined up like stair steps.

"You have four sons?"

"Had four. Had. God didn't see fit to let me keep them all. The best get taken young. You know that? The best always get taken young. Homer, the baby, he got polio. Five years old."

Lettie entered with a tray. She handed Mrs. Stanhope a tall glass with a sprig of mint, and handed me one just like it. The

210

usual, I thought, tasting it cautiously. I blinked in surprise. Gin and bitter lemon, more gin than lemon.

Lettie put coasters and napkins on end tables, then left without a sound.

Using the cane again, Mrs. Stanhope pointed to another studio picture, this time to a handsome man with a mustache. "That's Carly, Carlyle, my husband. He was a shiftless no-account, but I told Daddy that if I couldn't have him, I would drown myself in the bayou. He died . . . Lettie knows when he died. Ask her. She knows. Never did a lick of work in his life. Played with the boys like a boy himself. We danced. . . ." She took a long drink.

"Homer got polio and Tadpole got shanghaied. Next to Homer he was the best. I thought I would get to keep him, but he was shanghaied."

"What do you mean?" I asked.

"Don't you know what *shanghaied* means?" she said crossly. "He went to San Francisco and then he was taken by a Chinaman. That's what they used to do, and still do, I imagine. No one talks about it. They pretend it never happened, but it did. That's Tadpole. Such a good boy."

She raised her glass, and I stared at the studio picture she had pointed to. Slowly I stood up and went to the mantel and looked harder. I was looking at a picture of Hollis Jasper.

I looked from it to a studio portrait of Carlyle Stanhope, and the resemblance was unmistakable. The man I had thought was Holly Jasper was actually Thadeus Stanhope, Tadpole.

She was talking. "We called him that because when he was born his head was so big. Nearly killed me, giving birth to him did. He grew into it. He grew into a beautiful boy and young man. But he was taken, too. Angel in heaven. Never raised his voice to me, never said do this or do that. A good boy. The best get taken young. Always has been, always will be like that. Polio, shanghaied, dead and in heaven. When they can't row or do whatever their masters tell them, they get thrown over the side."

I sat down again and took a large drink of gin and bitter lemon, my thoughts in a spin that made no sense at all. Mrs. Stanhope talked on: the flower gardens her mother had maintained, the abominable animals Billy had brought in—"They wander around at night, you know"—the fields of Louisiana irises, even red. . . . Carly, Billy, others whose names I didn't know.

I paid scant attention, nor did she require any acknowledgment; she talked on.

"Ask Lettie. She can show you the dining room. Cypress burl table. You don't see cypress that big anymore, not burls like that."

Her head nodded, and then she leaned back. "Lettie will show you the rest of it. Tell her to show you . . ."

I stood up and left the room quietly. Lettie met me in the hall. "I think she fell asleep," I said.

She nodded. "She does this time of day. I'll tuck her in."

She would sleep now, I thought, as I left the house and motioned to Casey, who was sitting on a bench near a green bear. With her in character, keeping a discreet distance behind me, I headed toward the front of the zoo, toward the elephant, thinking: sleep now and keep watch at night when the animals roam and the invaders bring in buckets of fire ants.

I was on a bench near the green elephant with my eyes closed when Bruno yelled, "Hey, Sherlock, wake up. Time to go."

I stood up and stretched, and even yawned, although I had not been sleeping, but rather weaving an invisible tapestry with myriad, strange threads. The emerging picture was terrifying.

I waved at Bruno and Bill Stanhope, and walked toward the Olds in the parking lot, with the ever faithful Lionel following. Under my breath I said, "I'll make it up to you, Casey. Another place, another time, I'll carry your burdens."

In the car, heading out the twisting driveway, Bruno said, "Time to wash our faces, have a cup of coffee, and then hightail it to a cocktail party. I can interview the great man himself for a very short time. Dumarie flew into town this afternoon, and he's due at a reception or something tonight, with just a brief stopover for an interview. How about that?"

"Hold it, Perillo," I said. "How many stories do you already have? I can see a series shaping up. The old preacher and his scrapbook. William Tully and his German wife, Ilse. The Jaspers, from rags to relative riches through their own efforts. Dumarie's rise from obscurity to a national figure. The Klan and the lynching. And I have another one for you."

He looked at me suspiciously. "The zoo?"

"That could be part of it. Up to you. It's the story of the Stanhope boy Thadeus, or Tadpole. He vanished in San Francisco; his mother says he was shanghaied by a Chinaman. But I saw his picture in the Eugene newspaper and he was called Hollis Jasper, and his son, Kevin Jasper, was murdered. Question: Where is the real Holly Jasper?"

For a time Bruno did not move, perhaps did not breathe, then he exhaled softly. "Tell me, Sherlock. Tell all."

I told him about Mrs. Stanhope, what she had said about Tadpole. "I didn't ask questions. She's as batty as a cave, but I saw his picture, and he calls himself Hollis Jasper and lives in Eugene, Oregon. And soon after he arrived there, money for the Jaspers dried up, and the Stanhopes had a reversal of fortune and began a massive remodeling project. Three young men took a trip to the West Coast, one of them returned to New Orleans. I think they killed Hollis Jasper, and Tadpole assumed his identity. He stayed in San Francisco or went back and forth several times, long enough to send some postcards home, make certain Bobby Lee was in the clear, and then, as Tadpole, vanish."

"It doesn't make sense," Bruno said after a minute. "Why Oregon? With that kind of money, he could have gone anywhere."

"I don't know why Eugene, Oregon."

"Hey, Perillo," Casey said from the front seat. "You know I've been slumming in Dumarie's database. The Northwest is a unit, a cell. They use code names for places and people, and that one's WIMCO. Washington, Idaho, Montana, California, Oregon. Probably just the northern part of California; there's another cell for L.A. Anyway, WIMCO's coordinator is called Frog."

"I'm scared," I said in a low voice. I was facing the side window, gazing at swamps filled with cottonmouths and alligators. I did not want to be on a road like that after dark. "This is too big, and it just gets uglier and uglier. We have more than enough already. Let's leave it, let Willy use real investigators, or do whatever he does to get the complete story. With so many leads, so many different threads, there's enough material to keep a whole battalion busy for months. I want to get out of here."

"Amen," Casey said.

"Tomorrow," Bruno said. "I'll call the airline when we get back to the motel. First flight out tomorrow. And tonight we won't stay more than half an hour, just a few questions, a picture or two, and we'll duck out. An interview with Dumarie will wrap it up. Everything spins around him, the eye of a hurricane, something like that."

I shook my head. "I don't want to go to Mystic Gardens. I won't go there."

"No. No. It's in town. His reception is in a hotel downtown, and he'll give me half an hour on his way to it, no more than that. We'll meet him in Robert Lee Fontaine's house."

23

Fate. Destiny. Karma. Whatever it was, I felt trapped. If I had told Bruno in the first place that Geneva was my grandmother, I wouldn't even be in New Orleans, much less fated to meet her brother, Bobby Lee. I didn't look like the description they had of me, I told myself firmly, and any picture they had must have been an old school picture, long blond hair, gray eyes.... Watching television one night, Geo had said in disgust, "Why do all those women look alike? I can't tell one from another."

"Young white women in their twenties who have regular features look like that," Tess had said.

True, I told myself. Young white women with regular features, no distinguishing marks ... Wouldn't I arouse suspicions if I didn't show up? Why would the faithful, dogged, obedient photographer who meekly took verbal abuse from the project boss fail the biggest assignment, a photo op with the big man himself?

Purloined letter, I reminded myself; hide behind the camera. Brazen it out with a goofy, innocent smile.

At seven, when Casey pulled into a wide circular driveway to a house hidden from the street by shrubs, I got out with Bruno and walked halfway up the front stairs, but then I chickened out.

"I can't go in there," I said. "You can take a picture or two, and there are pictures on file. You don't need me. I'll wait with Casey."

Bruno scowled furiously, but I thrust the camera at him and turned. A tall man blocked my way. He had one hand in his coat pocket.

"Ah, the reporter and his charming photographer. I'm afraid everyone's running just a little late, but come in, come in. I just got here myself. Robert Lee Fontaine." He grasped my arm and ushered me up the rest of the stairs. "The door's unlocked. Just push it open."

Bruno pushed the door open, and at the same moment I heard a car start and looked around desperately in time to see Casey leave.

"You can't count on help these days," Robert Lee Fontaine said. "No matter, we'll call a cab when you're done here." He closed the door with his foot. He was over six feet and weighed twenty-five pounds more than he had in the pictures I had seen, and his hair was as white as it had appeared in the overexposed shot. I would have recognized him in a crowd of six-footers.

Still holding my arm, he began to walk through a wide entrance foyer. "Walter's running late also, I'm afraid. We'll wait a few minutes in the sitting room. It won't be long, I'm sure."

He opened a door and we entered the sitting room, where a woman was standing by a tall window, her face in shadows until she stepped forward. I stared, and she stood still, gazing at me. It was like looking into a time-distorting mirror that did not reflect what was, but what would be in forty years.

"Eerie, isn't it?" Bobby Lee said. He steered me to a sofa. "Just make yourself comfortable."

"Why did you come here?" Geneva demanded. "You're a fool!" She sat in a chair across a coffee table from the sofa, still gazing fixedly at me. Her fingers glittered with many rings; her hands were thin, the skin looked translucent. I could see a tracery of pale blue veins. Her hair was still blond, but her face was that of a woman in her sixties.

"Will someone tell me what is going on?" Bruno said harshly.

He didn't see the resemblance, I realized with surprise. Bobby Lee and Geneva did, but he was blind.

"She inherited the magic eye," Bobby Lee said, amused. "Who would have thought it would pop up again like that?"

Not a Landorf gift, I thought distantly, but one from my grandmother, a Fontaine gift.

"I think it's time for us to get the hell out of here," Bruno said. "Come on, Sherlock. We're leaving."

"I'm afraid not," Bobby Lee said. He pulled a handgun from his pocket. "Sit down by her, Mr. Perillo, close together, so I can keep you both in sight. I'm afraid you have to be our guests for a short time. Excuse me while I make a call." Bruno sat next to me on the sofa.

Bobby Lee kept the gun leveled at us when he picked up the phone from a side table and hit an automatic-dial number. He asked for Mr. Stanhope, and after a short wait he said, "I guess you'll have to come by for me, after all."

They had planned it, I thought, the trap, the signal if Bobby Lee's suspicions proved right, and now Bill Stanhope would come, probably with help, to finish this messy business. I looked at Geneva, whose face had become masklike.

"Why?" she said, as if wondering out loud. "Why betray me after all these years?"

"He didn't. He's in England. He doesn't know I found the film or anything else about this. He never betrayed you."

"That's a lie," Bobby Lee said. "We had pros go over that house from top to bottom."

"I found everything," I said, keeping my gaze on Geneva. "I turned over most of it to the newspaper, but not all. He protected you and your brother. I didn't give them the pictures of you two. They're still hidden."

Bobby Lee made a harsh snort of disbelief. "Bullshit!"

Without looking at him, Geneva said, "Bobby Lee, hush. Let her talk."

She could still use that big-sister voice of command on him, her little brother, I realized. I ignored him and kept my gaze on her. "You took most of the pictures, didn't you? You're only in two or three of them. You took the ballroom pictures, too, didn't you?"

She nodded. "Yes. I had a camera in a pretty purse. I fixed it myself, as a joke, a lark, or something. You're on *Candid Camera*, something like that."

"Without your pictures, no one can implicate you and your brother in anything," I said desperately. Beside me on the sofa I could feel Bruno's arm tensing. He was still holding the camera I had thrust upon him. Bobby Lee had come around the coffee table, pointing the gun at my face.

"You, shut your mouth," he said to me. "She's a lying bitch," he added, glancing at his sister.

"She isn't lying, and she's right," Geneva said after a moment. "I took pictures of men acting like fools in sheets and hoods. What can they prove about men they can't identify? Everyone knows the Klan was still meeting then."

"Don't be stupid! They sent her to locate the ballroom, the room where we met before . . . before. Traipsing around all week looking at old houses, taking pictures of ballrooms, other rooms. You could spot exactly where those pictures were taken, and I could, and so can she. If Bill had a brain in his head, he would have known from the start and this would all have been over on day one. If those pictures and her pictures get compared by experts, it's all over for Walter. That's the bottom line."

"I don't give a damn about Walter and his schemes," she

snapped. "I'm willing to save your worthless neck if I can. Let him sink or swim. I couldn't care less."

She stood up, a slender woman, a foot shorter than her brother, a hundred pounds lighter, and she said in an imperious tone, "Put that damned gun away. They're leaving, leaving the state. The film stays here, of course." She turned to me. "And if you ever come back, you will be killed on sight."

"You move and I'll kill you both right now," Bobby Lee said. "I won't wait for Bill." His gaze shifted from Bruno and me back to Geneva, back and forth, and the gun wavered in his hand. Suddenly he looked past us on the sofa, startled, and at the same moment Bruno threw the camera and hit his arm, spinning him around just as he fired. Everything happened at once: Bruno dived forward off the sofa toward Bobby Lee, and a second shot sounded almost instantaneously. Geneva screamed and fell backward into her chair, and Bobby Lee fell heavily to the floor. I jumped up and twisted around. Casey was in the doorway, holding a gun with both hands, and her gun did not waver.

Geneva made a rasping noise, pressing her hand over her shoulder. Blood was running through her fingers. "Give me the telephone," she gasped. "Hurry!"

Bruno dashed over and put the telephone in her hand. "Nine one one," she said in a hoarse whisper. "Hurry!"

Casey had gone to Bobby Lee, who had rolled to his side and was trying to get up. She kicked the gun out of his reach.

On the phone Geneva said in a barely audible whisper, "I'm Geneva Fontaine. My brother, Robert Lee, shot me. He went crazy and shot me. I think I killed him." She dropped the phone. "Wipe off that gun and give it to me," she said to Casey. "And the telephone. Your fingerprints. Then get out of here. All of you. Get out and keep running. If Bill comes first . . ." She was as white as death; the blood was gushing through her fingers and frothy blood was on her lips. Bruno took the gun from Casey and put it in Geneva's hand. "Hold my arm up," she whispered. "I can't lift my arm."

He held her arm, and she fired the gun once at her brother. He jerked, then stopped moving. She let the gun fall to the floor.

I ran to her and cried, "She's bleeding to death! Do something! A towel or something." Her lips moved again, and although I could hear nothing of what she was trying to say, I knew what words she formed: "Bobby Lee. Bobby Lee."

Bruno grabbed my arm and yanked me away from her. "You can't do anything for her. The medics are on the way, and so are the cops and Stanhope." I resisted, and he tightened his grip and pulled me harder, then yelled to Casey, "Grab her stuff and let's move! Can the gun be traced to you?"

Casey shook her head and snatched up my camera case and purse. Bruno picked up the camera and we ran, Bruno pulling me, stumbling and resisting, after Casey, who led us outside, through the shrubbery, out of the yard.

"I parked around the corner," she called over her shoulder. The Olds was partway down the street. We piled in and Casey started to drive.

"Keep to side streets if you can," Bruno said. The sound of sirens was all around us.

"Right." She zigzagged this way and that until we finally came out on a wide, busy street with a lot of traffic.

Bruno leaned forward. "We have to get to the motel, clear out our stuff. I told them we were leaving early in the morning. So it's a little earlier than I thought. Help her throw her things into a bag or something. Do you have to pick up anything at your place?"

"Nope. Got everything I need in that duffel."

"Good. Then we're out of here. Where? Mobile?"

"No. It's close enough, but Stanhope will probably cover that route. I'd say head north and get out of the state as fast as we can."

I felt as if I had been far away, no part of the frantic conversation, the insane dash to the car, and only then was I forcing myself back through layers of curtains that had to be ripped apart one by one as I drew near.

"Not in this car," Bruno said; his voice sounded strange, as if I had not made the trip back all the way yet. "We should do what we did in Portland, put this car in long-term parking, rent something else. They'll be watching the arriving flights in San Francisco." He kept looking out the rear window.

"And we won't be on any of them," Bruno said. "Snap out of it, Sherlock. We do have a little time," he said then. "I suspect the cops and ambulance arrived at the house before Stanhope, and he walked in on a scene of complete madness. He won't know what happened unless he goes in. For all he knows, we are the bodies on the carpet. Okay. He won't sic the cops on us. He doesn't want them to grab us any more than I do. And it will take him a little time to get his troops organized and out beating the bushes for us. With me so far?"

"Go on," Casey said, driving toward the motel.

"With any luck, they'll assume we hopped a flight to the West Coast and they won't look too hard in their own backyard. But they will look some. So we get a car and head north. We need a map, a destination. And a way to get our sweet little asses to California without being spotted on the way. And as soon as we've put this burg behind us, I want a telephone."

An hour later we pulled off Interstate 55 into a restaurant/gas station complex where Casey headed for the nearest rest room with her duffel bag and Bruno vanished into a telephone booth. I went inside and ordered fish and chips for three to go. And three big containers of coffee. I picked up a six-pack of Cokes and some potato chips at the gas station, and we all met back at the rented van. Casey had gotten rid of the Lionel garb. She was wearing her own trim jeans and a black turtleneck jersey with strands of gold chains.

Bruno got behind the wheel and moved the van to the edge of the parking area. "Let's eat, and then head up the road," he said. "Willy wants me to call him back before we reach Jackson, Mississippi. He'll make arrangements from his end."

"What did you tell him?" I asked in a low voice.

"Just what happened back at the house, and that we're on the run. But, Sherlock, you have some explaining to do. We'll let Casey get some rest in the backseat, and you and I will sit up front and you'll tell me a story. Right?"

"I can't."

"Sherlock, let me get you started. She was your grandmother, your grandfather had pictures that incriminated her and her brother, and those pictures are still tucked away somewhere. Look at that as chapter one, or maybe just the prologue, and take it from there."

When I shook my head and put down the piece of fish I found I couldn't eat, he reached over and took my hand. "Back at day one, or day ten, whenever the hell it was, I told you that you could trust Willy to keep his word. Remember? You can still trust him. He said that nothing about your grandfather would be in our story. That still goes. His word and mine. But I have to know what I'm dealing with. We damn near got killed back there, and I want an explanation." He released my hand. "Now eat something, it's going to be a long night, one way or another."

I looked at Casey helplessly, and after a moment she nodded.

"I think Perillo deserves to know the score," she said. "The whole score," she added, and picked up her last piece of fish.

We finished the food, and then in the van heading north, I leaned back in the front seat and closed my eyes and told him about it, starting with the first night I heard the ice cubes hit the roof. I told him everything except where the crypt was. He didn't ask.

When I stopped, he said softly, "Jesus Christ, you and Casey? You two did that! No questions asked, ever."

"Prather knows. They all know."

"They aren't going to tell. You didn't stop to think that your grandmother and her brother had the same kind of memory you do? That they might recognize you?"

"I never intended to meet them," I said. "I didn't know she would be there. Remember, I wanted to back out, not go into that house. But, no, it never crossed my mind that I got this kooky memory from that side of the family. My family is gifted: My grandfather, my mother, my father . . . and my brother is a genius. I just thought that when the fairies got to me, they ran out of goodies. I've never done anything right in my life, never finished anything I started, a washout with a strange memory."

For a time no one spoke, then Bruno sighed melodramatically. "Okay. That's the best story of all, but my lips are sealed. Casey, how the hell did you manage to come over the hill like the cavalry in the nick of time with a gun?"

She sounded lazy and sleepy when she said, "Oh, that. The day I bought the car in Mobile, I went looking for a gun. Wasn't hard to find. I took it out in the country and made sure it worked, and I kept it in my duffel bag, just in case. Company I've been keeping, you never know when a gun might come in handy. And when I saw how that dude grabbed her arm, with his other hand in his pocket, I thought, goddamn, that day's come. Prescient, I guess. I skedaddled because I thought the next act in that little play would be for someone to come out to the car and tell me I was needed inside. So I left. If the door hadn't opened, I was going to go around the side and break in through a window."

I was thinking of her impassioned words: "You don't know! You can't know!" It was true. She knew things I could never know, and I would have given anything in my power if I could have undone the past so that she had never learned them, either.

24

Bruno stopped again outside Jackson to call Willy. When he came back to the car, he said, "We're to hole up somewhere and get some rest, then deliver Casey to the airport around five to catch an early-bird flight to Chicago. Ms. Casada has been visiting old pals in Chicago and is on her way to a high-tech trade show in Las Vegas. You have a motel room reserved, Airport Sheraton in Chicago, and call Willy from there for the next flight number."

"What about you guys?" Casey asked.

"He couldn't get us together on a flight out of Jackson, so we push on to Memphis and call again. He's got people working on it. I have to stick to Sherlock like a tattoo, no separate flights for us. So, it's twelve-thirty and we get to rest until five. Good luck."

He moved the car away from the rest rooms and telephone in the rest area, and we tried to get comfortable enough to sleep. But when I closed my eyes, I saw Geneva bleeding to death, and when I dozed off, I dreamed she was dying and her blue-veined hand was reaching for me; she called me Bobby Lee.

We said good-bye to Casey at the Jackson airport, then flew first to Memphis then Detroit, to Denver, and finally to Las Vegas.

We were both reeling, punch-drunk with fatigue when Jeremy met us in Las Vegas and herded us to an SUV for the drive across the mountains, on to San Jose. Jeremy took us to a high-rise condominium, where Casey met us and, after one look, took me by the arm to a bedroom. I might have been asleep before I got my shoes off.

They said I slept for fourteen hours, and probably I did. I roused a time or two, rolled over, and went back to sleep, but finally hunger forced me up. I felt as if for half my adult life I had eaten only airplane non-food, or terminal food. I showered and found my own clothes nicely cleaned and folded, and then, dressed, I followed the sound of voices from the bedroom, down a hallway, and into a living room, where a group of people were seated.

They all got up when I entered. Bruno was there, and Willy, and Jeremy was leaning against the wall by a window, his usual pose. The other four people were strangers. One, a man in his fifties, with flowing white hair and a gorgeous suntan, came forward to greet me.

"My dear Ms. Reilly! It is an honor to meet you," he said, taking my hand in both of his. "Herman DeKalb, my dear."

I had never heard of him. Willy had lumbered over to me. "Our publisher," he said. He embraced me and kissed my forehead. "Good work, Sherlock. Very good work. If you're as hungry as Bruno was when he got up, you certainly won't want to put off food for the sake of being polite. I suggest you and Bruno beat it to the dining room and order up breakfast, or dinner as the case may be. But first, let me introduce our associates."

He introduced the other men, editors, and then DeKalb said, "I will be on my way, then. I really delayed until I had a chance to meet you, Ms. Reilly, and offer you the use of my condo-minium for the time being." He made a sweeping gesture that was all-inclusive. "Please make yourself at home here." He kissed my hand, and left.

Bruno rolled his eyes and said, "This way. I could use some more coffee."

Willy walked to the door with DeKalb; then he said to the other editors, "Right back," and followed Bruno and me to the dining room.

I eyed him suspiciously when he came in behind us and closed the door. "Why do I get the feeling this is a prison?" I demanded.

"Not a prison, a safe harbor. Some of Dumarie's people are in the area. Keeping an eye out for you? Possibly. We want to make sure you're nice and safe until they find something else to do. Bruno will fill you in; meanwhile, I have a council of war going on in the other room. I say we should let them know the eagle—or should I say skylark?—has landed: others don't want a word to leak yet. So, impasse for the time being. You can order up anything you want, day or night, and you are perfectly safe here. This is a very high security building."

I sat down. "It's not over yet?"

He regarded me for moment, then said, "We're in a war. A battle ends, and this is a very important one, but almost immedi-ately others rise to replace the fallen. It's never over. I'll come back when we finish up out there."

"Like the man said," Bruno said when Willy left, "order any-thing you want to eat. Just a warning: If it gets complicated, it takes longer."

According to my watch, it was four o'clock, and since the sun was shining, it had to be afternoon, too late for breakfast, too early for dinner. Irritably I said an omelette, and Bruno called to order coffee, a spinach omelette, salad, sliced tomatoes, and a bowl of strawberries and cream.

"Where's Casey?" I asked when he hung up.

"In computer wonk heaven, one floor up. We're on the ninth floor and have this entire floor and the one above for our very own use. There's a terrace garden up there, penthouse stuff. She says she needs this or that, and presto, it appears. We have pretty good computer nerds in the office, but not a one of them can do what she's been doing, and they'd give a month's salary just for the chance to come see her, maybe touch her." Softly he said, "She's keeping the entire Dumarie operation under surveillance. That's one reason for the battle going on in the other room. A message she intercepted said, quote, the skylark is on the wing, unquote. We think you're the skylark. Some of them think that as long as goons are looking for the birdie, we can keep tabs on them. Others think that once they know the bird has landed with its treasures, they'll disperse. Time to break camp and do something else."

I swallowed hard. "Where do you come down in the argument?"

"I think the bird can stand a gilded cage for a time. I'm not all that sure they'll decide it's a lost cause. Some of them might think payback time is at hand. After the story breaks, they'll probably scatter to cover their own asses."

A waiter brought food and coffee, and I welcomed it like a Saharan traveler coming across an oasis.

"How long, Perillo? When will the story be printed?"

"Six weeks to two months," he said.

I shook my head in disbelief, and he said placatingly, "Can't be helped. Everything takes time. They'll get an affidavit from the guy who makes Dumarie's shoes, and he'll have to see the pictures before he can identify them as work his company did.

William Tully's brother has to consult a lawyer; they'll come out next week for a discussion of the best way to proceed. They'll want to reopen the investigation into Tully's death. Lawyer stuff. They want affidavits from the people Casey talked to about Tully's movements in New Orleans. Run down the full stories of those lynchings in the preacher's scrapbook. We need pictures of the Jasper brothers. Get a good picture of Hollis Jasper, get a good picture of Tadpole as a young man. That could be tricky. Run them side by side. Maybe the caption should read, WILL THE REAL HOLLIS JASPER PLEASE STAND UP? It appears that the guy who calls himself Hollis Jasper has always been quite a traveler, gone as much as he's around. He's gone now. No forwarding address. I guess he knows what's in those pictures."

He paused, then said, "Enough of the big picture. More to the point, I have stories to write. You have pictures to develop and print. And so on." He poured more coffee for both of us. "In any event, they won't run it until after the election. It would just look like more dirty politics coming before."

"You and Casey? Are you prisoners, too?"

"Not prisoners, Sherlock. Come on. It's not that bad. I have an office here, and Casey couldn't be happier. Maybe just for a week, maybe longer. They'll decide."

When Willy joined us later, he looked harried, redder than ever. "Here's how we'll play it for now," he said, picking up the last roll from the bread basket. "We're setting up a darkroom for you, and you're in charge of all that film, everything."

"You have people with more experience than I have to do that."

"Sure. But you're good enough. What we don't want is a leak anywhere along the pipeline. Damn few people know the full scope of this story, and we want to keep it that way as long as possible. You did fine with the ones you already developed and printed." He ate the roll.

"Okay," he said then. "Next item. Your mother called and you have to call her back. We have a cell phone for you to use, and as soon as you finish the call, that number will be discontinued. If they're tapping her phone, they can trace the number, but not the location. So that will work. Just let us know whenever you want to call and we'll have another number ready. Say you're in Montana meditating or something. The guys in your grandfather's house told her they'd try to reach you but that it might take a day or two. And your own personal makeup artist is going to shop for you. Give him a list. He has your measurements, and you know he's good. Anything else you can think of?"

I shook my head.

Willy stood up. "Gotta go. One other thing to think of for later. What name will you want to use? Kristi Reilly? Or just Kristi? I sort of like that. One name like Madonna. Think about it."

"You're not going to use my name!"

He gave me a long, hard look. "You still haven't grasped how big this story is, have you? You will before it's over. Just keep in mind that you have a six-month contract with us, and you might read it over. There's a clause that says you can't go with anyone else without consulting us first, giving us the opportunity to match any offer." He grinned. "See you later."

"What was that all about?" I asked Bruno after Willy left. "No one's knocking at my door to hire me."

"It means," Bruno said, speaking slowly and deliberately, as if to a dim child, "that you, Casey, and I jointly occupy a most choice seat. I believe they call it the catbird seat."

Tess was aggrieved that I had been so out of touch. "I tried to reach you," she said, "but some twit said you weren't available, that she would have you call back. Really, Lee, that's no way to treat family. You might at least let us know where you are."

"I read about Geneva Fontaine's death," I said. "Your mother. I'm sorry."

"Why? You never even met her, and I have absolutely no memories of her. None. Something happens when a baby is abandoned, darling. The cord is severed, and it can't be repaired. What a terrible thing, but they were both crazy, of course. Shooting each other like that. I called James and asked him to get in touch with whoever was in charge down there. Of course, I didn't go. Such hypocrisy that would have been, to pretend to be the grieving daughter. She didn't even know my married name."

James was her attorney. I closed my eyes listening to her.

"It's possible that there is a significant inheritance. James said she left it all to her brother, but since he died first, the next of kin will inherit. I suppose that's me. How much closer than mother and child could any kin be?" Tess rushed on. "The lawyers will benefit most, of course, but still, there may be something left over—"

"Tess, I have to go. I think a bear is nosing around outside. I'll call you in a week or two."

I spent long hours in the darkroom. Casey worked as many hours or more with the computer, and Bruno was writing his stories. Casey ordered duck terrine one day, and the cook came to talk to us, delighted with the choice. "But, Madam, it will take four days. Not today, not tomorrow. Four days. Is that acceptable?"

She considered it, then nodded. "Acceptable."

I suspected she was not sleeping very well: I wasn't. My grandmother's image haunted my dreams. And blood. There was always a lot of blood in my dreams. We didn't talk about that day in New Orleans.

If I told Willy I didn't know how to do something that he required, he sent someone to teach me. A one-on-one crash course in darkroom technique. He wanted enlargements of the special shoes, the woodwork in the ballroom, the scrolled pillars behind William Tully and Ilse. . . . I learned how to do enlargements.

Now and then Willy confided about new developments: In the fifties, he said, Hollis Jasper had invested heavily in a corporation called Horizons Unlimited, a land-development corporation run by William Stanhope in New Orleans.

"And what do you know," Bruno said, "the Stanhopes remodeled their little old shack in the country, built a new ballroom, and no doubt threw a party. Funny how things work out."

"Also," Willy continued, ignoring Bruno, "Hollis Jasper has acquired half a dozen land tracts in the Northwest, five thousand acres here, eight thousand there, and various very far right groups have leased those holdings and moved in and set up camp. If it can be demonstrated that the money he used in all those instances was not his money, each and every deal will be contested in court."

Early on, Willy had said we had an octopus in our grasp, and each leg led to a new connection with extremists or even Nazis. I had the feeling it was not an octopus, but a Catherine wheel with endless spokes. And at the center spinning the wheel was Walter Dumarie.

Usually Casey, Bruno, and I had dinner together and then watched a movie for a while, or just talked. One night Willy joined us for dinner.

"We have a schedule," he said when we were having coffee.

"The Sunday after the election. There will be a week of post-mortems about the election; then on Sunday all hell breaks loose. Every day for a week a new story, and the following Sunday a recap." He was very pleased.

I had lost track of time, I realized. It was mid-October, but whether it was a Monday or a Friday, I couldn't have said.

"Three more weeks," Casey said, then groaned.

I stood up and walked to the windows and gazed at the lights below. I had watched Casey exercising on the treadmill on the upper terrace earlier, and when she caught my eye, she had said, "It's this, or I jump over the edge. This is better."

We were stir-crazy, all of us. Three more weeks. Then what? My haunting dreams were not going away, not fading. If anything, they were getting more and more detailed and frightening, as if I were under a curse to relive again and again that night in Geneva's house. I kept seeing Geneva bleeding to death, and Casey holding a gun in both hands, Bobby Lee jerking on the floor. What did Casey dream? I was afraid to ask.

I turned from the window and said, "Willy, I have to go back to Grandfather's house. There's more. I didn't give you everything."

"Jesus Christ! What are you holding out?" His red face glowed redder than ever.

"It won't change anything. It's just more, but it has to go in. I have to retrieve it."

"Where is it? I'll send Jeremy."

"No. I have to get it myself. And I have to be in the house alone when I do."

Bruno was on his feet, shaking his head. "You can hold out a little longer, Sherlock. Just three more weeks. We've got enough stuff to fill a book. We don't need any more."

"I have to get it, and you have to add it to the rest of the material. And I have to talk to my mother. Not on the phone. I have to go to her condo and talk to her."

"No way!" Willy yelled. "Not until we hit the stands!"

And Bruno said at the same time, "You're out of your mind!"

Casey didn't move, but she was watching me, and she said, "Baby, you've done enough. More than enough. Leave it alone."

"Next week," I said. "Tell your people to let me in and clear out for a couple of hours. That's all I'll need. Then I'll come back."

Willy was sputtering angrily. I ignored him.

"Afterward, I have to go down to Bel-Air and talk to my mother. First Grandfather's house, then hers."

"Forget it," Willy managed after sputtering some more. "You're staying right here where you're safe. Period. Finis."

"I stayed here voluntarily," I said, still at the window. "You know as well as I do that if I decide to leave, I'll find a way. It would be better if you arranged it."

Late that night, sleepless, I wandered through the dark condominium and came to a stop at the same window where I had stood earlier. The city lights were beautiful, all colors, a kaleidoscope with moving traffic, red and white lights coming and going. Lights blinking on and off, green, red, yellow.

"Bad night?" Bruno asked from the doorway.

"Yeah."

He crossed the room to stand by me. "Want to talk about it?"

"No."

"Couple of nights ago I held Casey's hand; this is better." He put his arm around me, and after a moment I rested my head on his shoulder.

We didn't talk, and we stood there for a long time watching the lights blink on and off.

25

The next day Willy brought in a lawyer to talk to me. Mr. Perlman represented the newspaper and was also DeKalb's personal attorney, Willy said. As a staff member of the newspaper, I would be represented by him, too.

"Why? For what purpose?"

"We have to establish your name. Just Kristi. Lots of famous people go by a pseudonym, you know. It's legal as hell. And if you get called as a witness, to authenticate those photographs, testify that you took them as part of an assignment, he'll guide you through that."

I stared at him, aghast. Witness at a trial? He was still talking.

"Plus, once this story breaks, the FBI, Justice Department, God knows who all, will be around asking questions. And no answers from you unless Perlman's at your elbow. He'll tell you the score, what to expect."

I looked at Bruno. He grinned his lopsided grin. "You're off the hook, Sherlock," he said. "You don't know nothing except that you had an assignment to get some pictures, and if they matched the ones Willy already showed you, so much the better. They'll go after Willy for his sources, and we all know what a fight that can turn into. He'd rot in prison before he revealed a source. Wouldn't you, Willy?" His grin was sardonic.

"I'm not going to prison," Willy snapped. "I got a package of stuff from an anonymous person, and a sharp-eyed photographer noticed some peculiarities. So I sent a green reporter and a

234

greener photographer who's still on probation down there to see if anything could be verified. If I'd thought there was anything big, I would have sent a seasoned crew. That's the story. The truth and nothing but. So sue me."

Bruno laughed.

"Have you made arrangements yet for me to go to Grandfather's house?" I asked, ignoring Bruno and the lawyer.

"Sunday. You and Jeremy will fly up to Eugene in DeKalb's Learjet. Jeremy will drive you to the house, then back to the airplane, and you'll fly home. We want you in and out before they have time to put two and two together, in case they're keeping an eye on his plane. But they probably aren't. That plane comes and goes two, three times a week. Satisfied?"

I could tell he was unhappy with the plan, and Bruno was furious and anxious, but I was relieved. I had thought of terminals, the wait for boarding time, seeing Prather at the other end. . . . Or else spending two days on the road each way, which would be even worse. This sounded like the best of all possible solutions. Besides, I had never flown in a private plane before. I nodded and only then turned my attention to Mr. Perlman, who had been waiting patiently.

He was a fussy little man with oversize glasses, gray hair, and a gorgeously tailored silk suit. He talked with me for an hour, coaching me, rehearsing me, guiding my answers to his questions ever so deftly. Then he smiled. "I don't think you'll have to take any witness stand, my dear. I believe any adversarial attorneys would be happy to stipulate that you indeed took the pictures that bear your signature."

"Why? I thought I was doing okay."

"You are a wonderful witness," he said. "And they wouldn't even try to trip you up, I'm sure. A jury would frown on any misbehavior on their part. No, they'll suggest we stipulate, and we will protest and insist that you be called, and they will insist that it would be a waste of time and that a stipulation would be in the interest of both parties. With very bad grace, we will accept it."

He didn't actually rub his hands together, but in his mind I was certain he was doing just that. "Moreover," he said, still very satisfied, "when the federal agents want to talk to you, I will represent your interests. Willy will arrange any interviews with them, and I suggest that they should be held right here, where you are comfortable."

The trip to Eugene on Sunday was almost anticlimactic. I went down in the elevator with Willy and Jeremy. A black limo was waiting in the basement parking garage, and Jeremy and I were whisked to the San Jose airport, where the Learjet was ready to take off. It was exactly what I had visualized, down to the glove-leather-covered seats. We got in, buckled up, and took off for a smooth, uneventful flight of less than an hour. Then a drive to Grandfather's house in another limousine, with Jeremy driving. He talked about his basketball-playing days and fishing, and he didn't seem to mind at all that my end of the conversation was an occasional nod or a noncommittal grunt. I thought, as I had before, that he had the sweetest smile I had ever seen on an adult male.

At the house my "dear old school pals" Alison and Buck opened the door for us and then went shopping, and Jeremy went back to wait for me in the limo. All as planned. I took a swift look through the house, marveling at the order of the many books, apparent even in that quick look. Then I got a flashlight from a kitchen drawer and went to the darkroom, closed and locked the door, dismantled the light table, and went down into the crypt again.

I knew what I wanted, and it did not take long: the pictures of Bobby Lee with and without his hood, and those of Geneva. I found the pictures and the negatives, then hesitated over the sheet and hood. I had gone back and forth about taking them, but decided not to. What was the point? I left them in the metal case, went back up the ladder, and reassembled the light table. Leaving the darkroom, I heard the doorbell. It rang, stopped, rang again longer. First I needed an envelope for the pictures; I ran to Grandfather's study to find one. I put Geneva's pictures in my purse, the others in the envelope, then rushed to the door. The bell was still ringing, stopping, ringing.

"What is it?" I asked, opening the door.

"We'd better take off," Jeremy said. "I mean like right now. Come on." He took my arm, hurried me toward the limo.

"What happened?"

"Some guy came down the driveway, looked the car over and wrote down the license number, then ran when I said, 'Hey.' I don't like it."

We got in the car, and he headed out the driveway fast.

"I didn't lock up the house."

"Forget it. We're out of here. How long would it take to get here from Jasper's house in Eugene? Crest Drive."

I had to think. "Fifteen minutes, maybe ten."

He sped down Mason Lane, out to Franklin and toward the airport, and kept an eye on the rearview mirror. Then on Sixth Street he picked up a car phone and pushed a number, waited a few seconds, and said, "Rev her up. We're on the way, ten minutes."

"What did that guy look like?" I asked. "It could have been one of the neighbors, just wondering about the limousine."

"Maybe. Tall, skinny, ponytail."

The flower boy, I though in dismay. Someone could have paid

him to keep an eye out, make a phone call if I showed up or a strange car did. I scrunched down in my seat.

"Relax," Jeremy said. "We don't have a tail."

"Thanks to you," I said. "What if you had gone in with me, or just hadn't noticed him? Or if he had been more careful?"

"My mother taught me a long time ago not to play the what-if game," he said. "It's a no-winner."

I noticed that he was still checking his rearview mirror frequently. I couldn't help it, couldn't stop the what if scenarios. What if they had come while I was still in the crypt? Forced their way past Jeremy, killed him even, and found me down there? They could have taken everything out, left me there, put the light table back together. . . . I would have stayed there until Casey arrived to find me, if ever. No one else could have done it.

Faintly I said, "Jeremy, thanks. Just thanks."

He smiled his beautiful smile, then said, "When we get on the plane, this time let's raid the bar. They keep some pretty good stuff on board. You like champagne?"

By the time we got back to San Jose, I was tipsy, and not at all prepared for Bruno's fury when Jeremy reported what had happened.

"You idiot! You had to go there! Put yourself in their sights again. Can't you get it through that thick skull of yours that you could be in danger? You could be killed?"

"Hey," Casey said, "you know what you sound like? Just like Ma did when I'd come in late. She would blow her stack. You'd think she'd have been glad and relieved to see her little girl safe and sound, but mad! Man, could she blow!"

Moving with great care, I opened the envelope and dumped

the contents onto the coffee table. "This is Bobby Lee Fontaine," I said, picking up his picture, enunciating my words carefully. "He was my great uncle."

No one spoke or moved for what seemed a very long time. Then Casey said, "What we need is some coffee. And you need something in your stomach," she added. "I watched you at breakfast. You picked up a piece of toast and put it back down half a dozen times."

"What I've been saying," Willy said. "You don't eat." He took the photograph from my hand and sat down. "Geneva Fontaine was your grandmother," he said. "Good God! Why didn't you tell me?"

"Food first, then the rubber hose," Casey said firmly. She went to the phone and ordered ham and cheese on rye. Jeremy cleared his throat, and she said, "Make that two." When Bruno held up his hand, she sighed. "Just bring a bunch of sandwiches. Five of us. And coffee right now."

She hung up and took my arm. "And you need to wash up. Come on."

She pulled me along to one of the bathrooms, where she closed and locked the door, then stood with her back against it, glaring at me.

"What the fuck are you up to? Is your grandmother's picture in that bunch?"

"No. Just his. He was part of it. He was Dumarie's memory, his right-hand man all these years. He has to be included."

"You're dragging your own family into this shit!"

"Tess isn't responsible for her uncle. She never even knew him."

"Jesus. She'll be dragged in, and so will you. Maybe your grandfather . . . Why? For God's sake, why?"

I shook my head.

"Oh, wash your hands."

We heard Bruno and Willy yelling at each other in the dining room when we left the bathroom. Jeremy was standing apart, regarding them with a placid expression. Coffee service was on the table. I went to it and poured myself a cup, then sat down. Everyone had become silent when we entered the room.

"You can't go to Bel-Air," Bruno said, jabbing his finger at me.

I looked at the finger, then at his face; he was flushed with anger. "Put that goddamn finger in your pocket! And stop telling me what I can do." He jammed both hands into his pockets and swung around. Jeremy moved out of his way briskly.

Willy sat down across from me. "He's right for once," he said. "Deal's off."

"You gave your word," I said furiously, pushing my chair back.

"Listen to me, Sherlock. Calm down and just listen. Okay?" He poured coffee for himself and added sugar and cream, then kept his eyes on it as he stirred and stirred. "That was a close call in Eugene. Too close. We figured in and out before they got wind that you'd gone anywhere, and we were wrong. They could have someone on the payroll down at your parents' place. It's just too big a risk."

"Why? What do they want with me now? You have all the pictures, the negatives, everything. You don't need me anymore, and they must know that."

He stopped stirring and tasted his coffee, added more sugar. "Let me give it to you straight. Dumarie's got friends in very high places. If we go to the feds with what we have, they could put a cork in the bottle within a couple of hours. We don't know that they would, but we don't know that they wouldn't, either. It's happened before. But until we have everything out in the open, and an official statement from you, signed, witnessed, notarized, all the rest of it, all we've got is a bunch of pictures and a story or two. We've seen smart lawyers tear into photographs like tigers going at lambs. They'd have their expert witnesses testifying about faked photographs day after day, and they can be convincing. There are faked photographs, God knows. And by the time anyone got around to confirming the woodwork, the paneling, the storefront pictures, remodelers would have been at work. So until those photographs are certified as legitimate, you're at risk. If you were out of the way, they'd make a case of politics as usual, the liberal/pinko smear technique at work, and Dumarie would come out of it smelling like a rose. There would be suspicions, but there have been suspicions for twenty years, and he's still running for president."

"Willy," I said, "for God's sake, bring in a notary, witnesses, whatever it takes to get this over with."

"Can't," he said morosely. "We can't use anyone in the inner circle or being paid by the newspaper. See, we need the feds, and we can't rope them in until the story's a wrap. Rock and hard place. But that's how it is."

I leaned back and closed my eyes, thinking hard. I should have held on to Bobby Lee's pictures; I kept coming back to that. I should have held on to them until the second part was done.

"Here are the sandwiches," Jeremy said. No one spoke again as the waiter set the table and uncovered a platter of sandwiches and crudités.

After the waiter left, I said, "If I can't go to her, you have to bring her up here."

"Will she come?" Casey asked doubtfully.

"She has to. I can't let her see that story without warning her first."

Bruno and Jeremy had come to the table and seated themselves, and we all reached for sandwiches. I stopped as a new alarm hit hard.

"Willy, is she in danger? Would they try to get to me through her?"

He shook his head. "We talked about that and decided, all of us this time, no. Dumarie's got smart people working for him: They know that any threat like that would send us straight to the FBI with what we have. And to press within hours. I imagine they had late-night powwows about it, too. Remember, they don't know exactly what we have. Your grandmother knew, and she must have told her brother, but they're both out of it. No one else can know exactly what shots she took. That film wasn't developed until you got your hands on it, remember. They might think we're still digging for more. As far as Dumarie knows, all we have on him is possibly the fact that he associated with others who were in the Klan when they were young and wild. They have since been born again, renounced hatred and violence, and so on. His spin doctors must be working overtime to keep him clean."

That afternoon I called Tess on a new cell phone. She rambled: Geo was expecting a call from Washington and might be gone for several weeks this time; she was considering a villa in southern France. They had thought about Rome, but it was so congested. Her new lecture tour—

"Tess, stop. Listen to me a minute. I have to talk to you."

"Well, darling, I know that. I've just been waiting for you to realize—"

"Will you just listen! I found some things at Grandfather's

242

house. Things that involve the Fontaine family, and I'm working for a newspaper. They have certain material that involves the family. I have to talk to you before they print the story."

There was a long silence. Then she said coolly, "I had no idea you had a job. It wouldn't hurt you to keep in touch, let us know where you are, what you're doing. If you want to discuss things with me, I'll be here most of this fall."

"No, Tess. I can't go down there. I can't take this material to you. You have to come here. You have to see what it is yourself, or you'll be deeply humiliated and embarrassed when the story breaks. So will Geo. It will hurt you both professionally."

"I have absolutely nothing to do with the Fontaine family," she said after another long pause. "I never knew any of them, including my own mother. If you have anything to tell me, just say so, tell me."

"If you don't come up here, you're going to be dragged into the same mud as Bobby Lee," I said. "My editor will make arrangements for you to be picked up and driven here, and then back home. You won't have to drive yourself. Whenever you say. But this coming week. It has to be this week."

"What did you find?" she said in a harsh whisper. "Just tell me what this is all about."

"Not on the phone. You have to see it. Will you speak with my editor?"

"Lee, this isn't like you. What's happened to you? You're like a stranger—"

"Will you speak with him?" I cried.

"Yes! Yes. For God's sake. Put him on."

I walked across the living room to where Bruno and Willy were seated on matching sofas, pretending they hadn't heard every word. "She'll talk to you," I said, and handed the phone to Willy, then went to stand at the window. Fog was moving in.

I listened to him speak soothingly to Tess, explaining that this was a very delicate and sensitive matter that had to be handled discreetly at all costs. I was startled when Bruno touched my arm.

"Want to go upstairs and watch the fog roll in?"

We left Willy talking and went to the terrace garden, where we could see the fog envelop the city.

26

Bruno was writing and rewriting stories constantly, revising, adding new material; I was developing film, making enlargements, working to bring up details, isolating faces or sections and enlarging them. But I never had a clear idea of what Casey was doing, and when I asked her one time, she shook her head.

"Baby, you don't want to know. Let's leave it at that."

I knew she was meeting with Perlman and Willy, sometimes with others, but that was all. Whatever she was up to was illegal, that was certain. I came across a doodle of hers, a spider web with X's marking where the vertical strands were connected to horizontal lines. At each first intersection several more vertical lines formed to link to the next horizontal line. When Casey saw me looking at it, she said, "Pretend the X's are labeled A, B, C, and so on, and the center is point zero. They know they're connected to point zero, but most of them don't have a clue about who else is, or even if anyone else is. Communications go up and down, and nothing goes around and around."

"Can't they get in touch with one another directly?"

"Doesn't look like it. Everything goes through point zero. Suppose you are building up an arms cache down here somewhere." She pointed to one of the intersections. "They know at point zero, and they tell others on a need-to-know basis, as near as I can figure out. Into the center, rerouted, back out maybe."

"Smart, but also risky," I said after a moment. "Pretend this X is Frog, and these lines coming off him go to Little Frog One, Frog Two, Frog Three, and so on. And none of them knows anything about the others. Great, they can't betray one another. Frog can't rat on Scorpion, or Rattlesnake, or any of the other X's, and each Little Frog knows only its own members and Frog. But if point zero collapses, they're all on their own. If Frog collapses, all the Little Frogs are on their own."

She nodded. "You've got it. Smart and careful."

I shook my head. "It doesn't make sense. Accidents happen, heart attacks, whatever. They must have people ready to step up and fill in." I was remembering what Willy had said, that Dumarie's son was waiting in the wings. And how many others?

"Right. And I'm looking for them. Now forget it." She picked up the doodle and tore it into many little pieces.

I had printed the new pictures I had given to Willy, made private prints and copies of those with Geneva, and suddenly I was done. Now it was up to the writers and editors and layout team.

The terrace garden had been fitted with glass panes and was a warm solarium filled with greenery and very private, like being on another planet. On Wednesday afternoon I was sitting there, brooding about my mother's visit on the following day when Bruno joined me.

"Simon Legree looking the other way?" I asked. Willy was driving him hard with his incessant demands for rewrites. I had read most of Bruno's stories and thought they were extremely good: major-league stuff, I had told him, to his pleasure.

"The way he's bouncing back and forth between here and the office, it's a wonder he doesn't lose a little weight," he said. "He's gone at the moment."

"I think he gets something to eat every time he turns up here. Does he have a kitchen and cook at the office?"

"Fast-food take-out stuff and chips." He looked at me, then quickly away. "I have to ask you this," he said. "Why are you dragging your family into it? What good can come of it with Bobby Lee dead, your grandmother dead? They're beyond punishment or redemption, on this plane, at least." He glanced again at me, then away. "Do you hate your mother that much?"

"Is that how it looks?" I asked, surprised. I had not thought of how others might see it.

I realized how carefully he was choosing his words when he hesitated, then said slowly, "Well, from what little you've said about her, I get the impression that she was a pretty absentee mother. And your brother was the favored child all the way."

"Oh, good heavens! I'm not jealous of my brother," I said. "He deserves all the help they can give him: God knows he's earned it. All his life he's worked like the devil, and now he must be putting in twenty-hour days as an intern. I, on the other hand, never did anything much. Read a lot, if that counts. And it doesn't. I don't hate Tess. In fact, I love her. I think I was always a little afraid that she might not come back, and I was overjoyed each and every time when she did. We all knew how her mother went away and didn't come back, of course. I was a little jealous of her. She has so much drive. That's where Ben got it, I guess, and I never had any to speak of."

I talked on and he listened without interrupting. Was he satisfied with my answer? I couldn't tell, but my answer had been truthful. I did love Tess and Geo, and I knew they loved me. I never doubted that. They were bewildered by me, uneasy, because I had always been so aimless, and they didn't know how to steer me into anything useful or anything that I would really apply myself to. And neither did I. I smiled, telling him about some of the games we used to play, my family around a table playing Risk. I always lost early, and I always wondered why the three of them cared so much. They were fiercely competitive at games. But if we played cards, I usually won because, without trying, I could remember every card played.

"I'm an automatic card counter," I said. "I should have gone to Las Vegas, and cleaned up."

"But you never cared enough," he said.

"That's it, all right. I never cared much about much."

"Until now," he said.

I looked at his crooked grin, and he said, "What's wrong? Catsup on my chin?"

"No. I was thinking a fishhook on the side of your mouth, attached to a line pegged to a nerve center at the scalp, so that when one side goes up, the other follows. Or maybe on the other side, attached to your collarbone, to keep one side down as much as the other. I think I'm onto something. I'll work on it."

He laughed a long time.

The next day Tess arrived at three o'clock. She was elegant in a red suede coat with shoes, handbag, and gloves exactly the same shade. She nodded to Casey and did not offer to shake hands with Willy or Bruno when I introduced her. This was not a social call, her attitude clearly stated.

I took her to my room, where I had a tray with a bottle of Jack Daniel's, ice cubes and water, and a wine cooler with a very good chardonnay in it. On another table I had a coffee carafe and cups. Ready for anything, I had thought when I arranged things. My room had a queen-size bed, and a nice grouping of furniture around a low table at tall windows. There was a folder on the table. We went to the windows and I helped her off with her coat. Her dress was silver-gray, sleek, and as elegant as everything else about her. She looked much more at home in these surroundings than I did in blue jeans and a T-shirt.

"You and your roommate have certainly come up in the world," she said tightly. "Even redone your hair. It's lovely like this."

"It's temporary. Tess, this is going to be very hard to explain; please be patient and hear me out."

She sat very straight on the edge of her chair, her legs crossed, her foot swinging back and forth.

"Your uncle Robert Lee Fontaine Jr. was a member of the Ku Klux Klan," I said. "He participated in the lynching of a man back in 1947. The man's wife died from a beating the Klan gave her at that time. Basically, that's the story that will be printed in the newspaper."

She lifted her chin and appeared to become even more rigid. "I don't see what that has to do with me. I can express my regrets if anyone brings it up. But no one will. I never even knew him."

"They came to Grandfather's house," I said. "Bobby Lee, Tadpole, and Holly, and they got into a big fight with Grandfather. Aunt Lu told you and her sons to go to your rooms, but you sneaked out again and went to the sitting room and listened at the door. You heard what they were shouting, and you became terrified. The next day your father said he would see you dead and buried before he would let you leave with your mother. You were nearly eight years old, Tess. You know what you saw and heard. You've always known."

She stood up. "I don't know what you're talking about! This

is all a fantasy. I don't know what Bobby Lee did or didn't do, and I have no recollection of my mother. I think it's time to stop this nonsense. If that's all you wanted with me, I wasted a whole day for nothing. I'm not to blame for the sins of my uncle."

I opened the folder and took out the three pictures I had prepared for her. Bobby Lee and the others in their sheets and hoods in front of the tree with the hanged man. Bobby Lee and Geneva, with him holding his hood. Geneva with others in front of the hanging tree.

Tess stared at the pictures as if hypnotized, then she sank down into the chair again. She was the color of putty. I mixed her a drink of Jack Daniel's and water and put it down in front of her.

"You gave them those pictures?" she whispered. "My God, how could you do such a thing?"

"They don't have Geneva's pictures," I said. "They don't know about her."

She took a long drink and put the glass down, then picked up her mother's picture and began to tear it up. I thought of what Aunt Lu had said: She looked at the postcard from her mother, and then tore it up and threw it away. Now, watching the pieces get smaller and smaller, Tess said, "I listened at the door. My mother said, 'When I tell them what you have, they'll come and kill you. You, your precious sister, her filthy kids, Tess, all of you, and burn down the house. And I won't lift a hand to save any of you.' I peed in my pants."

She could tear the print no more; it was like confetti. She picked up the other one and began to tear it. "I thought I heard them coming that night, every night. I could hear them coming to kill us and burn the house. I hear them sometimes in the condo, in hotels—no matter where I am, I can hear them coming to kill us." She took another long drink.

"I know it's all over. It's been so long, everyone's forgotten. Then I hear footsteps in the night."

She finished her drink, stood up, and went to the table to pour another one. When she came back, she pushed all the scraps together into a pyramid. I was glad she didn't have a match.

"She was always looking for the pictures," she said, her gaze on the pile of scraps. "She would take books off shelves and leaf through them, go through Dad's briefcase, look in the pockets of his raincoat . . . always looking for them. And you found them. Where were they?"

"That doesn't matter. I found them, and the story is going to be printed. That and others."

She closed her eyes for a moment. "But not her picture, her part in anything. Not my mother, your grandmother."

"That depends on you, Tess. I have the negatives, of course. You have to renounce that inheritance, give it up."

"What are you talking about?"

"The Fontaine fortune—all those plantation fortunes were made of cotton on the backs of slaves," I said, using Beverly Jasper's words. "You don't need it. Tell your attorney to set up a trust with it, with a board of directors to decide the best use for it."

She looked at me as if I had sprouted horns. "You're out of your mind! There could be millions of dollars. My mother inherited Bobby Lee's estate. That and her own money, it could be three million dollars or even more."

"All the more reason to put it to good use," I said. I got up and poured myself coffee and continued to stand across the room. "I want you to make a public statement renouncing that money and have your attorney set up the trust, naming Angela Casada as the chairman of the board of directors."

"That's it! She put you up to this insanity, didn't she? She sees a way to line her pockets!"

"She doesn't know anything about it. No one does. They don't have Geneva's pictures yet, but if you don't do this, I will hand them over. You don't need another house. You can't get one far enough away to stop hearing those footsteps in the night. You can shrug off an uncle you didn't know, but your own mother smiling in that picture? That will be harder."

"You'd do this to us, your mother and father?" She jumped up, disbelieving, and even scornful. "You know what something like that would do to Geo? I don't believe you. He'd never let me turn over that money to such a trust. I couldn't even if I wanted to."

"It's your inheritance, not his. You can do exactly what you decide to do. You've always done what you wanted. Think how magnanimous you will look, you and Geo, trying to right a terrible wrong. That statement has to be made by next Wednesday. All the stories have to be finished by the end of next week. That one is still incomplete."

"I don't believe you!" she said harshly. "I don't believe you could do a thing like that." She took a long drink and set the glass down hard.

"Look at me, Tess. No, not just a glance. Really look at me. You believe me because I'm your daughter. And you know that what I'm saying is what I'll do."

She stared at me as if she had never seen me before. She looked old, I thought in wonder, and terribly frightened.

"Talk to Geo. Tell him everything. Then both of you talk to your attorney. And, Tess, talk to Dr. Sandersson, and this time tell him the truth, all of it."

"You're no longer my daughter," she cried. "From now on you're a stranger to me. Do you understand what I'm saying? I won't be coerced by my own child. I'm leaving. Don't bother to call or write."

"Next Wednesday, Tess. By noon Wednesday."

Without a backward look, she snatched up her coat and walked from the room, as stiff as a wind-up doll. I went back to the chair by the window and sat down. I touched the pyramid of scraps, then scattered them across the table. After a moment, I started to cry.

Friday. Saturday. Sunday. Endless days. Casey and Bruno were wary, polite; they didn't ask anything, but watched me until I wanted to scream at them to go to a movie, go to a football game, do something somewhere else. Instead, I retreated behind Proust, starting at chapter one.

On Monday Willy called me from his office. My father was in town and wanted to see me. I nodded, then said, Send him around.

Willy brought him in person; he was not exactly deferential, but he was very polite.

"Hello, Geo," I said, standing in the middle of DeKalb's plush living room. I doubt that Geo noticed a thing about the condo, the room, Willy, or anything else. His gaze was fastened on me.

"Can we talk?" he asked.

"Yes. My room." I led the way. Inside my room I started to go to the window chairs, but he stood by the bed, and when I looked back at him, he opened his arms and I went to him, to be enveloped and held tightly. He had always done that after returning from a trip when I was a little girl, or when I came home after a prolonged visit with Aunt Lu. He had opened his arms and held me, stroking my hair. He stroked my hair now.

Then, fighting tears, I took his hand and we crossed the room to the windows and sat at the table there.

"She's very upset," he said. "She wouldn't say a word about it until last night. Do you have copies of the prints? I'd like to see them."

I got them from a bureau drawer and put them on the table before him. He looked at them a long time, then pushed them back, away from him.

"I understand," he said. "Her uncle, her mother. All these years . . . I never thought of ours as a dysfunctional family. You and Ben seemed to be thriving, not into drugs, not suicidal or homicidal, none of those things we're warned to watch out for in our offspring. I was busy, maybe too busy, and Tess, she lit up anything she got near. God, I looked at her and marveled that she had settled for a stick like me. But I always knew she loved me, loved you and Ben passionately. I was blind," he said. "Blind."

I wanted to touch him, to hold his hand, comfort him, but he was oblivious, facing the window, his eyes unfocused, or focused on the past.

"She used to jump out of bed in the middle of the night sometimes. I followed her a time or two in the early years, and she said something had occurred to her, she had to make a note or she would forget. She was always so vibrant, so vivacious. Like a lightning bolt, here, there, then gone for a time. I never suspected she was driven by fear, by footsteps in the night."

"Maybe if she faces it, talks about it, maybe she'll stop running," I said.

He pulled his gaze from the window to me and nodded. "I hope so. I have our statement. We'll release it tomorrow, election day. Fitting somehow, isn't it? Is your friend Casey up to a job like that, chairing a board responsible for so much money?"

"She'll get her doctorate this year, and she will have to get good advisers, but she's up to it. Would you be her financial adviser?"

He looked startled, but nodded. "If she'll have me." He took an envelope from his breast pocket and put it on the table.

"Will Tess forgive me?" I asked in a low voice when he stood up.

He hesitated, regarding me soberly, then shook his head. "I don't know. Not today or tomorrow. In time, perhaps. I just don't know."

"Geo, I'm sorry. I hurt her so much, and I'm sorry I had to."

He came and put his arms around me and kissed the top of my head. "You said the magic words, you had to. Strange, isn't it? I'm supposed to be the one preoccupied with money, its power, its attraction, how to make it and keep it."

"But this would have been hers," I said. "That makes a difference."

"Yes, it does," he said. "I know."

Casey shrieked, "You're out of your mind! I don't know shit about a board of directors!"

Willy read the statement, then yelled, "Jesus Christ, you're still holding out on me!"

Casey moved to my side, and Bruno slouched over to join us.

Willy glared at the three of us and threw the statement down. "I've got work to do!" He stamped out, redder than I had ever seen him before.

And Bruno, scowling with his eyes closed nearly to slits, said in a low, incredulous voice, "Holy shit! You blackmailed your own mother!"

27

The statement was very good, brief and to the point: "Mrs. Donne was setting up a trust. . . ." She even used the phrase I had borrowed from Beverly Jasper: "fortune made of cotton on the backs of slaves." There would be no further comment until the board of directors was chosen and issued its own mission statement.

The statement was lost in the welter of election news, and I supposed Tess's attorney had wanted it like that. But it was done. I went to my room and burned the prints with Geneva, as well as the negatives, then flushed the ashes down the toilet.

We watched election news into the night. When I went to bed, the latest estimate of Dumarie's tally was at 4.7 percent of the vote. The numbers played in my head as I tried to go to sleep. Four point seven percent of a hundred million, 4 million plus something. I couldn't do the zeros and decimal points without a calculator, or at least paper and pencil, and I gave up, and tried hard not to think of Tess for a very long time, and tried harder to stop the image of Geneva with her smiling lips morphing into bloody lips, back and forth.

On Sunday Jeremy came in with a stack of newspapers, a complete issue for each of us; he was grinning like a cherub. We sat around the living room reading the stories. I stared at the front-page byline: Story by Bruno Perillo, Photos by Kristi. I felt disoriented, strangely disconnected from it. Lee Donne was dead; Kristi had replaced her, and I didn't know Kristi. I felt that I had vanished without leaving a ripple, the way Hollis Jasper had vanished.

Casey came down from her office that afternoon and said, "My job's kaput. Over and out. After a certain amount of confusion, chaos, and disarray, an order went out to close down all systems, scrub hard drives, get rid of everything, prepare to dig in and wait out the storm. I assume that's what the order said because that was the immediate result."

Very late in the afternoon Willy came by. He couldn't stay, he said; his phone was ringing off the hook. Dumarie's lawyers were on the line with the company lawyers. "They're going to sue the hell out of us," he said. He was ecstatic.

That night Casey, Bruno, and I watched Marx Brothers movies and ate popcorn.

It all seemed dreamlike, the tension, the fear, the hours of work in the darkroom, the parks, parade routes, mansions, all a dream. Or more like a child's anticipation during an endless trip to Disneyland. Are we there yet? Are we there yet? a receding destination, unendurable anticipation, and suddenly you're there on the inside, and only later do you realize that the anticipation was as important as the main event. Now, having arrived, I felt deflated and as aimless as I had been in June.

The FBI arrived on Monday and wanted to take away all the films, negatives, prints—everything. Perlman explained why they couldn't do that, and they argued about it. In the end they requested, very politely, copies of everything. Their own technician would make the copies in my darkroom. Perlman, just as politely, said that would be satisfactory; one of the newspaper technicians would assist. After I identified which photographs were mine, and signed a long statement concerning them, they paid very little attention to me, a lowly staff photographer who had simply done the job assigned to her. When they asked what Casey's role was, she said that she was my chaperone.

Bruno moved back into his own apartment, although he didn't ever seem to be there. Casey spent two days in an FBI office. She told me about it late the second night. "See, I have my own lawyer now. I'll need him for the trust, and God knows I needed him yesterday and today. Willy's springing for his fee for now, then I'll be on my own with him. Willy stayed awhile just to get things cleared up. I have immunity, and the guarantee of anonymity. How about that!"

"Immunity from what?"

"I'm also sworn to secrecy, but shit, you already know more about this than I do, so here goes. I'll use Hollis Jasper as the example, since we know who he is. Mostly I just have code names. He's Frog. He's respectable, keeps a low profile, isn't openly anti-Semitic or a racist, does nothing to draw attention. He sees to it that groups get established here and there, in Idaho, Montana, like that. He buys the land; they lease it for a dollar a year, something of that sort. Or maybe it's just a city councilman he finances, or a judge, someone like that who heads the unit. They in turn begin to educate the locals. They intend to create a true Aryan nation with grassroots support in place and ready to take up the cause when Dumarie runs next time."

"I thought there was already an Aryan Nation group."

"There is. Out in the open, known and watched. Dumarie's been setting up his Liberty Party out in the open, populist, libertarian, you name it. And in secret he's building his own version of an Aryan nation, tiers on tiers, and most of them hidden." She dew in a breath, then went on slowly. "They don't instill hatred," she said, "they seek out little worms of baseless fear and anxiety, give them a cause, and then feed and nurture them until they're strong enough to make it on their own."

She paused, then said in an even lower voice. "It's really scary, how much they've done in the past ten or fifteen years. Talk about future planning!"

"You found all that on the computer?" My awe must have shown.

She grinned. "Sure. And now the FBI has it all. I found things they not only hadn't dug up yet but didn't suspect were there to be dug. They're impressed. Wondered if I was looking for a job. No way, José. I intend to become a computer millionaire and buy my folks a house. You know."

They would want another session or two with her, she said, and then she was free as a bird. "Home for Thanksgiving, and I have to talk to Pop about that trust. Start getting ideas."

It appeared that I was the only one asked to stay in the gilded cage. I complained to Willy about it.

"You need an apartment of your own," he said, "but it might take a few more days. I have people at the office keeping an eye out for something."

"Why? The story's over, finished."

"You're still on the payroll, and you will be for months. You will have assignments just like everyone else. No interviews, speeches, nothing like that. It's in the contract you signed. All such things come through our office, not over the phone. Okay?"

I was taken by surprise. "I thought this would end now. You mean I really have a job with the newspaper, not just this one shot? You know I'm not really a photographer."

"With any luck, and a hell of a lot of patience, maybe we can turn you into a newspaper photographer," he said.

"There's one more thing I have to do," I said then. "I have to go to Grandfather's house at the end of the month and stay a few days. I have to tell him what I did."

He threw up his hands. "Okay. Okay. But that's it. No more demands. You're a staff photographer. If I say it's the dog show, off you go to the dog show. No prima donna stuff. Understand?"

I nodded. "Yes, sir. Dog show, cat show, county fair, whatever you say."

"Good. You're off until the first Monday of December. You'll get an apartment, get a car, take care of things with your grandfather, but be in the office at nine o'clock on Monday. Got that?"

"Yes, sir. You know I didn't finish college? Does that matter?"

"Good God!" He stamped out.

Two weeks later I entered my own apartment with another load of stuff—pots this time. I stopped inside the doorway and smiled at my home. I loved it. I had a living room with some cushions on the floor, a bedroom with a bed and a chest of drawers, a bathroom with a tub, a kitchen with a stove, a microwave, refrigerator, and even a dishwasher. I had a card table and two chairs in the kitchen. Even if I had had more chairs, there was no room for them, so that was all right, too. There was a tiny balcony off the living room. And now I had enough pots to cook something beside microwavable frozen dinners.

And in my own parking space was my own car, a four-year-old Honda Civic. All mine.

Of course, I realized, when I paid rent, car payments, insurance, utilities, and phone bills, I might not have enough left over to buy food to go in the pots, but I had decided to worry about that later. For now I was content.

Bruno came by while I was scrubbing the new used pots. I opened the door and eyed a plant he was holding.

"What's that?"

"A houseplant," he said. "A house without plants is like a desert without sand." He put the plant on the table.

"I sort of suspected it was a plant," I said. "Do you know what kind of plant?"

"Nope. It has red flowers. Does that help?"

I laughed. "A house without plants is like the sea without water. Thank you."

"I rehearsed *my* line all the way from the florist shop," he said.

"What are you doing roaming around this time of day?"

"Vacation. I missed my vacation in August, you know. Taking part of it from now until the first Monday of December. Let's go eat tacos or something."

"You can't keep feeding me," I said.

"Tacos are cheap."

"Dutch treat," I said after a moment. "Or I stay home and heat up yesterday's leftovers."

He grinned. "Let me tell you about leftover frozen dinners. Been there, done that. You're on. Dutch treat."

Later, in a small Mexican restaurant, he said, "What are you doing for Thanksgiving?"

I took a sip of wine: It was cheap and surprisingly good. From Chile, the waiter had said when he suggested it. "Nothing. Getting my house in order. What about you? Going down to your folks' place?" I had assumed that was why he was taking his vacation now. I had not been invited home for Thanksgiving. In fact, I had heard nothing from Tess and Geo.

"I thought I might skip it this year. Actually," he said, "I thought we might do something together." He looked uncomfortable, almost shy, and he took a big drink of the wine. "What I thought I'd suggest is that we drive up to your grandfather's house together and spend a little time there. You know, get things ready for his return, make sure the heat's working. Like that."

I picked up my fork, put it down, at a loss.

"I don't expect anything," he said hurriedly. "I mean, I'm not trying to rush you into anything. Buddies. Like that, like before, in New Orleans. Just talk, eat together, maybe go watch the snow fall in the mountains, hike. . . ." He was flushed almost as red as Willy.

"I don't think I'm ready for anything more than that," I said. "Pals. Like in New Orleans. Except you don't get to order me around."

He grinned happily. "We'll make a turkey."

"Can you roast a turkey? Really?"

"Nope. Can you?"

"Are you kidding?"

"So we'll do something simple. I can fry chicken."

"A man of many talents. I know how to make candied sweet potatoes with marshmallows. They're awful, though."

"We'll exchange childhood secrets. You know, what we fantasized about doing, about becoming. You have to promise not to tell anyone, though."

"I'll show you my secret hiding places," I said. "Ben never did find me in that house. You won't, either."

"Want to bet? Five?"

"Done."

"We should leave early Tuesday, get there by midday Wednesday, in plenty of time to shop for dinner."

I had never seen him look so happy.

28

Sharing a motel room on Tuesday night was not like camping out with my brother. We tried to get two rooms, and had to count ourselves lucky to find one. Holiday traffic was fierce on I-5. Hearing him breathe in the other bed made me want to hold my own breath. I did not like to think of falling asleep, probably snoring, knowing that he was awake and aware of my every movement, just as I was aware of his. He fell asleep first, and then I began the drift downward.

I dreamed, as I did most nights. Bad dreams, frightening ones, filled with mummies turning and twisting in their wraps; Geneva's lips covered with blood; being locked in the crypt; Spanish moss writhing and twisting in the wind, turning into men . . . I came awake. Bruno was holding my hand.

"You were tossing and moaning," he said.

It was very dark in the room; I couldn't see him. His hand was warm. "Dreams," I said. "Sorry."

"Every night?"

"Most nights." I tried to withdraw my hand, but he tightened his grip.

"When I was twelve," he said, "I went to this summer camp, six weeks for young actors. I was a misfit, of course. The camp was in a mountainous area, and we hiked up and down hills a lot. I liked that part pretty much. Except that when we got high and the trail was near the edge of the cliff, I'd freeze. Fear of heights. Pretty bad case of it. The director who was trying to teach us how to act took me aside and said, 'Kid, everyone's afraid of heights, but most of them don't know it. You *should* be afraid of heights. Your body knows you don't belong up there and it's trying to tell you something. Most people aren't paying any attention. They don't get the message.'" Bruno laughed softly. "Crazy as it sounds, that helped. I still don't like high places much, but I don't freeze. Everyone's afraid, but they don't all know it." He tightened his grip a little more.

"Sherlock, you've seen things no one should witness. Your body's telling you those things are inhuman, it doesn't want to have any part of such inhumanity. Maybe it's afraid you'll go hunting danger and death again, and it's saying, Don't do it. Your body's speaking to you, it's trying to make sense of what can't be rationalized, because it's inhuman. Just listen to what it's telling you and let it all go."

He lifted my hand and I felt the warmth of his breath and the light brush of his lips, then he put my hand down and pulled the cover over my shoulders.

"Go back to sleep, Sherlock. Pleasant dreams."

When I woke up the next time, the room was bright with sunshine and my bed was not a tangled mess of sheets and covers.

It was snowing when we got to the Siskiyou Pass. Traffic was at a near standstill as drivers pulled over and put on chains, then crept back into traffic, inching along. We stopped, but after Bruno put on the chains, we played in the snow like children until we were soaked and freezing.

It was a slow drive all the way, with frequent stops: to take the chains off, to find some dry clothes in our bags and change, for coffee, for lunch. Our wet things had started to steam from the car heater. We traveled on the inside of a cloud. In the valley it was raining, sometimes a drenching downpour, then sprinkles, then a brief bit of sunshine. Oregon winter, I explained, and Bruno nodded and said that made sense now, didn't it?

Our last stop was at a supermarket in Eugene. And then we headed for Grandfather's house, which was now empty. As soon as the story began to run, Willy had called in the two substitute house sitters. "What's left to steal?" he had asked me, and then muttered, "I hope we have it all." He told Alison and Buck to put the key on a hook behind the downspout at the corner of the garage, where there had always been a spare key, and to leave the security system off. No one would be bothering that house again. Besides, who was left? Hollis Jasper or Thadeus Stanhope, whatever he was calling himself these days, had run, and there was a flunky closing up the law office.

I was very surprised at how glad I was to see the house. I thought of it as coming home, another surprise.

We put the groceries in the kitchen; I turned up the heat and then showed Bruno through the house. I gave him Aunt Lu's old room, the one Casey had used.

That night we ate hamburgers and deli slaw, and sat before the fire on the floor in the sitting room, talking.

"After you get the Pulitzer, will you stay on at the newspaper?" I asked. "I expect people will be clamoring for you all over the country."

He blushed. "Let's not count our prizes before they're hatched. Anyway, we all know that if a prize gets handed out, it should go to you. Your story from start to finish."

I shook my head. "What you said that first day was that there wasn't a story yet, just pictures and stuff. You made the stories."

"You don't forget a thing, do you? Let's drop it. Will you hang in there after your contract is up?"

"I guess so, if Willy will renew it."

He laughed. "Sherlock, he's practically adopted you. He knows what he has in you, and he'll keep you forever if he can. And you could do worse for the next few years. Willy is a great editor, and a great teacher. I'm not going anywhere else for a long time. I'm still learning my trade at the knee of a master. He already told me I have the follow-up assignment on the various stories as they continue to develop. Trials. Stanhope's trial for the Jasper murder, if he's ever caught. Tully's murder."

"After the way he yelled at you, made you rewrite and rewrite all the time, you'll stay on? Your stories were wonderful, but he's never satisfied."

"He yelled, and I guess I did some, but he was right every time. If there's a deadline crunch, he just does it himself, but given time, he makes us do our own work. And he's right."

"He isn't going to last long, the way he eats. He'll have a coronary or something."

"He doesn't eat quite that much unless he's under a lot of stress. He doesn't drink much, and he has to shake the tension somehow. He uses food."

"What do you use?" I asked.

He was silent for a time, then he said, "Cold showers? Doesn't work quite like they'd have you believe, though."

He was staring straight ahead at the fire, and I kept my gaze there, too. I had nothing to say for a time. Then in a low voice I said, "You realize that I've had a couple of boyfriends. You know. Nothing ever lasted. I think I tended to get involved too soon, before I really knew them. After I got to know them, over. A control freak. Jealous. A mama's boy. He wanted to take me home and meet his folks after three dates, and he kept wanting to take me home to show his mother, or get her approval or something. Over. I was a slow learner."

"Ah," he said. "My instincts were dead-on. When I told Mom

I'd spend Thanksgiving with a new friend, she said to bring you along, and I said nope. Moving too fast. Dead-on. Aside from that, any girl I ever took home saw Rog, and I was dead in the water. We'll take it nice and slow and easy. Right?"

I laughed.

He talked about his brother—he was very proud of him—and I talked about mine, equally proud. We talked about music and books we had liked, movies. . . . The fire died down, and we were both yawning when he said, "Seriously. A serious question. Will you level with me?"

"Maybe," I said.

"Good enough. If sweet potatoes with marshmallows on top is awful, why would you put them there?"

I considered it, frowning, then said, "Because."

"What if you left off the marshmallows, maybe put a little butter on top, would that be better?"

"No doubt."

"Let's forget the marshmallows tomorrow."

"Sounds like a plan. I have a question for you. Honest answer, right?"

"Maybe."

"Good enough. Have you ever fried chicken in your life?"

"Well, maybe not me exactly, I mean maybe I wasn't doing the actual cooking, but I've seen it done. Nothing to it."

"Ah. I've seen it done, too. I'll help."

We went through the house turning off lights, then we said good night and he went into his room and I went into mine and we both closed our doors. I was smiling.

On Thanksgiving we hiked up Mount Pisgah, where the view was of fog and rain mist. "On a clear day you can see your hand

before your face," I said. Then we went home and started to prepare our feast.

"Do you even like cranberry sauce?" he asked, eyeing the can
dubiously.

"Not really. Do you?"

"Nope. I wonder why we bought it."

"Because it's Thanksgiving?"

"That must be it. Maybe we can just leave it in the can and
look at it from time to time."

The chicken was soggy; the sweet potatoes were very good
and swimming in butter; the green beans were tough; the salad
was wonderful. We both knew how to make great salads. We
declared the dinner a success—if not the best ever, then very
close.

We watched television and talked and planned the next few
days. I had to pay the property tax, and see if other bills had come
in that would now be overdue. He said he would clean the gutters. That afternoon it had rained and water had cascaded over
the edge of the roof; the gutters were clogged with fir needles.

"Cross-country skiing?" he asked. "You up for that?"

"We should watch the weather report. I don't know how
much snow has piled up in the mountains." Of course, I
thought, he would not want to do downhill skiing, not with a
fear of heights.

We did not stay up as late as we had the previous night. All
that hiking, all that cooking, Bruno said, plumb tuckers you out.
We both hesitated outside our doors, then I said, "Good night,"
and he grinned and said good night, and we went into our bedrooms. I realized he would wait for me to make the first move,
and I was smiling again.

———

A dense fog moved in overnight, and the house seemed like a ship at sea, becalmed in featureless fog. I wrote the check for the tax, and looked over other pieces of mail that had not been forwarded to Grandfather, letters to Resident, to Homeowner, sales flyers . . . junk. I tossed it all; otherwise, I told myself, it would stay on his desk for the next ten years or longer. I was on my way to the kitchen when the doorbell rang.

Mrs. Hawkins, I thought. She had not come on the holiday, and here she was. I opened the door and saw the man who had posed as an FBI agent, who had called himself David Prather. He was smiling, and he was pointing a gun at me.

29

"What do you want?" I whispered.

"At the moment I just want to come in out of this fog. It's cold." He motioned me back, and when I took a step away, he entered and pushed the door shut with his foot. "Now I want your friend— Never mind, there he is." He was looking past me, but the gun did not waver and I did not move. "Put your hands on your head and walk forward very slowly," he said to Bruno. "I think we'll go into the parlor. Stop at the door. That's right. Turn around, Ms. Donne, and join your friend. Very slowly."

I turned and saw Bruno standing at the door to the sitting room with his hands on his head. I walked to his side.

"Now, we'll all go in," Prather said. "Stop by the coffee table."

We stopped at the table.

"Empty your pockets, Perillo. Just put everything on the table and then step back until I tell you to stop."

He told Bruno to stop in the middle of the room. "You may join him there," he said to me.

"What do you want here?" I cried. "I don't have anything else. I handed it all over to the newspaper."

"I don't think so. I want the case. Where is it, Ms. Donne?"

I shook my head, numb with fear. My nightmare, I thought distantly. He would make me go down into the crypt and then close it.

"Ms. Donne, don't lie. Just tell me where it is: We'll collect it, and I'll go away. Simple as that."

I shook my head again. "I don't know what you're talking about."

"Perillo, take three steps to your left. Hands on your head, if you will."

I watched the gun shift to follow Bruno.

"See, the first rule of gun safety really should be never to carry one unless you intend to use it. I took it away from Kevin because he had no intention of shooting you, but he fired it anyway. But I do intend to use it if I have to. Where is the case?"

"I gave them everything!" I said desperately. "No, wait! There was something else. A diary. My grandfather's diary. It was in the same box."

Prather looked at me as if considering this. "We'll start with the diary then. Where is it?"

"I put it in a safe-deposit box at the bank. He wrote about the lynching. It has names—my grandmother, Bobby Lee, Walter Dumarie, Tadpole, others. I didn't want anyone to see my grandmother's name like that. It's in the safe-deposit box."

The gun shifted again, this time back to me. Prather's mouth was a tight, hard line.

"If you kill her, the cops will open that safe-deposit box," Bruno said. "You're Dumarie's son, aren't you? Brandon Dumarie. Did he send you out here to pick up all that stuff? He must be disappointed in you."

"Another word, and you're dead meat," Prather snapped.

"If you kill him, you have to kill me, too!" I cried. "I won't go to the bank and sign for the box."

"We'll all go to the bank. Pick up your keys," he said to Bruno. "You drive. Which bank? Where?"

I told him the credit union on Eleventh, and he nodded. He made me get my raincoat and put it on a chair, then back away from it while he patted the pockets. Then he did the same with Bruno's jacket. When I picked up my purse, he told me to open it on the table and back away. He glanced inside, then closed it and tossed it to me.

"You both sit in the front seat, both hands on the wheel, Perillo. Your hands in your lap," he said to me.

Then, with Bruno driving, we headed for the credit union. "No heroics," he said when Bruno started. "No speeding, erratic driving . . ."

I felt his hand on my neck and stiffened, then gasped when a stab of pain shot through my neck, up into my head.

"See," he said. "You behave, or she gets punished."

Bruno drove with extreme care, and Prather talked.

"Ironic isn't it? Her grandmother took the pictures; she developed them after all those years. Geneva had everyone convinced that her ex had forgotten all about them. Then in February last year, after Walter announced his candidacy, she confessed to Bobby Lee exactly what she had taken pictures of, and she was afraid that Landorf probably still had them. And if he saw Walter's name and picture in the papers, he might remember. She knew she would have remembered, and so would Bobby Lee, and they assumed any normal person would. So Kevin and I came to find them."

Think! I kept telling myself. *Think!* But he kept talking, and I realized he was doing it to prevent thought.

"It was Kevin's idea to drive you away, and it really should have worked. We wanted to avoid violence, you see. We were all quite surprised when you didn't run. It would have ended there. If we hadn't found things at that time we would have waited for your grandfather to return, but you would have been out of it. Later, you really should have called the number I gave you, not the FBI office. Again we misjudged you. You have been a surprise all down the line, in fact."

I was groping in my purse with my left hand. His hand still rested on my shoulder and when I started to move my right hand, he told me to sit perfectly still, and there was the jab of sharp, burning pain in my neck again. I felt tissues, sunglasses . . .

"We really want the case," he was saying. "No intrinsic value, you understand, just a family treasure, passed down from father to son for generations. Geneva gave the film to Walter, and he put it in the case with some other things. Then the young men all went out on the town. A few days later when he went back to retrieve the case, they couldn't find it. Landorf had found it. He stole it."

"Why didn't they kill him then and there?" Bruno asked.

I felt the shell casing, then my fingers closed over the Swiss Army knife Casey had given me years before. "Never go out unarmed," she had said. It was a joke of a weapon, a two-inch blade, scissors, screwdriver, corkscrew. We were passing the university grounds.

"They should have killed him on the spot. But they were young, eighteen, and their parents didn't know they had Geneva take the pictures, much less that they had lost them. I believe they might have been a bit afraid their fathers would not take it well if they found out. In their own way, I expect they were being chivalrous, protecting Geneva. Her father had a fierce temper, I've been told. Anyway, however that went, Landorf had the case and the film, and he took Geneva and left town. Stay on the left ahead, turn left at the Eleventh Street exit."

I couldn't open the blade with one hand, but I started to work the corkscrew out as we entered Eleventh Street, just a few blocks from the credit union.

"The next corner," Dumarie said a second or two later. "Turn left, then into the parking lot." His hand tightened on my neck. "What are you groping for in your bag?"

I started and jabbed the corkscrew into my thumb hard. "A tissue," I said.

"Stop. Both hands in your lap, and keep them there until we get out. Now!"

I tucked my thumb in and made a fist and put my hand in my lap with my other hand. Bruno pulled into a parking space.

"Hand me the keys over your shoulder," he said to Bruno, who passed the keys over his shoulder. "Get out the key to the safe-deposit box," he told me.

I felt for my keys and pulled them out.

"When we get out, I'll hold your arm, and Perillo stays in front. One false step, Perillo, and I'll kill you, and then her and anyone else who interferes. I'll get away and join Holly in seclusion. That's already planned in case it's needed. You're both playing for time, playing for a break. Keep it that way. We'll all go into the vault with the safe-deposit boxes. If anyone questions that, tell them you have to show me something, and not another word. Let's go."

We did exactly what he told us to do, and inside the bank I went to the customer-service desk and said I had to get something from my safe-deposit box. The woman behind the desk nodded and asked my name. Her nameplate said Patricia Juarez.

"Lee Donne." I showed her my key with the box number on

it, and she nodded again. If she thought it strange that someone was holding my arm, she did not show it.

"I'll get your card," she said. She pulled a drawer out at her desk and riffled through a card file, brought out the card I had signed months earlier. "Now I'll just get the ledger for you to sign," she said pleasantly, and got up and took the few steps to a cabinet from which she took a ledger. "If you gentlemen will please stand back just little," she said, "Ms. Donne can come around and sign the book for me."

I pulled free from Dumarie's grasp and took two steps around her desk, held the ledger with my left hand, and wrote swiftly: *he has gun*. Blood dripped from my thumb onto the ledger.

Patricia Juarez glanced at it, then put the card down on the book. "Now the key," she said. "Excuse me." She brushed past me to go back to the cabinet and began looking for the matching key to my box. Her telephone rang, and she returned to the desk and picked up the receiver. "Hello, this is Pat." She listened a moment, then said, "Yes, I can do that, but can I put you on hold for a minute? I'm with a customer right now. It won't be more than a minute or two. Thank you." She smiled at me and said, "It never rains but it pours. One thing after another, but always all at once. Now, let's get that key."

She found the key, then unlocked the vault door and swung it open. "Are you all going in?" she asked in surprise.

"I have to show them something," I mumbled.

"Well, it's going to be a tight fit. We can open the box and I'll get out of the way so they can enter."

She went in and I followed. The vault was small, two walls of boxes with an aisle between them. She found the box and unlocked one lock with her key, waited for me to fumble with the second one and get it unlocked, and then pulled the box out partway. "There are shelves," she said, and pulled one out to show me. "You can place the box on a shelf in order to open it all the way. When you're finished, replace the box. There's a button on the wall by the door. Just push it and I'll open the door for you. You can't open it from the inside. Any questions?"

I shook my head. She smiled again, then left, and Bruno and Dumarie entered. "Like I warned you, it's going to be a tight fit," she said. She closed the door.

"All the way back, Perillo," Dumarie said.

Bruno squeezed past me to stand at the far end of the vault.

Dumarie pulled out a shelf and motioned toward the drawer. I pulled it out and placed it on the shelf, and he opened it. He took out the diary and glanced through it. "You were telling the truth," he said, as if in surprise. He started to put the diary in his pocket, but it was too wide. He handed it to me. "Put it in your purse and let's get out of here."

With the diary in my purse, the drawer back in place, the shelf pushed back in, he motioned to Bruno to move past us and be the first one to exit. "Just like before," he said. "You in front, and I'll help Ms. Donne along. Just like before. Push the button."

Bruno pushed the button and time stopped. What else could I do? The answer came back: nothing. I could think of nothing. Paralyzed with fear, my brain had stopped functioning. He would make me tell him about the case, about the crypt. He would make Bruno bring it out and then make us go back down, and he would close the top, put the rods in place, leave. I shuddered.

"Don't you go faint on me," he grated. "Push the damn button again!"

"She's on the phone," Bruno said, but he pushed the button again.

Finally the door swung open and Patricia Juarez said apologetically, "I'm terribly sorry about the delay."

Silently our little parade walked past her to the exit. No one was paying any attention to us, I thought in despair.

Outside, we had just cleared the door when Bruno yelled, "Sherlock, drop!" He swung around and lashed out at Dumarie, and hit me with the same motion, knocking me to the ground. He fell on top of me, and the world exploded all around us.

There were screams and sirens and men's voices shouting. Then Bruno heaved himself up and grabbed my arm to lift me. "Are you okay? Did I hurt you? Christ! You're bleeding!"

Dazed, I sat up; then Bruno and a uniformed officer helped me to my feet. Blood was running from my thumb where I had jabbed it with the corkscrew.

They took us to the police station, where a doctor looked me over, cleaned my thumb and bandaged it, and pronounced me as good as new. Then a captain asked us questions. The holdup man was dead, he told us. They didn't know yet how many shots he had taken, enough. He sighed heavily. "Why don't you tell me what was going on?"

"He came to her house and said he was looking for something," Bruno said. "A shell casing that he had dropped there last summer. She told him she had found it and put it in her safe-deposit box, and he pulled a gun and made us go to the bank to get it."

"A shell casing? Ms. Donne, why don't you tell me about it?"

"You must have records," I said. "Last summer I called the sheriff because someone was harassing me, stalking me or something. He shot a gun at my house. They didn't find the shell casing, but I did the next day."

"You have this shell casing?"

"He told me to put it in my purse. It's still there." I found it and handed it to him.

"And you," he said, turning to Bruno, "how did you know there were police all over the place out there?"

"I covered a story last year about an attempted bank robbery. The teller kept her head and did exactly what Ms. Juarez did, she rang the silent alarm to security, and when they called her back, she used almost exactly the same words that Ms. Juarez used confirming that a holdup was in progress. We didn't print that part," he added. "No point in broadcasting the fact that they have a system in place that works." He shrugged. "So I was looking. Parking lot emptied, no cars in line for the drive-up window, no pedestrians in sight. And I spotted a uniform."

The captain nodded. "Juarez kept her head, and you kept yours," he said to me. "That was good thinking to get blood on her book and write that message instead of your name." He shook his head. "If it hadn't worked, you'd probably all be in the morgue instead of him. If he had noticed that blood or that message . . ."

"Ms. Juarez put the card down on top of it," I said. "I didn't even think she had noticed, she was so cool about it."

He asked a few more questions and then said, "We'll have to get formal statements, but not now. Tomorrow, or the next day. I'll give you a call. I read your stories about the Klan, about Dumarie, all that. Good work on your part. Do you think this is connected to those stories?"

"I don't know," Bruno said. "I read about the Kevin Jasper murder, his being wrapped in a sheet, something like that. Could that have been Klan-related? You know his father was a Klansman, and he probably killed the real Hollis Jasper and took his place, and he was involved in that lynching years ago. Ms.

Casada, who was visiting Ms. Donne last summer, is non-white. Could that be related?"

The captain gave him a hard look, started to say something, changed his mind, and very soon after that told us we were free to leave. He would have someone bring the car from the bank and get us out the back way if we wanted to avoid the reporters waiting outside. We said we wanted very much to avoid them.

We drove a few blocks, then Bruno said, "Rubber gloves. Latex, I mean. Where do we get some?"

"Why?"

"That case. What's so special about it? You do have it, don't you?"

"Yes. I know where it is," I said guiltily.

"Okay. So we don't want more fingerprints on it than those already there, and we don't want to destroy anything, but we want to examine it. Right?"

"Right."

"And, God, I need a telephone. Willy will go atomic with this. Dumarie's son shot dead by Eugene police."

"You didn't tell them you think that's who he was."

"They do their work, I do mine," he said. "They'll find out soon enough. Where did you say a store is?"

I showed Bruno the secret of the crypt, and we took the case up to the darkroom, where we could examine it under a good light. I had not lifted it before, merely opened the lid, but now I saw a leather handle, and under it was engraved CLAUD DUMARIE, 1849.

"How in hell did your grandfather hide something like that from his wife?"

"I bet he boxed it up and shipped it home the way he did his army stuff and college books. Aunt Lu would have put it in his closet and never given it another thought. And when he came home again, he built the crypt for it."

Bruno considered it, then nodded. "I bet you're right. Did you touch any of the inside surfaces?"

I shook my head. "Just the top."

"And probably your grandfather didn't, either. What for? But Walter Dumarie might have left a print on the inside somewhere. We'll wipe the outside and let the fingerprint experts have a go at it."

He examined the sheet and hood carefully. It wasn't really a sheet at all, but a cotton robe with slits for the arms: the lower edge was stained. "It could be blood, or just dirt," Bruno said. "They can tell in a lab. If it's blood, and if it matches up with William Tully's . . ." Very carefully he folded the robe and returned it to the case. "Anything else?"

I knew he meant, Was I holding out anything else? I could truthfully say no. He knew about the diary and had not mentioned it a single time, and he wouldn't. I knew that, too.

"Okay, telephone. It might be a long call. Let's put this away again and leave it until Willy decides the next step."

I listened to him say to Willy, "The same anonymous person who sent you all those pictures has another present for you. You can decide how you actually received it. And I have a little story. Today in Eugene, Oregon, the police shot to death Brandon Dumarie. . . ." I left him in the study, talking to Willy.

I sat down in the family room and closed my eyes. I was sore from top to bottom, both knees were scraped and hurting, my thumb was throbbing, I had a lump on my head, my breasts were sore from my fall. . . . But I had not seen Dumarie die. I did not have that image in my head with the other inhuman images, and I was grateful that my nightmares, already overfilled with death scenes, would not have that one.

Last summer, I thought, if I had called that number Dumarie gave me, he would have come back and I would have handed him the film and the negatives, and he would have forced me to give him the case. Then he would have killed me. Today, after he had the case, he would have killed both of us. I was as sure about that as I was that Bruno would never tell about the diary.

I thought of what Casey had said: *You don't know. You can't know.* She had been right. I didn't know what it would be like to be Casey or her parents living in a world owned by men like Dumarie. I would never know that. Just brushing against them had made me feel unclean.

Now one more task, and I dreaded it. I didn't know how Grandfather would react: like Tess, and disown me? Or like my father, and be forgiving? Maybe he would give the investigators his diary, or maybe he would burn it. I didn't know.

He had escaped the horrors of war only to confront new horrors, and he had closed his eyes and walked away. Would it have been a foolish bit of bravado to do otherwise? An open secret made more open? To what end? Would anything have changed then? Did he ever regret that decision? Had he even felt that he had a choice back then? I didn't know, and I couldn't know, I realized tiredly. His inner world, the interior landscape he traveled, was his alone; no one else could ever know it.

Bruno came in after a long conversation with Willy. "He's sending Jeremy up by plane to pick up that case. He said to put it in a pillowcase and not to handle it any more than we have to."

279

He sat down beside me, not touching, but I could feel the warmth of his body. "He said," he continued, "if you're holding out anything else, he will wring your neck. He said, Good story. And he also said, Why didn't you at least get Brandon Dumarie's picture?" He looked at me and grinned. "Like you said, he's never satisfied."

"I have his picture. I took several last summer at Crater Lake. Jeremy can take them back with him."

Bruno stared at me, then laughed. "He also said that we're a hell of a team."

Hesitantly, I put my hand on his on the couch. "Like you said, he's right every time."

ABOUT THE AUTHOR

KATE WILHELM is the author of more than three dozen books, including such novels as *The Deepest Water, The Good Children, Justice for Some*, and *Where Late the Sweet Birds Sang*. She is the author of six Barbara Holloway thrillers: *Death Qualified, The Best Defense, Malice Prepense, Defense for the Devil, No Defense*, and *Desperate Measures*. Her fiction has been translated into many languages and received such honors as the Prix Apollo, the Kurd Lasswitz Award, and several Nebula Awards. She and her husband, Damon Knight, received an honorary doctor of humanities degree from Michigan State University in recognition of their many years as instructors for the Clarion Workshop in Fantasy and Science Fiction. Ms. Wilhelm lives in Eugene, Oregon.